RITES OF THE HEALER

F.E. Osborne Jr. High

RITES
of the
HEALER

BY

ANNE GRAY

SUMACH
PRESS

LIBRARY AND ARCHIVES CANADA CATALOGUING IN PUBLICATION

Gray, Anne (Anne Elizabeth)
Rites of the healer : a young adult novel / Anne Gray.

ISBN-13: 978-1-894549-59-2
ISBN-10: 1-894549-59-7

I. Title.

PS8613.R386R58 2006   jC813'.6   C2006-904345-0

Edited by Marg Gilks and Jennifer Day
Designed by Liz Martin
Cover art by Charmaine Lurch

*Sumach Press acknowledges the support of the Canada Council
for the Arts and the Ontario Arts Council for our publishing program.
We acknowledge the financial support of the Government of Canada through
the Book Publishing Industry Development Program (BPIDP)
for our publishing activities.*

ONTARIO ARTS COUNCIL
CONSEIL DES ARTS DE L'ONTARIO

Printed and bound in Canada

Published by

SUMACH PRESS
1415 Bathurst Street #202
Toronto ON Canada M5R 3H8

sumachpress@on.aibn.com
www.sumachpress.com

In Memory of My Parents
Atrice W. Gray
and
Roy O. Gray

Acknowledgements

I would like to thank all the teachers and friends who
have helped and encouraged me since I began writing,
but I am particularly grateful to my friend and first
reader, Gillian Chan, who has been with me in this
project from the beginning when she read a story
and said, "This has to be a book." Here it is.

And Edlena, the Silver Goddess, descended in a fiery cloud, and in great travail was delivered of her four children; after them, she gave birth also to divers beasts and birds and fish, and to plants of all manner. And the four children divided their inheritance and went out to defeat the giants and take possession of the land.

And it came to pass that the Sacred Land where Edlena gave birth, which had in the beginning been given to the son Technol, did tremble and quake, and the children dwelling there separated; some fled to the hills, some to the plains, some searched for their brothers of the sea, while some remained among the broken stones of The Krashite.

And the brothers and sisters of the hills did welcome the displaced children of Technol and shared with them their corner of the land, but what happened to the other children of Edlena is lost to us.

From *Edlenal Tales*

One

APPRENTICE DOVELLA STOOD AT THE WINDOW OF THE Engineering Building and gazed at the sky, an endless stretch of blue without a wisp of cloud in sight. How long would the drought continue? The flowers in the park across the way had long since withered, and the young leaves of the trees hung limply from drooping branches. Near the edge of the road, a scruffy black dog scratched behind his ear. His thumping leg churned up puffs of dust.

Two years already, she thought. Now, for reasons that mystified even the Master Engineer, the machine that supplied power and water to the Village no longer worked properly. The flow had diminished steadily over the past year quarter, and acres of once fertile farmland lay parched. And the rationing wasn't working. They had diverted as much water as possible to outlying fields, but still it wasn't enough — not nearly enough.

She turned to Narlos. "It's as bare as if it were mid-winter, not time for Festival."

Her fellow apprentice grinned. "Thinking of celebrating with Jael, are you?"

Dovella felt herself blush. True, she had been hoping that Jael would notice her, but she hadn't realized that anyone might have seen her looking at him. She'd thought she was being discreet.

Narlos laughed. "I don't think he's noticed your lingering glances."

"But you did."

"I'm the noticing type. He's more the acting type."

"You'd think he ought to be a noticing type too, being a security apprentice."

"Oh, I'm sure he is where his work is concerned. He just hasn't realized that you might be a security danger." Narlos wagged a finger at her.

"There won't be much celebrating if this drought continues."

He shrugged. "Drought or not, if we can't get the machine working properly there's going to be trouble. Jael will notice that quick enough."

Dovella's shoulders slumped. "But we've checked everything time and time again."

"There has to be something wrong, or we'd have more water and power."

All too true, but what she'd said was true as well: they *had* checked. Again and again. Dovella could usually feel it in her hands when there was a problem, could almost visualize where the trouble lay, but not this time.

Narlos bent back over the manual he was studying. Watching him, Dovella thought of the old books she'd discovered in the archives. Reading through them had gotten her thinking: what if the fault lay elsewhere? The books spoke of something called the source, a lake beyond Hill country.

Before she could mention her idea, the bell sounded. She snatched up the olive green robe she'd tossed over the back of a chair. "We'd best rush or the Master Engineer will have my head."

Narlos laughed. "She's only harder on you because she's afraid others will say she's favouring you."

"Because I'm her daughter," Dovella finished for him.

Narlos shrugged. "You're good and she knows it. But she also knows you'd suffer more than she would if it looked like she was being easy on you."

She stopped and stared at him for a moment. Could that be true? Dovella performed the maintenance routines perfectly, but Master Avella was always more critical of her work than she was that of the other apprentices.

Master Avella was frowning as Dovella and Narlos rushed into the triangular maintenance room. Few people would have placed the small, fair-haired woman with the ivory skin as Dovella's mother, for Dovella was tall and lanky, with golden-hued skin and shoulder-length hair that was as straight and shiny as polished blackwood. Only their eyes were the same brilliant blue.

They took up their containers of oil and went to their positions. With Master Avella at the centre, Dovella, Narlos and a third apprentice traced a spiral pattern around the room before each one peeled off and walked exactly nine steps to their set of dials on each of the three walls. It took a long time to master walking the spiral properly.

When Master Avella called out, "To the centre," they each put a drop of oil in a small hole at the base of the centre dial on their wall. Following her words, they continued in an intricate pattern, until each dial had received its drop of oil.

Dovella had once asked the reason for the routine: "Why can't one person just go through and oil each of them in turn? It would require far fewer people."

Master Avella had looked angry for a moment, then she'd

shrugged. "I've often wondered the same thing myself, as I'm sure others have. But this is the way we are taught to do it, and it works. It may be that the way the machine is set up, different parts need oil at exactly the same time. And we have to calm our minds so we can control the amount of oil we put in each dial. In any case, the machine is too important for us to take chances with the routine."

When they had finished the oiling, they returned the remaining oil to the vat, carefully twisting their hands outward as they tipped their containers. Dovella caught a quick nod and smile from Avella before her mother's face returned to its usual professional repose.

Dovella stepped back and listened. She was sure the machine was working properly. So why were they getting such a small flow of water? It didn't make sense. Perhaps those performing the routine for cleaning the equipment later in the day would find the problem, but she didn't think so.

Her shift completed, Dovella hung up her robe and changed into tunic and breeches before rushing from the building. She had some herbs to make into a tincture before she went to the afternoon Council meeting. As she hurried down the cobblestone road toward home, worries about her healing ability replaced those concerning the machine.

Dovella had chosen to apprentice with her mother as an engineer, but she was also a gifted healer and often went with her father, Healer Safir, to assist in his work. As a somapath, Dovella took into her own body the wound or disease of the people she touched; she absorbed the injury, transmuted it and sent back waves of healing energy. This was an ability unheard of among Village healers; according to Safir, even the Master Healer could not heal the way she did. Safir couldn't explain her power.

"Keep your gift secret," he'd warned her, "for there are those who would hold it against you."

His warning had frightened her even more than the awareness that she possessed such a healing ability. Was her gift somehow shameful? But how could it be, when she returned people to health?

It had been a hard decision, choosing between being a healer and an engineer. Both vocations had called to her. In the end she had chosen engineering simply because as an engineer she could still help with healing, but would have found no place in engineering had she chosen to apprentice as a healer. And the machine called to her just as strongly as people in pain.

Well, maybe that wasn't the only reason. She had also known that as long as Healer Plais was Master Healer, she would never be fully accepted in Healer's Hall. He couldn't deny her the teaching she'd asked for, couldn't refuse her the Rites of the Healer, even though she was an engineering apprentice, but had she apprenticed as a healer, he could have kept her from going beyond apprentice level, and would surely have done so. According to him, women didn't belong in Healer's Hall, even though he supported women in other high positions. In any case, she wouldn't have been able to keep her healing gift a secret if she'd apprenticed with Plais. And Safir had said she must keep it secret.

Again Dovella shivered, wondering why, as she hurried through the front door and clattered up the stairs to her room. It wasn't much larger than a cell, with space only for a small oak desk and chair, a narrow bed and an intricately carved cabinet for her clothes. The stone walls were bare except for two small tapestries — one in shades of green that she had knotted herself, and a blue one done by Avella. Both of them had been made as Fourteenth Spring projects. An alcove contained a tiny work space, for Safir insisted that she prepare her own herbs.

Using the circular motion she'd been taught, Dovella began pulverizing the herbs for her tincture. She didn't understand why they had to be crushed in such a manner, nor why it should be necessary always to take up the powder using thumb and middle finger. But any time she asked Safir, she got the same kind of answer she got from Avella about the machine: "Following traditional routines keeps us from getting careless and making mistakes."

A few toutile roots for healing oils would help as well, she thought wistfully as she crushed the dried collitflower blossoms. She'd used up all of her oil, and Safir had only a very little left. The toutile plant had once been plentiful in the woods around the Village, but two years back, a disease had seared them, and where toutile once flourished, nothing now grew except scraggly weeds.

That was something else that didn't make sense — unless the blight was connected to the drought. According to the deedstellers, never before had the village suffered such a drought. Some said the gods were angry, but that was just nonsense spread by New School fanatics.

A tap at her door interrupted her work. "Yes?" she called, and her father entered.

He was a tall man with the same dark hair and coppery skin as Dovella, only his eyes were as black as his hair. His smile warmed her. "I've just received word that Councillor Wraller needs to see me," he said.

She immediately put aside her work to join him. She had assisted in Councillor Wraller's healing, and still didn't understand what ailed him.

"The New School physician will be there," Safir warned as they descended to the street. "You must be very careful around him."

New School indeed, she thought, her mouth curved in a sneer. A name they'd chosen, no doubt, to link themselves to the Schoolmen, another group of fanatics who had almost brought destruction on the Village two centuries earlier. And their aims were the same: return to the ways of the Founders. Though no one really knew what the Founders had believed, the New Schoolers had an answer for that: they would determine what the Founder ways were.

Safir paused at the door and gazed at her when she didn't reply. "The New School physician knows me. He will believe I only use healing oils. Even if he doesn't like it, he can't say that the Old Books forbid the use of tinctures and oils. But he can object to ... other ways of healing. Besides, I have the Guild behind me, and that still counts for something." He hesitated, then added urgently, "You know the Guild won't help you, not until you have gone through the Rites."

Reluctantly, Dovella nodded. She was used to having to pretend she was only using herbs and oils rather than her healing gift, but it still chafed, even though she understood why she had to keep her gift a secret. It was dangerous and ... perhaps, even shameful.

As they walked along, she kicked the toe of her boot against a loose stone in the road, then stooped down to shove it back in place. She knew she was acting more like a child than a young woman of sixteen springs; besides, destroying road work wasn't going to influence the Guild. But she hated the pretense.

Until she went through the Rites of the Healer in a few days, the Guild considered her Unbound, and while it could not prevent her from assisting in healing, it would not help her if she got into trouble. "They are absurd rules," she said.

They walked past small shops whose jutting display shelves were filled with Festival decorations. She gave them barely a glance. Although Festival was usually Dovella's favourite season, she felt there was little to celebrate this year.

"Do the Founders' books forbid the use of healing powers?" Dovella didn't know where she got her gift, didn't understand how it worked, but she couldn't see why the New Schoolers should object to it. They should be pleased that healers were able to make people well.

"I don't know. I never had any reason to consult the Old Books before, and now — it's hard to know where to start."

"But if their medicines don't work ..."

"It isn't that they don't work. The Founders' medicines used to work, at least I suppose they did. But who knows whether the New School medicine is the same as that of the Founders?"

They crossed the road to avoid the workers out cleaning and repairing shop walls in anticipation of the coming Festival. The men shouted good-natured instructions and encouragement to one another. Dovella looked around and frowned. By next week, the stone streets would be dry-scrubbed and patched and the dirt roads repacked. Right now, however, they were all filthy and full of holes. Still, it was better here than in the newer parts of the Village; the people here still showed some pride in their shops. She smiled and nodded at the shopkeepers as she and her father walked by.

At Wraller's house, Safir reached for the knocker, but before he could lift it, a young woman flung open the door and motioned them in. Macil, the councillor's younger daughter, the one who had called Safir when the New School doctors had been unable to cure her father, stood clutching at her apron. "Doctor Cagema is here," she whispered. "He's very angry."

With her dark hair and eyes, Macil was clearly of pure Village blood, the same as Safir. Not that it would help her, Dovella thought; not if the New School took over.

Councillor Wraller was propped up in a padded wicker chair, a red pillow pushed behind his head. His arms, once stout and firmly fleshed, lay limp across his thin chest. He had been struck by a virulent fever, and Dovella had feared that she would be unable to heal him. His mouth still held the pinched look of an invalid, but his cheeks had begun to show a tinge of colour.

"You are looking much better, Councillor," Safir said.

"Thanks to you." Councillor Wraller smiled at Dovella, then tilted his head toward the window where a tall man dressed in a black tunic stood looking up at the sky. The man didn't turn, but Dovella noticed his shoulders stiffen slightly.

Dovella and Safir approached the chair, and both touched the councillor's temples, but it was Dovella who gave a slight nod. "The fever is gone," Safir said, "but it will take some time for you to regain your strength. We'll just rub in a little more healing oil, then it's a matter of good food and rest."

He took a vial from his belt and handed it to Dovella, who poured a drop on her fingertips and began massaging

Wraller's temples, focusing her healing powers to strengthen the sick man's own natural defences. Safir always stood beside her so that she could lean against him if the healing drained too much of her energy. Now, to protect her from the threat posed by the New School physician, he examined the councillor.

"I must get back to Council," Wraller said. There was a slight catch in his voice which had become higher, thinner.

Dovella glanced at the other visitor, then back to Wraller. Maybe that was the answer. Councillor Wraller was one of the most outspoken opponents of the New School, and without him, the Council would be more easily swayed. She had never completely understood his fever; it had been quite unlike anything she had ever felt before. She wondered if it could be something induced by the New School physician.

She remembered then that Councillor Wraller's elder daughter and her husband, who had insisted that his father-in-law be tended by a New School physician, were recent converts. She must ask Safir whether the illness might have been caused by tainted food. She didn't like to think a child could do that to her own father, but Dovella knew that the New School demanded complete obedience.

"We all know how much he is needed." The man at the window turned and strode toward Wraller's chair. His sharp nose jutted out over bloodless, twisted lips. "But *we* would like to be sure that he is cured, and not just made to feel better by some hypnotic weeds." He smiled at Councillor Wraller, and his voice softened. "Going back to Council before you are completely healed may well bring about a relapse." He looked at Safir as if daring him to argue.

"The herbs I used are not hypnotic," Safir replied calmly.

"Besides, all the oils we use have a long record of success."

"Our methods — the Founders' methods — were used for healing long before you started with this chicanery."

"The Founders' methods have been lost," Councillor Wraller said, his voice peevish. "It doesn't make sense to discard the medicines that have taken us forward."

"But we haven't moved forward!" Cagema's face went red. Dovella wanted to reach out and touch him, but she knew she must not.

"We've regressed to a misty realm of superstition that our Founders discarded long before they ever came to Edlena." As he spoke, Cagema's long, bony fingers moved constantly, plucking at the folds of his tunic.

"Cagema!" Councillor Wraller's voice, though weak, still had the power to cut through the other man's words. "Do you think that I am unacquainted with the Old Books of our Founders?"

As Master Archivist, Wraller knew what was in the books better than most. He sat forward. "Of course the Founders were a highly advanced people; we can see evidence of that all around us. Our housing, our electricity — none of that would have lasted till this day, otherwise. Deciphering the Old Books can only benefit the Village. We have lost too much of the wisdom and knowledge the Founders brought to Edlena."

Doctor Cagema nodded. "Yes! Yes, and we —"

"But," Councillor Wraller went on, clutching weakly the arms of the chair, "the people cannot study what is hidden from them." He lifted a pale hand and pointed at Cagema. "It is you, you New Schoolers, who want to forbid study of the Old Books."

Cagema's face grew ever redder, and Dovella and Safir moved a few steps away. They couldn't intervene in this confrontation, for anything they said would only make matters worse.

"The Books should be freely available to all," Wraller went on, his voice faltering. "Then we could choose what we want to recover."

"There can be no choice." Cagema's eyes took on the frenzied look found in so many New Schoolers. "All the knowledge of the Founders must be restored. Villagers must return to the Founders' ways. And we intend to see to it that they do."

He stormed from the room, and Councillor Wraller fell back against his pillow. Dovella rushed forward, but the councillor waved her back. "I'm all right, Dovella." He smiled. "I think the fight did me good." Then his face grew grave. "But now you see how vital it is that I get back to Council."

"Yes," Safir said, "and you should be able to return soon. But Cagema is right about one thing: you won't do any good by going back before you are well."

Dovella stepped forward, looked at Wraller. "I never have understood this fever." She hesitated. "I'm not accusing, but ... I have wondered if you've been given something."

"Don't worry," Councillor Wraller said. "I've asked myself the same question. I, too, am loath to make accusations. But Doctor Cagema wanted to take blood today, as he did several times previously. I refused, and it made him very angry. Could he have injected something when he took the blood before?"

"Thank the gods you didn't allow it," Safir said. "I don't know what he might have done, but you don't need to lose blood."

"And he would have tried to blame you. I won't accept any more medication or treatment, except from you. And I'll eat only the food that Macil prepares." Wraller looked at Dovella. "If I'm not mistaken, you are due at Council. You had best run along. Your father can see to me now."

Dovella touched fingers with the councillor, then rushed from the room. She could just make it, if she hurried. She didn't want to run into trouble by being late.

Two

TWELVE BLACK-ROBED MEMBERS OF THE COUNCIL SAT around a polished grey table, its centre inset with three interlinked gears in a darker grey wood. Apart from the table and the thirteen straight-backed chairs, the room was bare, cast in an artificial twilight created by the filters in the window glass that blocked direct sunlight. Nothing could be seen of the surrounding buildings.

In her place by the door of the chamber, Dovella stood at attention. She wore leggings and a tunic of olive green, embroidered with an emblem much like the symbol in the centre of the table. As she scanned the circular room, assessing the mood, she felt the tension; like swamp fog, tentacles of fear and malice reached out to encircle first one councillor and then another. She took a deep, steadying breath.

Usually the councillors engaged in a great deal of bickering, but today they remained silent, some looking down at their hands, others smiling smugly, as Havkad, the Associate Engineer, spoke. He stared at Master Engineer Avella, who returned his gaze with apparent calm.

"We need to renew the rituals of the machine, bring meaning to them again," he said. "Our devotion to the gods demands it."

Dovella's lips pursed with scorn. Again she scanned those

seated around the table. Pandil, Master of Security, would have spoken, but as she was chairing Council meetings this season, the rules demanded that she take no part in debates, and vote only to break a tie. And Councillor Wraller's chair was empty. But the others? Cowards, all of them. Or, worse yet, in league with Havkad. She curled her hands into fists and glared at him.

Havkad shifted in his chair, and it rasped across the burnished floor. "There are times when change is needed." His eyes, hard and predatory, moved slowly around the room before returning to Avella, and his mouth twisted into a smile that made Dovella squirm.

Around the walls stood other apprentices, among them Carpace, also bound to Avella. Carpace watched Havkad with avid eyes, a faint smile curving her lips. Perhaps she felt Dovella watching her, for she turned her head, and when she met Dovella's gaze, she stiffened and looked away.

"Would you hold back progress?" Havkad's voice was soft, but Dovella felt her heart beat faster; that control made him all the more dangerous.

Avella's blue eyes glittered. "What you suggest would take us back into some dark age of superstition." She smoothed a strand of fair hair behind one ear, a gesture that told Dovella her mother was fighting to govern her temper.

"You deny there are gods?" Havkad's voice was sly, wheedling, but Avella was too shrewd to fall into so obvious a trap.

She threw open her hands and smiled, a wide, innocent smile. "The gods I do not deny." Then her face hardened. "But I've seen no evidence that you and your cultists speak for them."

Havkad and his followers had worked hard to convince people that the New School represented a return to the true religion; they had recruited followers from the educated and wealthy as well as from the poor. Havkad had kindled a fire in his devotees with his talk of the Village opening new territory, perhaps even invading the lands of the Hill Folk again. He had also managed to convince the more fervent that the gods were displeased with the current leaders. He would not forgive Avella for dismissing the New School as a cult, nor would the other New School supporters who sat on Council.

Havkad's dark eyes went flat and he clenched his fleshy hands on top of the table, but his voice remained calm. "If it's evidence you want —"

"I'm sure you could manufacture it," Avella broke in. "But as long as I am Master Engineer, I will not allow the workings of the machine to be made into more of a mystery than they are already; nor will I and my apprentices become cult priestesses and priests."

The two stared at each other for a moment, then Havkad flicked his hand as if swatting away an insect. "And have you ascertained the source of the machine's problem?"

The *source*. That reminded Dovella of the Old Books she'd read. Could the problem really be at the source?

According to New School teachings, the failure of the machine was a sign of the gods' displeasure. Unless Avella could suggest measures for restoring water flow, she would lose her position as Master Engineer; and without her influence, the Council might well be swayed to support the New School, especially if Councillor Wraller's illness persisted.

Dovella shivered at the prospect. Already people were afraid, and only the strongest resisted the New Schoolers' constant intimidation — witness the silence of her mother's supporters today. If the New Schoolers convinced enough people that only they could fathom the sacred mystery of the machine, they would be able to do whatever they wanted; no one would dare speak against them then. And it would go ill for those like Avella and Pandil who had dared fight them. Indeed, it would go ill for many people: healers, archivists — anyone that Villagers held in esteem. Anyone who did not support the New School.

They couldn't let that happen! But she and everyone else in the Engineering Guild had been over the machine a hundred times, and found nothing wrong. Nothing wrong *here*. An idea began to form. What if she went to the source?

Havkad heaved his squat body from the chair, breathing heavily from the exertion, and smiled, a small, satisfied twitch of the lips. "I don't think you know anything about the machine."

"And you do?" Avella faced him without flinching.

"Two weeks. That is when we meet again." His black eyes moved slowly around the table before returning to Avella. "Unless you have restored power by our next assembly, I shall move that you be discharged from your position, and someone more suitable installed." Everyone knew who that would be.

Dovella crossed her arms, hugging her fists, as she watched Havkad stride away from the table, a smirk on his lips. Anyone not enslaved by New School fanaticism knew what would come of his elevation. He must be very sure of his support or he would never have threatened Avella in front of the Council.

Shifting in their seats, the other members of the High

Council sneaked furtive looks at one another, some smiling, others not, but all avoiding Avella's eyes as they stood and scuttled away, their black robes rustling. They avoided Dovella's gaze as well, all except old Councillor Staver. He met her gaze, his eyes filled with shame and fear. But at least he'd had the courage to face her.

After the councillors, the other apprentices filed out, Carpace smiling slyly. Two of Pandil's apprentices waited by the door. The younger one smiled at Dovella and she felt herself redden. She turned quickly, hoping Jael wouldn't see her confusion. This was no time to be thinking of how he made her pulse quicken.

She hurried over to the table where her mother sat with Master Pandil. During the meeting, she'd thought more and more about her idea; she would have to convince Avella to let her look for the source.

Pandil was shaking her head. Tall, lean and large-boned, Pandil looked more like Dovella than her mother did, except for her sable eyes. "What will you do?" she asked.

"There is little I can do." Avella's voice was heavy. "It has been ages since Master Engineer meant anything other than head caretaker. The workings of the machine have always been thought to be infallible, to need nothing but watching, oiling and occasional adjustment." She laughed wryly. "In fact, little more that the empty ritual that Havkad wants made part of his religion. We have manuals enough for that, but nothing that tells us how the machine works."

"May I speak, Master Engineer?" As an apprentice, Dovella took care to address her mother formally in public. Avella turned with a scowl, then nodded.

"I think I know what ails the machine," Dovella said.

"How is it that you know more than your Master?" Pandil's voice grated.

"I've been studying the Old Books." Curiosity had made Dovella start reading, and interest had sent her back on subsequent occasions. She had taken care not to let the old Engineering Archivist see her, not that he had shown much interest in what she read. He'd probably assumed that young people like her despised the old learning.

Avella and Pandil stared at her in dismay. The New School discouraged study of the Old Books by anyone except their own leaders; already they had begun taking careful note of anyone who showed too much interest in the archives.

"Were you seen?" Avella blurted out.

But before Dovella could answer, Pandil broke in. "What did you find?"

"I think the problem may be caused by the source water. For some reason, it no longer flows strongly enough."

Avella bit her lip, then looked at Pandil. "It's possible. I've been assuming there is something wrong with the machine itself, but the failure could be at the source."

Pandil studied Dovella's face. "You do know how critical this is?"

"I know what the New School people would like to do." What had happened to Councillor Wraller could easily happen to others. She told Pandil and her mother of her suspicions about his illness. "I would like permission to go to the source and find out what is wrong before they gain complete control."

Avella shook her head. "Even if what you say is true, repairing the fault is beyond us. Besides, we aren't even sure where the source water is." Avella pushed back her chair and rose. Pacing back and forth, she ran the palm of one hand across the knuckles of the other. "Havkad and his crew would have it that the water comes from the gods."

Pandil shifted in her chair and looked at Dovella. "Do you know where it comes from?" Her tone had softened; now she seemed ready to listen even though Avella clearly wanted the subject dropped.

"Not exactly. One volume of the Old Books — and I think it's the one that tells about the source — is missing; but according to the maps I've seen, the water comes from a lake beyond the mountains."

"You see! The Raiders would have you before you were a day's journey from the Village; and even if you managed to avoid them, you would still have to worry about the Outlanders." Avella's voice sounded unsteady.

"I've gone through self-defence training and ..."

Avella shook her head. "At the very least it would take ten days to get to the other side of the mountain."

Dovella fought to keep her voice calm. She wouldn't win her mother with emotion, only with reason. "We can't let the New School take over without a fight."

"Then I should be the one to go." Avella walked back and dropped into her chair. She ran her hands across her face and through her hair.

"I can't hold off Havkad alone," Pandil said. "Between the two of us, we might keep him from calling a hasty assembly of Council, but I could not do that without you. Even if Councillor Wraller is able to return in time, I need you here. Besides, you would be missed; even if you pleaded illness, some-one would find out. Dovella's absence could be covered up."

"And what would she do if she got there?" Avella asked.

"We don't even fully understand the working of the machine here."

Pandil laughed softly. "Why don't you admit the real reason? You fear for Dovella's safety."

Avella reddened, then rose and walked over to caress Dovella's face. "Of course, I do." Her voice trembled. "How can I not?"

"I understand your fear, but it's our only hope." Pandil smiled. "She's a resourceful young woman."

"It's far too dangerous." Avella's voice broke, and she looked away.

"Isn't the alternative even more so?" Dovella asked.

"You can't dispute that," Pandil said softly as she joined them. "I understand that you don't want your daughter to go into danger, but her position will be perilous if Havkad gains control." She touched Avella's hand. "She's no longer a child, Avella; she's a woman now."

"I know." Avella smiled and turned back to her daughter. "If it can be done, child, you can do it. You have a feel for the machine that the rest of us lack." Avella looked back at Pandil, then shook her head. "I doubt that she will get her father's blessing for this. In four days time she's due to go through the Rites."

Dovella moistened her lips and looked away. How could she have forgotten? Even though she was in training to be an engineer, she still had a healer's gift. A healer's obligations. For four springs now, she'd been looking forward to the day when she would finally receive the Medallion of the Healer. If she missed the Rites, she would always feel she had been deprived, and not just of the medallion, important as that was.

She couldn't miss the Rites. The journey would have to wait. Surely four days wouldn't hurt.

Dovella opened her mouth, then closed it. Of course, it would hurt; waiting four days meant that even if the trip went well, she wouldn't reach the source before two weeks had passed. If she didn't leave right away, the Village might not survive.

Blinking back tears, she clenched her hands behind her back. "I must try."

Avella gazed at her daughter for a moment, then smiled softly. "If your father will permit it, then you have my blessing."

Dovella trudged up the steep staircase to her father's workroom, wondering how to convince him that she must undertake this journey ... wondering how to convince *herself* that what she'd chosen to do was right. If she missed the Rites, she would never have another chance to become a member of the Guild. The Master Healer was far too rigid to make an exception, no matter how good her reason for being absent. In fact, he'd be pleased to see her miss the Rites.

At the top of the stairs, Dovella sank down on the stone steps and buried her face in her hands. But I have to go, she thought. There's no other way. Slowly she pushed herself to her feet, straightened her shoulders and shoved open the door.

Safir sat hunched over his books at the cherry-wood desk, his dark head propped on one hand. Through the narrow windows sunlight flowed, but Safir's desk stood in a shadowy corner. Red candles burned brightly in a tall holder on the desk and in polished wall sconces. Since the rationing of power first began, Safir had worked mostly by the light of candles, which he made himself. He was determined that no one could accuse Avella of using more than her share of power.

A fire burned on the grate, for even on late spring days like this, the tower still held the winter's chill. Dovella glanced around the familiar room, and her throat tightened. This had always been her favourite place. Rich carpets in vibrant blues and golds, ruby reds and creams warmed the stone floor, and bookshelves and tapestries in muted gold and peach and blue covered the stone walls. All these things had been in Safir's family for generations.

In an alcove stood his work table, with its vials of liquids and jars of herbs and salves, and a locked wooden cabinet with richly carved doors. How often she had played in front of that cabinet, running her fingers over the carvings of intertwined leaves and fruit.

Safir looked up and rose from his chair, his black eyes luminous with delight at seeing her, a delight that faded as she related what had happened at the meeting.

"Something has to be done," she said. Drawing a deep breath, she set out her plan, and he listened without interruption.

"It is serious if he dared threaten your mother," he said at last. "But have you fully considered both the dangers and whether you can accomplish anything?"

Dovella clasped her hands to her chest and looked away. She had asked herself the same question. "I know it may be for nothing." She looked at him again. "But I see no other way."

Safir walked over to the window, his lower lip caught

between a thumb and forefinger. The sunlight made his black hair shine. He turned to study her for a moment. "You may be right."

"What of the Rites?" she burst out. "Even if I have chosen to be an engineer, I still want to be a healer."

He came over, cupped her chin in his hand and lifted her face. When she raised her eyes, he smiled. "The Rites are designed by man, for man's purposes. The gift comes from the gods."

She felt her shoulders relax and reached out to take his hand. "Then I'll not lose the gift?" Much as she feared it, she wanted to keep it.

"The gift can wither, as your legs would wither if you didn't use them; but no one will forbid the use of your gift — unless the New Schoolers come to power; then all the rules would change."

"We have to stop them," she said; "but if I miss the Rites ..."

"Without the Rites, you won't be accepted into the Guild, so you won't get further teaching, nor have access to their supplies."

"Father ..." She hesitated, afraid that what she was thinking was blasphemy, yet unable to excise the question from her mind. "Are the herbs that important?"

She had expected him to show dismay, but he only shook his head. "A gifted healer such as you might well be able to heal without the herbs, but it's perilous. And therefore forbidden."

Safir led her to a wooden bench in front of a window, and pulled her down beside him. The sunshine warmed her shoulders. "Without the aid of the fruits of the earth," he said, "it is too easy for a healer to forget that the gift comes from the gods, and as a result grow proud. Such pride is fatal to the gift, and dangerous to both healer and the one in need of healing. Besides, the herbs do assist in some measure, though we don't understand why. Perhaps it is the gods' way of reminding us that they hold the power and that we, like the herbs, are only their instruments. Don't ever think of healing without them, Dovella. It will destroy you."

"Is that why the Rites are so important then — to gain admittance to the Guild?"

He hesitated for a moment, his eyes holding hers. "The experience of the Rites ... I can't tell you more, Dovella, but make no mistake, the Rites are important, as is the Guild, in ways I cannot begin to name."

Safir pulled her into his arms and kissed her forehead, then held her away and looked into her eyes. "As much as I should like to see you go through the Rites, I accept the need for this journey. But I don't want you to go alone. Take Zagoad with you, at least."

Dovella stiffened. Zagoad was a Forester that Safir had met a few years back on one of his forays into the forest searching for herbs. Dovella knew that the young man held her father's trust, but she had always found him intimidating even though he was only three years older than she.

"He's an experienced guide, and he knows the ways of the Hill Folk," Safir went on, giving her no time to object. "He might persuade them to give you safe passage through the mountains. That would shorten your journey."

Dovella drew back and stared at him. Everyone knew that the Hill Folk denied the true gods. They worshipped ancient idols and followed evil ways. Surely they were far more dangerous than the Raiders, or even the New Schoolers.

"Trust the Hill Folk?"

He smiled gently. "You fear them because you don't know them."

"They are our enemies!"

"Once they were our friends. When our ancestors had to flee their first home, it was the Hill Folk who gave them land here in the Village; they shared their food until Villagers were able to provide their own, and taught our healers most of what we know about healing. Even our Guild Rites began with the Hill Folk, and we still hold a place in the ritual to honour Khanti-Lafta, their Great Healer." He sighed. "I almost wish I could go with you. Perhaps I could find the herbs we need to replenish our medicine stores."

"They slaughtered Villagers!" She pressed her lips together, startled at her vehemence. How could he defend such people? And who knew what kind of healing practices they followed now? Probably theirs were even more dangerous than her own.

Safir looked at her sharply. "Where did you hear this?"

"It's in all of the deeds books. " Dovella stared at him, challenging him to deny her words.

"I am not a deedsrecorder, but I don't think you know the whole story. Ask Zagoad."

"Is he a deedsrecorder?" Knowing her father's regard for Zagoad, she tried to keep the scorn from her voice.

He laughed. "You know he is not. But a woodsman knows many things that are not in the records. There is much you can learn from him, and he would keep you safe."

"By giving me to the Hill Folk?" She could barely conceal her revulsion.

"Zagoad tells me they attack only those who invade their hills uninvited." His voice had taken on a sharper note, and

Dovella expected him to pursue the argument, but he only said, "I will give my permission if you go with him."

She crossed her arms, opened her mouth to protest, then shrugged. She recognized that her father had made up his mind. If accepting Zagoad as her guide was the only way she could gain her father's permission, so be it. But she was not going to allow the Forester to deliver her into the hands of her enemies.

Without waiting for an answer, her father went to his cabinet and began preparing a medicine belt. She watched as he drained his healing oil into a vial.

"I can't take the last of your oil, Father." Once it was gone, there would be no more unless they could find a way to cure the blight on the toutile plants.

Safir didn't reply. When he finished preparing the belt, he brought it to her. He kissed her brow and cupped his hands over her eyes. "The gods go with you."

She placed her hands over his and bowed her head. The gods should be sufficient, she thought, but if she must have Zagoad accompany her, then she must. Best to accept that and get on with her preparations for the journey.

Dovella stared at the things lying on her bed. There was very little, considering that she would be gone several weeks, but even this small amount would soon get heavy. She needed the cloak, for despite the sunny spring weather, it still got cool at night. The small bedroll, though it seemed like a luxury, was something her father had always insisted was worth the weight. "If you are cold and wet, you get little sleep; and rest is essential when you are making a long expedition through the forest," he'd said. "Fatigue is your greatest enemy." Besides that and her medicine belt, she had a waterskin, a food pouch, a knife, a tin for boiling water, a small drying cloth and two changes of clothes.

Zagoad was sure to think it was too much.

She looked at the knife and sighed. It would do for skinning the rabbits they would be eating for dinner, assuming Zagoad was as good a Forester as he was said to be, but it would be of little use against a real fighting knife. Of course, it was Zagoad's job to ensure she wouldn't need a fighting knife.

She knew she was being unfair. She couldn't fault her father for choosing a Forester as her guide. The men and women who worked as guides had a strong code of behaviour, and disciplined severely anyone who broke it. But she found it hard to be fair to Zagoad, even though she barely knew him. Partly it was jealousy of the regard Safir had for the young man — she knew that; but mostly, it was the way Zagoad viewed all Village women, as if they were good for nothing but sewing fine seams.

FALs, the Foresters named them, for Fine Aristocratic Ladies; but the word was usually pronounced *vols*, the name of a fat, lazy, farm animal. Maybe Village women didn't have Forester skills, but they worked hard, and many of them, like Avella and Pandil, held responsible jobs. Dovella resented the attitude she sensed whenever she was around him, and now she would be subjected to it for weeks. Well, he'd better possess superior skills, she thought spitefully; they were unlikely to make the trip without meeting Raiders, or at least renegade Outlanders.

It was then it struck her that she really was going to face the dangers her parents and Pandil so feared. Going to leave home. Would she ever see it again?

Three

DOVELLA SLUMPED DOWN IN A CHAIR AND GAZED AROUND her room, inhaling the mingled scent of wax and herbs, and had to bite her lip to keep from crying. She would miss all this, and no matter how brave she had pretended to be when she talked to her mother and Pandil, she had to admit she was frightened: frightened of Zagoad, of the trip, of what she would find when she got to the source water — if she ever did — and of what would happen here in the Village while she was gone. Most of all, she was frightened of running into the Hill Folk.

A rap at the door, a rap unlike the quiet knock of her father or the finger taps of her mother, startled her. "Yes?" She stood, smoothed her tunic and straightened her shoulders. The door opened, and Master Pandil stepped in, carrying a package under her arm.

Dressed in her grey Security uniform, her red cloak draped over her shoulders, she smiled and walked over to the bed to glance at the items lying there. She nodded, moved the chair from the desk over near the bed and placed her package on the floor as she sat down. She motioned for Dovella to sit. "Do you understand the dangers you will be encountering?"

"Probably not," Dovella admitted, knowing she had to be honest. "But Havkad is an even greater threat."

"And from what my people tell me, he's been dabbling in the black arts as well."

"Sorcery?" How could Master Pandil believe in such a thing?

Pandil shrugged. "Some of the original settlers had strange powers."

"Who?"

"They were called the Plains People. We've lost much of our knowledge about them. The Hill Folk might know; I understand their archives are in good shape."

Dovella sniffed. "Why should we believe what they've written?"

"You know the Hill Folk?" Pandil voice was sharp.

Chin jutting forward, Dovella said, "I learned about them in school."

"A plague on such school masters!" Pandil paused. "Look, I expect there was some truth in what you were taught, but I doubt that you learned the whole truth. In any case, I'm afraid that Havkad may have found a way to call up some power, or at least to convince his followers that he has, which is almost as bad."

Dovella looked away, embarrassed that Pandil could be so superstitious.

Pandil studied her for a moment. "You reject the idea of powers beyond ourselves?"

"Well ... yes. We have our minds and that's enough. We've lost a lot of our knowledge, but we could regain it, if we just put our minds to it."

"And your healing power, could we all have that if we put our minds to it?" She smiled at Dovella's expression of surprise. "Yes, I know about it, though few do."

"But I ... I don't know." Dovella felt herself flush. Her gift was not something she wanted to talk about. "I don't know why I have it."

"Exactly. It's a gift, a gift we don't understand. And there may be others with gifts we don't understand, gifts which may well be used for ill."

Dovella grimaced. "I suppose."

"No matter," Pandil said. "The important thing right now is for you to restore water flow."

She picked up the package she had brought with her, and pulled from it a knife and scabbard. "You've been trained well, but I doubt that you have a decent weapon."

Dovella gasped, for the knife was magnificent. The hilt of carved blackwood fit her hand as if made for it, and the blade was weighted and honed to perfection. "Oh, Master Pandil! It's the most beautiful knife I've ever seen."

Pandil smiled, then became serious. "Just remember, although you are well trained, you can't rely solely on that, because your opponents may be equally well trained. Watch your opponent, watch his eyes, his shoulders. Be ready for the unexpected, and be ready to do the unexpected."

She reached back into the parcel and drew out a pair of grey boots, stitched with intricate designs. "These are soft, but they're tough. And look here." She touched one of the designs and a little pocket opened revealing a thinner knife. "It's not as good as the fighting knife, but it is well to have something in reserve."

"Master Pandil, thank you. I ..." Dovella couldn't find the words.

"I wish I could send you with a magic amulet, but unfortunately I don't have one." Pandil laughed. "And no doubt you wouldn't believe in it anyway. Well, never mind. Go with the blessings of the gods, or whatever blessing you will accept."

"Thank you, Master Pandil. I will accept any blessing you give."

Pandil's fingers moved to her chest, lightly fingering something she wore under her tunic, but then she gave a little shake to her head. "I'm sure you will find your own blessings."

Awakened the next morning by a touch on her shoulder, Dovella struggled up onto her elbows, and blinked her eyes. In the candlelight, she could see Safir holding a steaming mug. She sat up and took the stoneware mug, inhaling the aroma. Macha, a mild stimulant, but one her father must have judged she would need. She leaned back against a feather pillow and held the mug against her chest. "Why are you using a candle?"

"Pandil thought it best not to draw attention with too much light."

Dovella went very still, then began to tremble. The need for stealth in her own home told her more strongly than anything else just what danger they faced. She took a sip of the hot liquid and tried to calm herself.

Safir touched her shoulder again, and she twisted her head over to rub her cheek against his hand. "Wash and dress," he said, "and then come to breakfast."

Dovella nodded, took another swallow of the drink and put the mug on the table. She threw back the covers and swung her long legs over the side of the bed. Shivering, she ran across the icy floor to the bathroom, the cold shooting through her feet. The bathroom was a luxury, she knew. Only the houses that had been kept in good repair still had baths such as theirs. It would be wonderful to have a leisurely soak in hot, scented water, but there was no time. Besides, she had already taken the one full bath she was allowed this week.

Standing on a fluffy rug, she soaked a cloth in the basin of soapy water and rubbed it over her body, then rinsed as well as she could; this might still be the best bath she would have for some time. Pandil had said that Zagoad would understand, but Dovella was sure he would think her need for cleanliness another sign of FAL frippery.

She raced back to her room to pull on breeches of brown tarvelcloth, tough enough to withstand the snag of briars and twigs, warm enough for the evening chill, yet still comfortable during the midday heat. A light shirt, a sip of macha and then a heavier tunic over the shirt. She brushed and braided her hair, gulped the last mouthful of macha and hurried into the kitchen.

Avella sat with her elbows resting on the table, her face buried in her hands, and Safir stood beside her, stroking her fair hair. When Dovella came into the room, they looked up. Avella's eyes were rimmed in red.

Safir smiled and pulled out a chair. "I know it's early, but you must have strength, and it will be some hours before it will be safe for you to break your journey for food."

Avella had prepared porridge with okerberries and had bought fresh oat bread, sharp cheese and thin slices of wild chofowl — all Dovella's favourite breakfast foods — so, despite the hour, Dovella found herself eating with relish. The sweet-tart taste of the okerberries increased her appetite.

"I've put the rest of the chofowl in your pouch," Avella

said. Shadows circled her eyes. "As long as you eat it today, it will be fine, but don't keep it until tomorrow."

"We'd best be on our way," Safir said.

"We?" For just a moment she felt a lightness of mind, followed by a cold lump in her chest when she realized that it could not be so.

"Just down to the park. Anyone hearing steps go down will hear steps return."

"Oh, dear gods, I wish I were the one going, or at least going with you, but Pandil says I mustn't." Avella looked away as her eyes filled with tears.

"You know she's right," Safir said.

"I feel useless. If I could just do something, but I dare not even send for books from the archives lest Havkad become suspicious of my sudden interest."

"Send Narlos," Dovella suggested. "You can trust him, and he's good at escaping notice."

"How do you know that if you saw him?" A brief smile touched Avella's lips.

"I was escaping notice too."

Avella laughed, and reached out to touch Dovella's hand. "That's a good idea. I'll send the apprentices."

"But not Carpace," Dovella said quickly.

Avella went still, and her smile vanished. "Why not? She's a good apprentice."

"I know, but ... I'm not sure, and perhaps I shouldn't say it, but I've got a bad feeling about Carpace. Something about the way she and Havkad are so careful never to look at each other at meetings, and yet I've seen them in conversation."

"She is an apprentice, and he's the Associate Engineer. And you don't exactly run to greet me when we're at work."

"No, but I don't avoid meeting your glance." She shook her head, unsure how to convey her suspicions. "I think she sees him someplace besides work. Sometimes she smells just like him."

Safir frowned. "Not everyone has the advantage of a bathroom, Dovella. You shouldn't hold that against them."

"I don't mean that way." She swallowed hard, hurt that he could believe she might think herself above others. "It's that scent Havkad wears." She turned to Avella. "You must have noticed it. He reeks of it sometimes."

Avella nodded slowly. "It's some kind of incense, something the New Schoolers use at their meetings, I think."

"Well, sometimes Carpace smells of it, too; and I don't think she could take on that much of the scent just from talking to Havkad. I may be wrong, but please be careful about trusting her too much. Please."

"Not all New Schoolers are fanatics. Still, if it will put you at ease, I promise to be careful."

But she wouldn't, Dovella knew. Avella was never swayed by vague feelings. She would trust Carpace unless Dovella could give her a good reason not to. And she had none to give.

"Now we really must go," Safir said. "You are supposed to meet Zagoad before it gets light."

She glanced at Avella again, then nodded and went to her room, pulled on her new boots, buckled her medicine belt and strapped on her knife. As she neared the door, she stopped, strode back to the desk and yanked open the bottom drawer. She would take her slingshot. Maybe she wasn't as good as Zagoad with his bow, but she could always bring down a rabbit or a fowl if she needed to. She wouldn't be dependent on him for all their food. See then what he had to say about FALs.

Avella was waiting at the front door. She embraced Dovella, then handed her the food pouch and waterskin. "The gods go with you."

Safir took up his staff and opened the door, then shut it behind them a bit harder than Dovella thought necessary. He went down the stairs with heavy steps, though he was careful not to let the staff touch the treads. No one could say later that there had been a furtive exit from the building.

"I had your mother put several packets of macha leaves in your pouch," he said. "You shouldn't drink it every day, but it's good to have some. There are also packets of assorted herbs. People you meet on your journey will give you food, and in some cases a place to sleep. They won't accept payment, but will be glad of some herbs."

"Thank you, Father. I should have thought of that."

"You have enough to think of. Now, I know you aren't fond of Zagoad, but once you get to know him, you'll see he's a good man. Just be patient with him, as you will want him to be patient with you. He'll take care of you. You'll have fresh food, for he's good with his bow."

Dovella sniffed. "I've got my sling."

"So you have." She heard the smile in his voice. "Well, between the two of you, you'll feast."

"Father." She hesitated. She didn't want to worry him with what Pandil had said, and yet she needed his assurance that it *was* nonsense. "Last night, Master Pandil was talking about sorcery. Surely there's nothing in that."

For a moment he remained silent. Then, "I don't know, Dovella. There are many powers we don't understand, and if they can be used for good, why surely they can also be used for evil." He put his hands on her shoulders, and looked into her eyes. "Just remember this," he said, his voice firm, "anything conjured by the mind can be defeated by the mind."

As they walked on, the old buildings gave way to newer structures, many whose facades were already crumbling. Frowning, Dovella looked around at the small shops they passed, with their half-rotten boards and missing bricks. More had been forgotten than just the technology that provided power and water. The house where they lived had stood for four centuries, but it was in better condition than these buildings of less than a hundred years old. And the newer buildings, further on, were shoddier still. Even these small shops, new as they were, had bricks missing, boards that were rotting or crumbling plaster. As they walked past the bakery, Dovella paused to inhale the yeasty aroma of baking bread, and her mouth watered. She glanced through the window, and by the dim light of the lantern hanging over the baker's board in the rear saw a pile of Edlenal wreaths. Then she stopped abruptly and stared — there on the wall of the shop, someone had scrawled the word "Heresy" in white paint.

She clutched her father's arm. "That's it," she said. "The Festival. Havkad's planning something for the time of Festival. That's the reason for his deadline."

four

Dovella pointed to the wreaths of bread. "The Edlenal."

Edlenal was a popular holiday, though few Villagers still believed in the legend of the Silver Goddess. For more than two hundred years, religious leaders had tried to discourage the celebration, saying that veneration of the Goddess was a heresy derived from the Hill Folk. They had stamped out such worship in the Village, making sure that only the unnamed gods were honoured, but Villagers clung to Edlenal. And the Edlenal bread was a constant reminder of the origins of the holiday. Made of four interwoven ropes of dough, each filled with nuts and seeds and dried fruits, tied into a garland and topped with tiny candied figures of animals and birds, it would always make people think of the four families born of the great Goddess, and the animals and plants born with them.

"With all the Outlanders coming to the Village, it will be an ideal time for Havkad to make his challenge."

"I've no doubt Pandil has thought of that," Safir said, "but I'll mention it to her all the same." He rubbed his chin. "We'll need to find another excuse for your absence from work. Despite your studies, people will be looking for you to attend a few parties."

Dovella felt a twinge of disappointment, for she had always enjoyed the dances at Festival, and she'd hoped to see Jael there this year. She felt herself flush as she remembered Narlos's teasing, and shook her head, as if to dislodge the thought. No time for that now. "What should we do?"

"Don't worry. I can make up an illness to explain your absence." He touched her cheek, and she reached up to place her hand over his. "You must concentrate on your quest. You can't do your job if you are constantly worried about the Village."

She nodded, but she knew it would be impossible. How could she not worry?

They crossed the stone street. Safir stopped at the edge of the park. "This is as far as I go."

She'd known he'd have to leave her, but even so it was hard to keep her voice calm. "Thank you for coming with me."

He embraced Dovella, then stepped back and handed her his staff.

"But, Father, you'll need it."

"I won't be doing any work in the forest for a while, and I don't use it around the Village. If it becomes a burden, leave it somewhere." He leaned over and kissed her on the forehead. "The gods go with you, Dovella, make your journey successful and bring you home safely." Then he turned and walked rapidly away.

Dovella watched until Safir disappeared, then pulling her cloak more tightly around her, she stepped onto the path. The darkness here was pleasant, almost soothing; but having to walk through the streets of New Village would be another matter entirely. Zagoad would probably have been willing to meet her on the far side of the park, but after she'd made such a fuss about being able to make the entire journey on her own, she couldn't admit that she was uneasy about crossing her own village. She touched the hilt of her knife; even if she did run into a troublemaker, she had nothing to be afraid of. Probably no one about anyway. The inhabitants of New Village were noted for carousing in the taverns and brawling in the streets until long after midnight and then idling in bed until the sun was high.

Once she entered the park, her apprehension melted away. Although it was even darker here than on the streets, she had Safir's staff to feel out the path and could immerse herself in the fragrances around her. The zalebush had the most powerful bouquet, but it didn't overpower the spicy perfume of the gold-flowered bakul and the wild roses. And mingled with it all, the resinous smell of the evergreens. She almost forgot time as she attempted to sort out the various scents, and only snapped back to reality at the other edge of the park.

She paused for a moment to listen before she stepped out, but the streets were silent, the only signs of life the feral cats scrounging for food. They scuttled away as she approached. At the best of times, very few streetlamps in New Village worked, but now, with the power shortages, they were all dark. Fortunately, bright Lucella was in the sky, though scarcely half full, and she could see a sliver of green Gaeltan. In two weeks, all three of Edlena's moons would be full simultaneously, something that happened only once every twenty-five springs. In such a year Festival took on added importance, another reason for the New Schoolers to have chosen this time to escalate their attack.

Dovella pulled up the hood of her cloak and made her

way along the cobblestone road, which was littered with garbage and animal droppings. She grimaced as she passed the houses she could barely make out in the darkness. They were bleak and shabby, she knew, for all that they were much newer than the ones where she lived. The small dirt yards were bare, though some had a straggle of weeds.

Noting a thin streak of pearly grey on the horizon, Dovella quickened her steps. If she was late, Zagoad would be furious, and that was no way to start the trip.

As she neared the end of the street, Dovella heard a scuffling coming from around the corner. She stopped and looked frantically for a place to hide. She darted into a recessed doorway, pulled Safir's staff close to her chest and pressed herself against the door.

First the pale glow from a lantern appeared, followed a moment later by two figures. Dovella let out her breath when they crossed the road. One of them was unknown to Dovella, but the stout one she recognized. She steadied herself against the wall. What was Havkad doing in this part of town, and before daybreak at that?

The two men approached a house further down the street; Havkad opened the door, and he and the stranger disappeared inside. This was something Pandil should know about, but Dovella dared not go back. She rubbed a thumb across her knuckles, trying to think of some plan. Waiting for them to disappear had delayed her just enough that she would barely arrive on time, and Zagoad would surely have some comment about FALs who couldn't get out of their beds.

About to step out of the doorway, she heard more footsteps approaching. She huddled against the door again and clasped the staff tighter. Her hands felt damp, but her throat was dry.

It sounded like more than one person, and they were in a hurry. Perhaps they, too, were late. Three Villagers came into view; Dovella recognized one of them — Avella's apprentice, Carpace. Gripping the staff tighter, Dovella wished she could bring it down on the girl's head. She should have tried harder to convince her mother that Carpace was in Havkad's camp. Avella had promised to be careful, but would she be careful enough, or would she dismiss Dovella's warning as jealousy?

When they too had disappeared into the house, Dovella stepped out and listened. Nothing, except her own breathing. She swallowed hard, and set off at a fast pace. The sky was still dark and thick with stars when she saw the wall looming ahead, but the streak of grey on the horizon had widened. Half wishing that she were still in bed, Dovella pulled her frielskin cloak tighter against the morning chill and increased her pace. She was almost out of breath when she spotted Zagoad, standing in the shadows.

He was only a little taller than Dovella, slender but wiry with long, muscular arms and broad shoulders. His people had been woodsmen for generations, acting as guides for Villagers such as her father on treks deep into the forest; supplying game to the Village for food and clothing; carrying messages to and between Outlanders; and probably, Dovella thought, acting as spies for the Council. Or, perhaps, for someone else.

People maintained that Zagoad was of Hill Folk blood, but they said that about anyone with fair hair and blue eyes, even Avella. That would be used against her, too, if Dovella was unsuccessful. But she would succeed, she told herself; she must. Not only for Avella's sake, but for the entire Village. And that meant she had to rely on Zagoad, no matter how she felt about him.

She waved and rushed forward, trying to pretend she was pleased to see him. The bundle he carried on his back was not much larger than her own, but he also carried two bows and a quiver of arrows, as well as two knives and a hatchet which hung from his belt. He, too, was dressed in tarvelcloth breeches and wore a brown tunic, open at the neck.

Although he looked impatient, he said nothing, only shushed her abruptly when she tried to speak, and gestured for her to follow him through a tunnel that had long since been half filled with rubble.

She touched his arm. "Zagoad, I have to go back."

"Quiet," he snarled. She could only follow, but she was determined to stop him when they reached the safety of the woods beyond. On the far side of the wall, he paused. "Why were you so late?" Although he spoke quietly, his voice was sharp. "It will be full light by the time we reach the edge of the forest."

She wanted to protest that he was being unfair, for she hadn't really been late, but her news was more important. "I had to dodge Havkad, and a stranger. I need to get word to Pandil."

He scowled and mumbled something she couldn't hear, but she imagined that it wasn't flattering. "Did he see you?"

"I hid in a doorway, but I've got to let Pandil know. And my mother. Carpace and two others were there too."

"Wait a minute." He held up a hand and drew a breath as if trying to control his words. "Who is Carpace?"

"Carpace is one of my mother's apprentices. I have to tell her."

"You can't."

"But I've got to." She had to warn Avella, now that she had proof that Carpace was involved in something. Surely this would convince her.

He studied her for a moment. "We'll talk about this later." Without waiting for a response, he turned and strode away, and she could only scamper after him.

When they reached the cover of the forest, he stopped. "All right," he said, "we need to get word to Pandil, but we can't go back, not if I'm to guide you."

She stared at him. How dare he refuse; he was being well paid. "Why not?"

"We can't be seen, and I want to get this journey over; I have my own errands. Anyway, I thought it was critical that we start right away."

It was clear he wasn't going to listen, and there was no use in arguing; she knew he was right. Every day counted. "But Pandil needs to know what I saw."

He nodded slowly. "I'll arrange for someone to get word to Pandil. Now come on. We've got to make up for the time you lost."

She wanted to scream at him that she had discovered something of value to Pandil in the time she had lost, but she knew it would be pointless, and besides, she would need all her breath at the rate he was walking. She would be worn out before they had gone an hour if he went on like this. But she was determined to keep up, and to do so, she would have to keep quiet. For the time being.

Pebbles skittered down the hill behind them as Dovella followed Zagoad up a steep and stony path, pushing past small bushes clinging to the rocky hillside. Their branches whipped at her face, but Dovella kept silent. Clearly Zagoad was no more pleased about accompanying her on the journey than she was about having him along.

Mouth tight, she glared at his back. However much he objected, he had no cause to sneer at her. She was strong, and she had made many trips in rough terrain with her father when he went searching for the rare herbs he needed. She was no delicate house maiden. Her resentment festered as she scrambled along behind him.

The exertion soon warmed her, and she pulled off her cloak, tucking it into the strap of her pack. She trudged on, but the rockier the terrain, the faster Zagoad went, and soon Dovella's breathing grew laboured. The muscles in her back and legs felt bruised and torn. She wiped her brow with her forearm and licked her salty lips.

Glad now that she had accepted her father's staff, she leaned on it more and more as her steps faltered; but her sweaty hands frequently slipped down the smooth wood, and the staff sent small stones skittering off the path. She ought to ask Zagoad to slow down, she knew, but she was determined not to complain.

It was fully light before Zagoad glanced back over his shoulder. When he saw how she was faring, he stopped and glared at her, his lips thinning in anger. "You won't last many days like this. Why didn't you tell me I was going too fast?" A vein in his temple pulsated.

She grasped the staff tighter. "Why didn't you try to find out?" Her voice lashed out like a whip, and he stepped back.

"You're *supposed* to be a responsible person," he snapped.

"You're *supposed* to be a trained guide. It's your job to know how I'm faring."

He flinched. She knew she had hit the mark. He hadn't

acted professionally, and he knew it; he had let his feelings about guiding her affect his work, and that went directly against Forester codes of conduct.

He turned and stalked on without responding, but he proceeded at a more reasonable pace, and soon Dovella could breathe normally. A little while later, he stopped again and wheeled around.

"All right," he said, standing with his hands on his hips, "I should have been more careful. But you have to take some responsibility for this trip, too. You would have said something to anyone else."

Dovella gripped the staff harder and silently stared at him with all the scorn she could muster.

"We're going to be together for many days, and it isn't going to be easy, so we've got to work together. I'll try to be more alert, but you have to speak up." He studied her for a moment, then his face relaxed and he smiled. "Actually, you've been doing very well." Then he looked away, his face closed against her again.

He's ashamed, she thought, and well he should be. Still, she recognized the justice of his words. She couldn't bring herself to admit he was right, but she knew she had to meet him part way. "I know I haven't a Forester's stamina."

"You haven't been trained that way. It's nothing to be ashamed of." He still sounded gruff, but she didn't sense any hostility. "Let's just accept that and get on the best we can."

It was only a truce, she knew, but it would have to do. She nodded, too weary to speak, and they started off again. Zagoad set a steady pace, and by the time the sun was fully up, they had reached a small glade well beyond the Village wall. Goldspikes and willowy blue bellflowers grew tall and thick, interspersed with blood red mallows, and jays scolded at them from a blackthorn tree covered with small white flowers.

They sat on the grass, opened their packs and pulled out loaves of bread and rounds of cheese. Dovella tore off a hunk of the dark bread, nutty and moist, that her mother had packed, and then ate it with a piece of the creamy cheese. But good as the food was, she couldn't enjoy it; she was too impatient to be on her way. Even so, she made herself chew slowly, knowing she must follow the pace set by Zagoad. He would be reasonable from now on, and she had to trust him.

A light breeze ruffled the flowers, and from somewhere nearby came intermittent bird calls. High above flew a golden grandin, searching for prey. Then the sudden squawk of a jackbird tore through the hush. Dovella cried out and dropped her bread.

Zagoad lifted his head and listened. "A marauding cat, I expect," he said. "That grandin will probably get it."

Dovella swallowed hard, ashamed of her outburst, and looked away, her hands clenched.

"There's no shame in being afraid," Zagoad said.

"I'm not afraid." Dovella snapped up her head and glared at him.

"Then you're a fool."

"Are you afraid?" She dared him to admit or deny it; either reply she could attack.

"Anybody who scouts these woods and isn't afraid, doesn't last long."

She looked away, ashamed. "I've been taught to master my fear."

"Fear makes a poor servant; it will rise up against you

when you least expect it."

"But if you let it control you ..."

He shook his head. "There's a third way. Acknowledge it and let it walk beside you; if it's left to lurk behind, you will always be looking over your shoulder; and if it races ahead, it will freeze your footsteps."

Dovella gazed at her hands. He'd spoken gently, but still she could not meet his eyes. "My parents taught me to be strong."

"If they didn't fear Havkad and the New School, would they have let you venture on this journey?"

She looked up and met his eyes. She saw no derision, as she had half expected; only honesty and concern. Perhaps her father had been right, she thought grudgingly; perhaps she could learn from Zagoad. She still couldn't feel a liking for him, but she would give him a chance.

As they walked on, Dovella wondered if she should remind Zagoad that he had promised to send word to Pandil; but she was reluctant to do anything to spoil the peaceful mood. Glancing at the sky, she noticed that the sun was on their right whereas before they had been walking into it. She stopped, feeling a chill creep over her. This wasn't the right direction.

Five

WHEN SHE SPOKE ALOUD HER THOUGHTS, ZAGOAD STOPPED and stared at her, his lips pressed into a thin white line. Certain that he had taken offence, Dovella added quickly, "I mean it's a different direction from where we were heading before."

After a moment he smiled, and Dovella, still puzzled, relaxed. He had clearly been annoyed, and yet he was also pleased. It didn't make sense.

"I'm glad you're noticing what we're doing," he said. "Lots of people don't. It will make things easier, knowing you are alert. I'm going this way so I can see someone I know about sending a message to Pandil." His face turned hard again. "You thought I had forgotten, didn't you?"

He whirled around and started off. Dovella followed, her own anger rekindling. Why couldn't her father have chosen someone pleasant?

They continued in silence for another couple of hours, and though the terrain became easier, the forest canopy thickened until she could barely see the sky. A rustle in the bushes sent her heart thumping. Slowly she turned her head, and caught sight of a deer; after a moment it bounded away, and she hurried on after Zagoad.

She studied Zagoad's stiff shoulders and suddenly became aware of the cramp in her own clenched hand. As she stretched it out and moved her shoulders, she tried to regulate her breathing. Such tension was not healthy. Especially not for a healer.

The trail narrowed and they came upon a clearing containing a small hut. The house had probably once been built entirely of dressed stone, but two crumbling walls had been mended with bits of rock and logs. The roof was thatched with rushes and leafy branches, and the yard was knee-high in weeds. In the shadow of a tree, a shaggy black dog rose and started barking.

An old woman, dressed in loose pants and a tattered grey tunic, opened the door as they approached. She glared at them, her wrinkled skin becoming even more furrowed by the deep frown; then the creases disappeared and she smiled.

"Zagoad! Good to see you, lad." She walked forward and put her hand on his arm. "The sun was in my eyes and I couldn't tell who it was at first." She glanced curiously at Dovella, but gave most of her attention to welcoming the guide.

"We need a place to rest for awhile," he said.

She nodded. "And something to eat, I'll wager."

Dovella started to refuse the offer of food, knowing that the old woman probably had little to spare, then pressed her lips together. Best to leave this to Zagoad. She tried to smile, but was far too tired to do more than quirk her lips.

"This is my great-aunt, Coraine." Zagoad took Dovella's arm and brought her forward. "This is Dovella. I'm taking her to the other side of the mountains."

"Oh?" But when Zagoad offered no more information, Coraine only nodded. Perhaps she was used to his coming and going without explanation.

Coraine stepped back into the house and held open the door. Once they were inside, Dovella could only stare. It was so different from what the outside had led her to expect. Probably that was the intention: if the exterior looked shabby enough, it would escape the attention of Raiders and marauding Outlanders.

The room was clean and tidy enough to please even Dovella's exacting standards. Blue, handwoven curtains covered the windows, and brightly-coloured rugs were strewn across the glossy floors. The furnishings were simple: a large wooden table with several chairs, and two beds, each tucked into its own little niche with heavy red drapes for privacy. Two other chairs, covered with frielskin, were drawn close to the fireplace.

Dovella glimpsed an iron stove and a crude wooden table in a side room; there was even a sink with faucets, so the house must be very old — and originally well-built — to have running water. If the water was still running.

"You would probably like to bathe your face," Coraine said. "Just go through there and to the right." She motioned toward the kitchen.

"Yes, thanks," Dovella said. She went through the kitchen and opened a door, then stopped short in surprise. Inside was a fully furnished bathing room. Hand pumps had been installed beside the pink stone sink and the deep tub. What she would have given to strip off and soak, but she dared not take that much of Coraine's water, and in any case it couldn't be hot. Even so, it felt good to be able to sluice water over her face. She removed her boots and washed her feet, then returned to the main room to find Coraine sitting alone.

"He's gone a'hunting," Coraine said. "I could have

stretched my bit of food, but he said he wanted some rabbit stew." She smiled.

How beautiful she is when she smiles, Dovella thought, admiring her delicate features. Her skin, though wrinkled, was still finely grained. Her greying hair had once been wheat-coloured, and she had dark blue eyes, like Zagoad, but she wasn't of Hill Folk blood any more that he was. Perhaps she was a descendent of one of the other groups that Pandil had mentioned.

"You must be tired," Coraine said. "Why not rest until Zagoad returns?"

Dovella awoke to a savoury aroma. Zagoad must have been successful, she thought, stretching lazily and yawning. She peeked around the alcove curtain and saw Coraine standing in front of the iron cook stove in the kitchen. She quietly pulled the curtain aside.

Just as Dovella swung her feet to the floor, Coraine looked around. "The stew is ready. We should eat so you can start off before it gets dark. The first part of the path is tricky."

Dovella opened her food pouch and took out one of the packets her mother had put in. "Here is a little chofowl," she said. "Mother said it should be eaten today."

Zagoad scowled. He's angry again, she thought. No doubt he believed she was trying to make a show of having wild chofowl, but she only wanted to contribute, knowing that Coraine didn't have a lot of food to spare.

Coraine smiled. "Your lady mother no doubt knew that you wouldn't be hungry so early in the morning, and looked for something special to tempt your appetite. It is good of you to share it." Coraine turned to Zagoad. "Have you heard any more about the expedition?"

"I've been accepted to join in ... if I get back in time." His voice was heavy. Coraine turned to Dovella. "There's a group going to look for the old Plains Folk," she explained. "I'm not sure if it's a good thing or not."

"If they are anywhere around, it's as well to know," he said, his voice sharp. "And it's an opportunity I may never have again."

So that's why he resented making this trip, Dovella thought. He didn't want to lose his big chance. She couldn't blame him for that, but he didn't have to take it out on her.

"Will you be able to get away?" Coraine asked. "From what you said, things are not good in the Village."

"We're hoping this trip will help. If it doesn't ... well, I'd still want to go."

"I don't know whether to hope you'll find them or not," Coraine said. "No telling what path the Plains People have followed since we lost touch with them." She hesitated, then went on more slowly. "I sense that someone has been meddling in things they shouldn't."

Coraine and Zagoad held eyes for a moment. Dovella looked down and smoothed her tunic, trying to hide a smile. Now what was that all about? Was Coraine talking about the 'black arts' Pandil had mentioned? Dovella was quite willing to concede that she didn't understand her own healing gift, and that — as Pandil had pointed out — others might also have gifts that Village technology couldn't explain; but this talk of sorcery was pure superstition.

"Something is stalking about in the woods," Coraine said softly, "something that shouldn't be."

There was silence for a moment, then Zagoad said, "I've

got my bow."

Coraine shook her head. "Your arrows wouldn't kill this."

Even though Dovella didn't believe it, she couldn't suppress a shiver.

Rising, Coraine walked over to a tall cabinet. When she opened the door, Dovella saw a bow and two full quivers. From one, Coraine drew six arrows and brought them to Zagoad. They were pure white, fletched with white feathers.

"These are made from Harving wood," Coraine said. "They will kill anything, no matter what evil possesses it. Take them with you."

Zagoad studied her, the skin between his eyes pinched. Then he nodded. "If you think I will need them, I accept them with thanks. But what about you?"

"I've enough for myself and some to spare." She shook her head and sighed. "I hope you won't need them, but what I've been hearing is worrisome." She turned away. "We'd better eat now, so you two can be on your way."

Coraine put out a platter containing nutty bread, cheese and the chofowl, then dipped up three bowls of stew. When they were seated at the table, Dovella said, "I never knew there were people other than the Villagers and Hill Folk until yesterday. They don't mention them in the deeds records."

Coraine smiled. "They've been gone so long, the school masters probably think they are only legends, and I expect others want to forget them. Those that stayed were good people, mainly, but they didn't always agree with the Villagers. Most left when the first Hill war started. I guess they didn't want to be drawn in, or perhaps they were afraid that the fanatics would turn on them next."

Maybe that was why she and Zagoad looked so different,

Dovella thought; not Villagers, for sure, and yet not Hill Folk either. "What kind of people were they?" She took another bite of the stew.

"The Plains People? Herdsmen or trappers for the most part, though some of them farmed as well. Mostly they lived in small clans."

"They had strange powers," Zagoad said.

Dovella felt her throat tighten. "What kind of strange powers?"

Six

Dovella still didn't believe what Pandil had said about sorcery, but if Zagoad and Coraine were also worried, she should at least listen.

Coraine shrugged. "They could read what was in someone's mind, and some of them could even put things into a person's mind. They could see afar, and a few could touch the minds of animals. There were different kinds of powers. Most of them were good, or could be good." She stirred uneasily. "It depended on the way they were used."

While they ate, Coraine and Zagoad related some of the legends of the birth of the people of Edlena. Dovella had heard a few of them, especially those connected with Edlenal, but she had never known anyone to take them seriously. Yet Coraine and Zagoad were saying that two of the four original groups were somewhere else on the planet.

"I don't really know anything about the Fisher Folk," Coraine went on. "They went their own way very early on. Many of the Plains People who had intermarried with Villagers or Hill Folk chose to stay behind when the clans left. We Foresters are said to be descended from them, and I expect it's so."

Dovella glanced at Zagoad, but he only laughed. "If there were any sorcerers in my family, the talent has long since died out, or at least, I didn't get it." He nodded toward Coraine.

"She did though."

Coraine studied him, looking amused. "Hush, you'll have Dovella thinking I'm worse than the New Schoolers." She took a spoonful of stew, chewed it thoughtfully. "I've a few talents, like making the arrows, but nothing powerful. Still, I can smell it when it's around, and it's around now."

"That man I saw with Havkad. He was definitely a stranger." He had looked like any other Villager, still ... "Could he have anything to do with this ... smell?"

"I don't know," Zagoad said, "but while I was out, I arranged for a friend to go see Pandil; she will sniff him out." He laughed. "So far as I know, she hasn't a drop of Plains blood, but she's as good a bloodhound as any Forester I've ever met."

Coraine smiled. "I don't know about Master Pandil, but I expect there are more Villagers with Plains blood than know it. Hill Folk blood too, for that matter."

Dovella looked down at her bowl, hoping no one would notice the flush she felt in her cheeks. Could her gift have come from the Plains People, or maybe even the Hill Folk? No; she was of Village blood. Only Village blood. "Were the Plains People the only ones with evil gifts?"

Coraine shook her head. "It's not the gift that's evil; it's how the gift is used. From the stories I heard when I was a child, the Founders had no magical gifts when they first came to Edlena, but something here changed them. Maybe it was their interaction with the giants and their Goddess, maybe it was the moons. Anyway, they developed different kinds of power. In later years, the old Schoolmen were determined to stamp out Goddess worship in the Village and elsewhere. They failed in that. But that's when the use of magic was banned in the Village and branded as evil."

"They just wanted to keep it for themselves," Zagoad said.

"Naturally," Coraine said. "But they had to make people believe there was no such thing, and that anyone who thought there was, and tried to use it, was evil. They succeeded pretty well in that, more's the pity."

Dovella wasn't sure what to say about that, so she turned her attention to her food and they finished the meal in silence.

Before darkness fell, Dovella and Zagoad were once again on their journey. Content to walk in silence, reflecting on what Coraine had said, Dovella followed along; but she kept her eyes on Zagoad, her senses alert.

They traversed a narrow ridge, and Dovella could see why Coraine had wanted them to leave before dark. She edged along, trying to ignore the drop to the river below. Thank the gods the path was dry; she wouldn't have wanted to navigate it when it was slippery. Twigs snagged on her cloak, and loose gravel shifted under her feet. She was greatly relieved when they finally reached a plateau.

Zagoad stopped and searched her face. "Can you go further?" No doubt he felt guilty about rushing her earlier. "There's a stretch just ahead that is not as thickly wooded as this, and we'll run fewer risks if we travel by night and early morning. But you have to tell me, Dovella. Don't let pride force you on."

Despite her rest, she still felt tired, but she knew he was right. If they could get across the open country without running into anyone, they had a good chance of reaching the great forest safely. "I'll make it." She was determined not to show her weariness.

They maintained a good pace, gaining the forest without incident. Though Zagoad was near enough that she could have reached out and touched him, Dovella could scarcely see his back. Sometimes he paused, then continued without a word. She wanted to ask him what he heard, but he had warned her against speaking unless it was necessary, and so she kept quiet. Occasionally she looked upward, hoping to see some stars or one of the moons, but here, too, the forest canopy was so thick that she could see nothing of the sky.

At first Dovella kept close on Zagoad's heels lest she lose him, for he moved too quietly for her to hear his footsteps. Soon, however, she fell into his pace and effortlessly kept far enough back not to trip over him when he stopped from time to time, yet not lose her sense of where he was. She would be glad when they could rest, though; she was almost breathless, and she had so many questions about the things she had heard at Coraine's house, questions she had been shy about asking there.

Dovella was still a little uncomfortable with Zagoad, but she was beginning to see him in a different light, and she was sure he would be able to satisfy her curiosity. She knew, vaguely, the Village legends about Edlena, how it had been settled by the children born of the Silver Goddess, though the priests taught that it was the gods who came in silver vessels and brought with them people and animals and plants from their own world. Mostly what they stressed was how the gods demanded obedience in return. That story she had dismissed as just a tale made up by the early priests as a way of controlling the people — as much a myth as the one about the Goddess giving birth to the four children. No doubt those priests were men like Havkad, who wanted power. And yet both Coraine and Zagoad had seemed to take for granted that the legends were in some way based on fact. This meant that not only were there other worlds but, of more immediate interest to Dovella, there were other peoples here on Edlena.

The ground was smoother now, the path well worn, so she could focus less on following Zagoad's feet. Ahead of her, Zagoad kept an easy pace, but then she sensed that he had stopped, and she halted so she wouldn't run into him. Peering ahead, she saw the flicker of a light through the trees.

"A Raider camp," Zagoad whispered. "It's further inside the forest than I would have expected, but I imagine they've gone to bed. Still, we'll have to go pretty far around, or they'll hear us."

She muffled a groan, thinking of the tangled growth, the brambles and small bushes with their sharp twigs, and the treacherous rocks that seemed to spring up from nowhere. But she was even less happy about the thought of running into Raiders.

As she started to reply, Dovella sensed movement behind her. Before she could turn, a rough hand pressed across her mouth. She rammed her elbow backwards into the person holding her, but before she could hit her captor a second time, the hand dropped from her mouth and her arms were gripped behind her. Something cold and sharp pressed against her neck.

"Zagoad!" she cried.

She heard curses and growls, the rustle of material and the grunts of a scuffle.

Her heart beat as if it were trying to keep pace with the struggle going on in the darkness ahead. Pinned closely to her captor, Dovella could smell the stench from his body; his breath sent chills along her neck. He let out a shrill whistle, and footsteps thudded toward them, stamping through the brush; then the glint of metal caught her eye.

"You'll get your throat slit," the man holding Zagoad snarled, "but the girl will die first if you keep this up." Silence, then a grunt of satisfaction.

Dovella struggled to move forward and felt her arms being pulled tighter together. The straps of her pack bit into her shoulder.

"I don't want to have to cut your throat, woman," a voice rasped next to her ear, "but if you don't settle down, I'll do it."

Her pulse pounding, Dovella realized that Zagoad was quiet, no longer resisting. She didn't like surrendering without a fight, but she suspected the man holding her would do as he threatened, and then, even if she didn't die, she would be of little use when they managed to escape.

That thought stopped her short. What if they didn't escape? But they had to; they just had to. And maybe the best way to escape was to play along with them. She made herself relax.

"What were you doing sneaking around our camp?"

"We weren't sneaking," Dovella snapped. "You were."

"Sharp tongue, haven't you? Best mind it in camp." The men laughed, and she felt the pack being yanked from her shoulders, then something rough scraped across her wrists, jerking her hands together. Her captor shoved her towards the light.

Dovella stumbled into the clearing and saw Zagoad, bound like her, being prodded forward by two men. There was only one other person in the camp, and he lay bundled up by the fire, his face pale and glistening with sweat. He moaned softly, and Dovella felt the tug to heal him. She looked away. She must not let them know what she was.

He needs you. Dovella steeled herself against the nagging inner voice. If the Raiders thought she and Zagoad were just a couple of ordinary people on a trek through the forest, they might not keep close watch on them; letting them know she was a healer could only endanger her mission. And the mission had to come before all else.

She straightened her shoulders and turned her attention to their captors. They were all of medium height and build, but one was running to fat even though he couldn't be much older than Dovella herself. In fact, none of them looked to be over five and twenty. From the smell of them, they hadn't bathed in days.

They tossed Dovella and Zagoad's packs and weapons down near a tent, then one of the men went to squat beside the sick man, while the other two prodded Dovella and Zagoad to the edge of the clearing and pushed them to the ground.

One man tugged off Dovella's boots. "Nice," he said.

"Forget it," the fat man tying Zagoad's legs replied. "You'll just have to give them up when Ancel comes."

The first man sighed. "I suppose so." He tossed them down beside Dovella and bound her feet.

"That'll keep you settled," the fat one said, and the two disappeared back into the forest, laughing softly.

The ground was cold and damp, and gnarled roots bit into Dovella's shoulder. She wriggled around until she found more level ground, then turned to look at Zagoad who lay a few feet away. "What do we do now?" She strove to keep her voice calm.

"Wait for a chance to get away. It won't be easy to get out of these ropes, but even if we can't, they'll have to loosen us eventually, if only to let us ... look after our needs."

It wasn't an answer that satisfied Dovella, but she had no better suggestion to offer. She settled back and began twisting her wrists, trying to see how secure her bonds were, but all she gained from her efforts was rope burns.

She heard distant hoofbeats, and soon after, three people rode into the clearing and pulled up near the fire. One of them was a woman. The two men swung down from their horses, and one of them went over to the woman. He reached up to help her alight, pressed her body to his for a moment, then took her arm and led her closer to the fire.

"Look after the horses, Keelow," he called over his shoulder.

Keelow led the horses a few paces away and stood silently watching.

The woman walked slowly to the figure bundled by the fire, her long dark skirt flowing softly about her legs, and knelt down beside him. As she leaned forward to lay her hand on his brow, her honey-coloured hair glowed in the firelight.

A healer, it seemed, and yet Dovella was certain that she was not from the Village; but neither did she have the look of the Hill Folk. An Outlander then, though they didn't usually dress in bright multicoloured bodices such as she wore. Nor had Dovella ever heard of healers among them. Unless this woman, like Zagoad and Coraine, was a descendent of the Plains People.

"Can you do anything for him?" the man who had helped the healer down from her horse asked. He had his back to

Dovella, but his voice was deep and clear, not like the guttural voices of the men who had captured them.

A Village man? Dovella knew that some Villagers had turned to raiding, but she had thought it was only ruffians or the uneducated, and this man was clearly neither. She wished he would turn her way so she could see his face. He was slender and tall, as tall as her father, and Safir was tall even for a Village man. Unlike the other men, he wore clothes that appeared to be clean and well made.

"The fever must run its course," the healer said, "but I will clean the wound to make sure it doesn't get infected. I'll need hot water."

"Raquim," the tall man said, "get her some water." The squatting man reached for a kettle and poured some water into a basin.

The healer reached into her pouch and took out something, but then the others huddled around her, and Dovella couldn't see what she was doing; all she could see was the woman's face lit by the glow of the fire. Calm and lovely, and yet there was a hardness to it that frightened Dovella.

Although she had known there must be others in the Raider troop, the arrival of the newcomers sent Dovella's heart racing. It meant she and Zagoad would have to deal with that many more people in order to escape. Working again at the ropes, she squirmed to one side and whispered, "What are they going to do with us?"

"Depends on who they are."

She stopped her struggle. "Aren't they Raiders?"

"Not like any I know. From the looks of the horses, they've come some way, and that woman is a healer."

"What does that mean?"

"Most Raiders wouldn't bother with a healer, let alone go some distance for one. If a person is sick, he either gets well on his own, or he dies and the others share whatever possessions he has. But more important, ordinary Raiders wouldn't have sentries roaming the outskirts of the camp. As to what they plan to do with us, I expect the man who just arrived will make that decision."

Raquim stood and said something to the tall man, then the two of them walked away from the fire.

The tall man glanced toward Dovella and Zagoad. "A Village woman? Are you sure?"

"I'm sure," Raquim said. "The man is a Forester, Ancel. What's he doing out here?"

Although he was facing them now, Ancel stood too far away from the fire for Dovella to make out his features. "Havkad will want to know about this," he said.

Dovella choked back a cry. If Havkad was behind this, there was no telling what was in store for her and Zagoad.

"We dare not take them into the Village though," he went on. "Let me look at their things." He and Raquim went over to Zagoad and Dovella's packs and stooped down to go through them. He held up Dovella's knife. "This is interesting. I doubt there are many knives like this."

"It's a beautiful piece of work," Raquim agreed.

"It's more than that." Ancel laughed. "I'll take it with me when I go; if I don't, Lovid and Mancil will kill each other for it."

Raquim spat. "Not much of a loss if they did. Raider trash, that's all they are."

"True, but right now we need them."

"I suppose. When are you going to see the priest?"

"I'm due in for a meeting tomorrow night." Ancel glanced toward the fire. "After I return the healer to her home, I'll go directly to the Village and find out what he wants done with these two."

Seven

İT WAS MOST UNUSUAL FOR MASTER SECURITY OFFICER Pandil to occupy herself with a drunken Outlander, but this one had started a fight with First Officer Maidel, her number one assistant, and everyone knew that she wouldn't tolerate anyone assaulting her officers.

As she stalked toward the interview room, her boots tapped out a hollow cadence through the chill hallway. Shadows from the green candles in sconces high on the wall danced across the stone floor. Those who saw her coming hastened out of her way.

Pandil smothered a smile under the grimace that was said to make men shiver. Her reputation saved her a lot of trouble. She knew that, and appreciated those who fostered the legend; but one of these days she might have to prove that she was as cruel as people thought. She dreaded that day as much as she dreaded the events that would bring it, and she feared that both would come sooner than she had ever dreamed.

She dismissed the guards and closed the door behind them, then turned and studied the prisoner for a moment. He was a big man, his black hair drawn back and tied with a red leather thong in Outlander fashion. She smiled. "You couldn't have found a less spectacular way to gain an interview?"

The man grinned. "Who's going to give any thought to

another drunk Outlander?"

"I expect you're right, as long as no one got a good look at you."

"They didn't, except for Maidel; but even if they had, same question. That's one advantage of being an Outlander. May well be the only advantage."

"I wish I could say you're wrong, but I can't." She pulled up a chair and sat across from him. After her apprenticeship, she'd spent two years training in the outlands, and Drase had been one of her best teachers. "I didn't expect to hear from you so soon."

"I had a visit from Zagoad today."

"What happened? Is?..." She stopped. Pandil trusted Drase as she trusted few people, but better to see what he knew before she mentioned Dovella's name.

He held up a hand. "Nothing's happened, but he had some information he thought you should know. Don't ask how he got it — Zagoad deals out words as if they were gold coins — and I hope you know what the message means because I don't, and he wouldn't explain. Just said to tell you that Havkad went into 73 New Road early this morning with a stranger, and that three others followed close behind, including the engineering apprentice Carpace. He emphasized that last bit. Wasn't in the best mood either, if that's of any interest."

Pandil nodded. "I expect Zagoad didn't appreciate how important that information is, and coming to see you no doubt took him out of his way."

"That would irritate him for sure."

She stood. "Thanks for coming in, Drase — even if you did choose a most unusual method for getting my attention."

"Always a pleasure," he said. "Might as well give you

the rest of my information while I'm here — which is just more of the same. Unrest; Raider attacks; anger; and fear or enthusiasm — depending on who you talk to — about the possibility of another war with the Hill Folk." He went on at some length, itemizing the houses that had been destroyed, the crops that had been burned, the Outlanders beaten or killed. "Cheery news as usual."

"And not likely to get better. Now, how are we going to get you out of here?"

"You could drive me out with a whip." He smiled. "That would enhance your reputation."

"No doubt, but do you really want to feel my whip across your back?"

He laughed, then tried to make it sound like a cry of pain. "I can't imagine you whipping anyone." His smile faded. "But someday you may have to — that or something worse. Make up your mind to that. Everyone does their best to build you up as being meaner than a mad varg, but reputation will only carry you so far."

Stepping from the Security Building just before dusk, Apprentice Jael had scarcely reached the road when he stopped and looked around. It was quiet, much too quiet, like the air before a storm. But inside his head, angry thoughts and violent yearnings roared. Their source was somewhere close by.

He had been taught to shut out the turbulent emotions of those around him, as he had been taught that he must never pry into the minds and emotions of others. That way lies evil, the elders had told him; that was the way of the old Plains People. "And while they are a part of our blood," they said, "we must never let their ways be ours." But sometimes, no matter how hard he tried, Jael found it impossible to shut out such turmoil. And now his Plains blood told him there was something greatly amiss.

The tumult in his head translated into the noise of a physical clash. He raced down the road toward it.

Jael rounded the corner to find a full scale ruckus in front of the Engineering Building. He had known the Villagers were angry about the lack of power, and many of them blamed the engineers, but he'd never expected the anger to boil over into a riot such as this. He recognized Councillor Blaint, a young, well-built man of old Village blood, who was defending himself against two men, and ably too. A weaver by trade, Blaint seldom spoke in Council, concerned, no doubt, that he'd be reported to the New School supporters in his Guild. But he was not holding back now.

Someone lay on the ground near the centre of the crowd. A tall man in a black tunic was kicking the figure, while several others struggled with a security man and a Villager who were trying to pull the attacker away. Jael ran toward the fighting men, yelling at a young boy who was watching, eyes wide and mouth agape, to run to the Security Building and bring help.

It usually annoyed Jael to see the New Schoolers sneering at those who didn't wear the New School emblem, a golden pin in the shape of a book, but now he appreciated the pins glittering in the light of the lamps outside the building; they made it much easier to know who to fight.

He heard the crack of a fist against bone, and winced. Without waiting for help, Jael hurled himself toward the man at the centre of the struggle, catching him square on the knee and sending him sprawling backwards. Whirling, he jabbed his fist in the stomach of the second man who had grabbed his arm. When the man doubled over, Jael slammed the edge of his hand down on his thick neck.

By then, the first man was on his feet again. Dark hair and eyes; an old-blood Villager. He grabbed Jael's wrist, but the young security apprentice twisted away and doubled his attacker's arm behind him. Before Jael could disable him, someone else was at his back. He turned to slam that one in the face, caught him with a boot to the knee, then turned his attention back to the other, who had grabbed him around the neck. The man was strong — a lot stronger than Jael had first judged. But Jael had an advantage the big man lacked: he had been trained by Security Master Pandil.

Jael grabbed him by the shoulder of his black tunic, then bent his knee and with a practiced move sent the attacker flying over his shoulder to slam against the cobblestone road. The man hit the ground head first with a solid thud, and lay there unmoving. Jael smiled. He didn't enjoy hurting people, but he could take satisfaction from a job well done.

He was vaguely aware that Pandil had joined the skirmish, but he couldn't spare her more than a glance. He knew that she didn't relish fighting any more than he did, except when pitted against an equal for sport or training, but when a fight was forced on her, she held nothing back, and the fool who had forced the encounter would have good cause to regret it.

He gave a quick glance around, worried that Dovella might have been caught in the fray, but he saw no sign of her. He saw her friend Narlos, and also Osten the knife maker, but some of those helping in the defence against the attackers he didn't recognize.

Newcomers flooded the square, some from Security, others just Villagers come to help. Among them Jael saw old Councillor Staver. The man was too old and too frail to do much damage and was far more likely to be injured himself. Despite that, he waded into the throng brandishing a cudgel.

When order was finally restored, there were five young men in custody — three of them little more than boys. The ringleaders had disappeared into the gathering darkness before they could be taken into custody. Three Villagers were badly wounded. One was from Security, the young man who'd tried to protect the person on the ground.

Together with Councillors Blaint and Staver, Jael moved closer to see who had been so brutally attacked. Master Engineer Avella lay crumpled on the ground, her blonde hair now dark with blood, her face battered. Blaint tried to staunch the flow of blood with her torn cloak. Old Councillor Staver cried out at the sight, and Jael led him aside, yelling for someone to run for a healer.

The agony of Avella's suffering slashed at him, and Jael threw up barriers against it, lest it disable him, something he could not afford to let happen. He had work yet to do this night.

He surveyed the scene, looking again for Dovella. He felt an unexplained relief that she had not been part of the fight.

Healer Safir felt his throat contract as he knelt by his wife, his face awash with tears. Avella's fine blonde hair was matted with blood, and her face was a bloody pulp. Pandil touched his shoulder lightly as she knelt beside him.

"Avella!" Pandil took her friend's limp hand and looked

up at Master Healer Plais, who stood nearby, his face also bathed in tears. "I never thought Havkad would go this far."

"You don't know that he was behind this." Plais's voice was sharp.

"I know those were New School foulheads," she snarled. "They'd never dare attack a councillor without Havkad's approval."

"You don't know that," Plais repeated. "He can't be held responsible for the actions of all the New Schoolers."

"He's responsible for the filth he preaches, and that's what caused this. So that makes it his responsibility."

Safir wanted to shout at them that this was not the time for arguing, not when Avella lay dying, but he couldn't choke the words out.

Perhaps Plais felt the same, for though his mouth tightened in the grimace Safir knew so well, the Master Healer said nothing more, only knelt beside Avella and laid his thin hand on her brow.

Her voice breaking, Pandil whispered, "Is she going to be all right?"

"I don't know," Master Plais said. His skeletal features were even more haggard than usual. "I've called for litter bearers to take her to Healer's Hall."

Safir looked up and saw a questioning look in Pandil's eyes. Knowing her as he did, he could almost read the thought: dared they let Plais take charge? He gave a small nod. Looking at the Master Healer's hand and how gently it stroked Avella's brow, how could anyone believe he'd not do everything possible for Avella? Besides, even if Plais were in sympathy with the New Schoolers, his oath as healer would never allow him to do less than his best for a patient. But, of course, Pandil didn't know Plais as Safir did.

Safir watched as his wife was gently transferred to a litter, wondering if anyone could heal her injuries. Dovella might have been able to. But she was far away by now.

Later, at Healer's Hall, Safir sat by his wife's bed, his hands clenched together. He'd never felt so helpless. He could sense that Avella was fighting something, for that was part of his healing talent, to sense emotions. It was this talent that had let him register the turmoil Dovella was undergoing as she felt torn between being an engineer and a healer, had let him understand how much she feared her own gift.

Safir had never envied her the gift before, knowing the dangers it entailed, both in its use and in others' knowledge of its existence. That's why he had warned her to keep it secret. But now he wished that he did possess it himself, so he could take on his wife's hurt and heal her.

He looked up when Pandil entered the room. "She's still unconscious."

"How bad is it?"

"She has at least three broken ribs, a lot of bruising and I'm sure there are internal injuries. Her head ..." He tried to speak calmly, the way a healer should, but his voice broke. This was Avella.

"Should we send after Dovella?" Pandil asked, her voice low enough that no one else could hear.

He felt hope jump in his chest, but fought it down and shook his head. "I won't deny that I would like to have her help but, in here, with all the other healers watching, it would be impossible to disguise what she is."

"But if she could help ..."

"Even if she could, it wouldn't put an end to this madness. Avella might be healed, but she'd be in no less danger, and Dovella would be in even more."

Pandil sighed. "I would have tried to locate her if you'd asked it, but apart from it taking too many of my people to find her, she is our only hope of defeating Havkad."

"I only wish I could know how she is faring."

"I received word from her today," Pandil said, and related what Drase had told her about Dovella seeing Havkad and his companion.

"Did Havkad see her?" This could mean that she was already in danger.

"I think not, otherwise Zagoad would have said so. However, there was something else. An engineering apprentice named Carpace was seen going into the same house a few moments later."

He looked down at his hands. "She was right then."

"Who was right?"

"Dovella. She ... she tried to warn Avella about Carpace, but Avella didn't want to listen. I think she was afraid that Dovella was jealous. Carpace is almost ready for her journeyman's exam."

Pandil bristled. "But surely Avella knows that Dovella would never behave like that. The girl might be far too quick to condemn the Hill Folk and ways she doesn't understand, but I can't believe that jealousy would bring her to speak false words about a fellow apprentice."

He brushed a hand through the air as if to wipe out her words. "Of course she knows, but she's so afraid of appearing to favour Dovella that she's apt to overlook what others do." He shook his head and smiled, thinking of his daughter.

"Dovella is a gifted apprentice, you know. Avella says it's almost as if she can feel what the machine needs. So that makes Avella treat her even more sternly, lest someone accuse her of teaching Dovella things she denies the others."

"Well, I hope she'll be warned now." After a moment she added, "We may be able to make some good of this. She can let slip to Carpace information we'd like Havkad to hear."

"When she's conscious, I'll speak to her, but you know she's not good at dissembling."

"She won't have to, except in treating Carpace exactly as she always has. Can you convince her to do that?"

He glanced at the pale figure on the bed. "I just hope I'll get a chance to try."

Pandil had scarcely departed when there came a soft knock on the door and Outlander Councillor Melkard walked in. He walked up to the bed and looked at Avella, shook his head. "I'm so sorry to see this, Safir."

Melkard had been a friend of Safir's and Avella's since their apprentice days, but of late they had seen little of him. Safir knew that Pandil believed the man had joined forces with the New Schoolers, and were Avella not lying here helpless, he might have asked Melkard why. But as it was, even knowing the importance of having Melkard's support, he couldn't bring himself to talk of Village politics.

"I know she's getting the best of care, but is there anything I can do?" Melkard asked.

Something burst forth then, something Safir had kept pent up since he'd first seen Avella lying on the dusty cobblestone road. "You can find the foulhead that did this, and turn him over to Pandil!"

Melkard stepped back and stared, no doubt astonished at

the anger he saw in Safir's eyes. He looked away. "Then she knows who it was?"

"No, the coward stole away in the darkness. Someone must know who it was, though; someone among the New Schoolers. If you want to help, find him." He gazed steadily at Melkard, challenging him to stand by his word. Melkard stared at him bleakly, then swallowed hard and turned away.

After Melkard left, Safir returned his attention to Avella. What was keeping her in this coma? As he watched, his anger flared again. He had always been a peaceable man, but now he found himself sitting with clenched fists, fists that ached to hit someone, if only he knew who to hit.

After leaving Safir, Pandil made her way to Security Hall. She'd barely had time to assign some security apprentices to the Engineering Building and send word asking Elder Engineering Master Quade to take over from Avella, before it was time to go to the Hall of Inquiries. As she'd expected, the room was already crowded.

Master Eilert of the Laws was pacing angrily. She was Havkad's cousin and, next to him, the most outspoken of the councillors on the New School side. How she thought she'd be able to keep her position as a councillor, let alone Master of the Laws, after a New School takeover, was something Pandil had always wanted to ask her.

As she waited for everyone to be seated, Pandil looked around the room. All the other New School councillors were there, as might be expected, except Havkad.

She sighed in relief when Wraller walked in leaning heavily on the arm of his daughter. Pandil knew that he shouldn't be there, but she was glad of his support.

When everyone was finally seated, Master Eilert turned to Pandil. "Why was I not allowed to see my clients when they were first arrested?"

"What makes you think they want your representation?" Pandil asked, her voice bland.

Eilert blinked. "Their fathers sent for me."

"Ah." Pandil took her place at the head of the court, nodding to one of her apprentices who opened the door behind him. The prisoners were led in. The tall one glared at her, but the others hung their heads, from shame or embarrassment.

"Your clients are all New Schoolers, are they not?" Pandil asked.

"And if they are? Does that make them guilty, and with no right to representation?"

"Of course not. But I naturally thought that as they are New Schoolers, they might want to follow the old Founders' laws. That is what you teach, isn't it? That we should return to the ways of the Founders?" Before Master Eilert could speak, Pandil turned to the prisoners. "Although I'm not a New Schooler, I'd be prepared to make that concession if you would like to have Founders' laws applied."

"Yes," they said as one, grinning.

At the same time, Master Eilert shouted, "No." Her squat body was shaking.

Pandil glanced around the courtroom, taking in the looks of puzzlement and anger. And the smile which Councillor Wraller was unable to hide.

"No?" She asked, looking now at Master Eilert as if she could not believe what she had heard. "Are you, a leader of the New School, saying you do not want the Founders' laws applied? And yet you are quick enough to teach that Villagers should return to Founder ways." She turned to the prisoners. "Are you sure you want Master Eilert representing you when she goes against your wishes to be tried under Founders' Law?"

They stared at Eilert, looking puzzled.

"Perhaps," Pandil went on, "you aren't aware of what the Founders' laws entail. And yet, if you are prepared to fight for the New Schoolers, surely you must know what you are fighting to bring about."

The prisoners' eyes slid back and forth from Pandil to Master Eilert. The tall young man, who appeared to be the leader, shouted, "We don't need you to teach us about New School law. If it was right for the Founders' time, it is right for us."

"I'm going to tell you, anyway," Pandil said. "Your fellow prisoners might like to know why Master Eilert objects. Our present law demands that you be aware of your rights and choices, so I'll go by that until you and your representative are in agreement. Under Founders' Law, however, I would be allowed to keep you without representation, until my case is ready. This is not allowed under present law. If I deem a public trial not in the interest of the Village, I can try you in private — again, this is not allowed under present law. If you are found guilty of attacking the three who are now at Healer's Hall, I alone determine the penalty. One person is still unconscious. Should she die, the penalty under Founders' Law is death by any manner I choose — something not allowed under present law. Do you understand what I'm telling you?"

The leader had turned pale. He nodded.

"I ask again, do you, as avowed members of the New School, wish to be tried by the laws of the Founders, the laws which you have publicly professed to be desirable?"

Each in turn shook his head except for the tall one. He stared at Master Eilert as if expecting her to deny the truth of Pandil's words. When Eilert looked away, biting her lip, he looked back at Pandil.

"I'm waiting for your reply," she snapped.

"No." His voice was scarcely audible.

"You'll have to speak louder so the court can hear you."

"No," he shouted, his face mottled.

Pandil stared at him, as if at a loss for words. Then, "I must confess, I find this beyond understanding, as I'm sure others in the courtroom do as well. How can you not want to be tried by these wonderful laws that you are so insistent we should reinstate?"

A titter ran through the room. One of the prisoners turned bright red. "No one told us what they were."

"No one told you? But have you no duty to find out for yourself what it is you are fighting for? Are you an animal, to silently follow the New School leaders without knowing what you are following?"

"That is not the issue here," Master Eilert broke in. "You are misrepresenting the Founders' laws."

"Am I, indeed? Perhaps you can explain in what way I've misrepresented them."

"As I said, that is not at issue here. We are now under present law, and I demand that it be followed."

"Oh, it will be," Pandil assured her. "We will have the trial in one week. The prisoners, however, remain in custody until then." She met Master Eilert's eyes and was pleased to see them spark with anger at having been so caught.

"Meanwhile, the witnesses to these attacks are under my

protection, as are all councillors and the acting Engineer. Anyone who attempts to harm or intimidate any one of them will answer to me personally." She paused for a moment, then added ominously, "Under present law."

She rose and swept out of the room, gratified at the rumble of voices behind her. She had given them a lot to think about, and news of the refusal of a prominent New Schooler to use Founders' Law would soon be travelling through the Village. Not a victory, by any means, but a small skirmish won.

Afterwards Wraller joined her in her office. "The madness has started," she said. "I suppose I knew it would come eventually."

"I'm surprised they waited so long." He sat heavily in a chair beside the desk.

She nodded. She wished they had waited forever before attacking Avella. "I can't help wondering why they waited. Perhaps I'll find out tonight."

"I won't ask what you're up to, but do be careful, Pandil."

"I'm always careful, old friend. But as you can see, it's more important than ever that we gain support for our side."

"I know. Especially if Avella doesn't recover. I know you don't even want to think about that possibility and neither do I, but we must."

Yes, she had to think about it; more than that, she had to unravel the reason for it. "It does seem that they are trying to pick us off one by one." She paced the small room. "First you, now Avella."

"So, have you given any thought to who we might persuade to join our side?"

Pandil shook her head. "Eilert I can understand — she's Havkad's cousin, and thinks that will give her a special position. But the others … I wonder what they have been promised." She shook her head. "The Healers' Guild will be attacked next, but will Master Healer Plais listen? Even today he refused to accept that Havkad had to be behind this assault on Avella."

Wraller rubbed a pale hand over his face, more drawn now than when he arrived. "I'll have a word with him."

"If you can convince him, well and good. The big problems are Melkard and the Master Trader. Both seem to be in Havkad's camp. Unless Avella recovers enough to attend Council, we'll be two short when it comes to a vote, even if we gain Plais's vote."

"The Master Trader, I think, is lost to us," Wraller said, his voice reflecting his weariness, "though I confess I can't understand the New School attraction for him. I would have thought that anyone of Forester blood would fight the New Schoolers, but apparently not. However, I think I may be able to sway Melkard. Whatever quarrel Outlanders have with the Village, they can have no love for the New School, and he is bound to their best interests. They could make life very difficult for him if he went against them."

She knew she should send him home to rest, but he was the only person she could rely on now that Avella was so badly injured. "We should just make a majority then."

"Assuming Avella recovers."

"I think we must assume that," Pandil said. "Otherwise we are lost."

The sound of raucous voices came from the hall, and she got up. Before she could move around her desk, the door was flung open and Havkad stormed in, his eyes like stones. Maidel stood behind him, ready to intervene.

"How dare you appoint a replacement Master, and shut me out of the Engineering Building!"

"Everyone but Elder Master Quade and my security people has been shut out."

"On whose authority?"

"On mine." She came around the desk. She knew her height irritated him, and she wanted to keep him off balance. She wanted to do more than that, but she knew she had to control her temper. "As you well know, you incited a vicious attack on Master Engineer Avella."

"I had nothing to do with that."

"You may not have directed them to beat her, but you had everything to do with the attack, and well you know it."

"Be careful, Master Pandil, how you accuse," he said, his silky voice menacing.

She smiled at him, but it was not a smile anyone would have found comforting. "If you wish to bring charges, I'll give you the same choice I gave your minions: the opportunity to enjoy Founders' Law."

"I heard about that. You have lied about the Founders' laws."

"Be careful, Master Havkad, how you accuse," she mimicked. "I can back up my words, you know."

Havkad turned to Wraller. "You, at least, should have better judgement than to defy the New School." He turned and stormed out the door, slamming it closed behind him.

Pandil looked down at her hands for a moment, then told Wraller about Dovella's journey and what she'd learned earlier from Drase. "I'm more worried than I can say about that stranger Dovella saw. If he isn't a Villager ... could he be one of the old Plains People? I've heard that Havkad is dabbling in sorcery."

He nodded, his lips drawn into a thin line. "We were well rid of them. It will be a bad day for the Village if one of them has come back with that filth."

"We may wish we had someone on our side with their power before this is all over."

"We have no need for that." He held up a hand. "No, I'm not a fanatic. I know, for example, that Dovella's healing gift is out of the ordinary, and quite frankly, I'd not be surprised to find out that you have some gifts yourself of which most of us are unaware. But the sorcery of the Plains People was something else entirely."

"I know, but this man worries me." She glanced up at the candle holder. She, too, had been sparing in her use of power. "The candle is half gone. You should be at home, and I must be on my way. I've a lot to do before I seek my bed."

Pandil shook her head as she made her way through the dark alleys. There was very little to be grateful for in the diminished water flow, especially with this drought, but the rationing of power meant that the streets around New Road were almost dark. Bright Lucella cast her light, but it was easy enough to dodge from shadow to shadow. It hadn't been wise to come on her own, she knew, but she didn't want to put the burden of what she might find on any of those in her tutelage.

Soon she stood at the back door of number 73. A more sophisticated lock than she would have expected in this part of town, but it didn't take long for her to get it open. Another benefit of studying with Drase. She paused, listening. The house was empty now, but she had to consider the possibility that Havkad and his mysterious stranger might arrive.

She parted the curtains on the back windows, letting in enough moonlight to see where everything was placed, then she drew them together again. If she had to leave in a hurry, she didn't want to leave any signs of her visit.

Though he'll know, she thought; that stranger will know, if he's the kind of man I think he is. But in that case, we're in deep trouble anyway.

She pulled a small candle from her pocket and lit it. Shading it with her hand, she went over to the table she'd spied in the moonlight. It was covered with scrolls, most of them dealing with the Plains People and their powers. Obviously stolen from the House of Archives. Wraller would not be pleased about that, and he'd soon ferret out who'd taken them.

She leaned over a small sheet of parchment with strange signs drawn on it in red. Red that looked very much like blood. She studied them carefully, trying to commit them to memory. Something vaguely familiar, and vividly repugnant, sent shivers through her bones.

The metallic scrape of a key in the front door made her freeze. Tearing herself from her near trance, she raced to the back door. She'd return; for sure she'd return. But first she had to discuss this with Wraller.

Pandil passed close to Healer's Hall on her way home, and decided to check on Avella. Plais was sitting by her bed when Pandil stepped into the room. "Still unconscious?" she asked, looking down at Avella.

Plais nodded. "I had to order Safir home to rest. He was near collapse." He shook his head. "Much as I dislike the idea, I suggested that he send his daughter, but it seems she is ill."

"Yes. She was with Safir when he attended Master Wraller. I've no doubt she picked up some illness there."

"Something caused by Havkad, no doubt." His voice was heavy with scorn.

"Wraller was in the care of a New School physician who was taking blood. It was only when Safir began treatment that he began to recover."

That made him stop to consider, but she knew he'd find a way to dismiss her suspicions. She could only hope that Wraller would convince him that his stand was short-sighted.

"How long do you think it will be before she wakes up?" Pandil asked.

He looked at Avella and Pandil could see the concern in his dark eyes. And perhaps the beginning of fear. "I don't know," he said. "Right now I ... I'm not even sure she will."

Very early the next morning, when Pandil knocked at Councillor Wraller's door, his daughter Macil answered, her night robe pulled tightly about her.

"I'm sorry to awaken you so early," Pandil said, "but I must see your father."

She'd scarcely spoken the words before Wraller appeared at the door. "What's wrong?" Without waiting for her answer, he drew her into the hallway and turned to his daughter. "Please make us some macha."

"I'm all right," Pandil assured him as she followed him into his study, "but I had to show you something. Do you have parchment?"

He motioned to the desk, then stood over her as she painstakingly drew out the signs she had committed to memory. When she finished, she looked up. "I can't swear to it, but I think it was written with blood."

His face turned white. Then, when she told him about the scrolls she'd seen, a flush of anger coloured his cheeks. "I'll look into that today," he said. "But this … this outrage leaves me trembling." He shook his head. "I never thought I'd say it, but I think you may have been right."

"About what?"

"That before this is over, we might well wish for the help of someone with the power of the old Plains People. Or at least someone who understands it. Whoever wrote this filth is dangerous. Very dangerous indeed."

Eight

DOVELLA WENT LIMP WHEN SHE HEARD THE TALL MAN speak of taking the knife to the Village. Havkad would surely be able to trace such an unusual knife to its maker, and from there to Master Pandil. No doubt he would quickly make the connection between Dovella's absence from her duties and the young woman being held by his men.

The two men walked back toward the fire. "Keep the prisoners secure," Ancel said, "and make sure no one bothers them." He paused for a minute. "I hope I make myself clear."

"No one will go near them except me," Raquim said. "I'll see to it."

"Make sure you do."

When the men reached the fire, the woman stood. "I've done all I can. He will recover, but someone needs to sit with him through the night."

"He's my brother," Raquim said. "Tell me what to do."

She pointed to a basin on the ground. "Bathe his face with that from time to time, and when he regains consciousness, give him a drop of this." She handed him a small vial. When she'd finished her instructions, she turned and headed for her horse. Ancel followed her.

When the two horses had disappeared, Keelow walked over to Raquim. "So you caught a couple of people tonight.

Who are they?"

"Forester and a Village woman."

"Village woman? Maybe I'll have a look." He started in their direction.

"You keep away from them, Keelow." Raquim's voice broke off, as if he'd surprised himself; then, "Ancel wants them left alone. Completely alone."

Keelow went still for a moment, a silhouette in the firelight, then he shrugged and turned back. "Never mind. I'll be content with a bottle."

"You know what Ancel says about that."

"But Ancel ain't here." Keelow crossed his arms. His voice took on a mocking tone. "He's gone off with the healer woman, and if I know our Ancel, he'll be having his pleasure before he sets off for the Village. If I'm to be denied the comfort of the Village woman, why shouldn't I have some other kind?" He walked a few steps toward the edge of the clearing. "Ho there, Mancil!" he called. "Lovid! Get over here."

The bushes rustled, then the two sentries burst into the clearing. "What's wrong?"

Keelow laughed. "Our valiant leader is off with his wild woman and won't be back for a few days; and while we were away, I managed to pick up some supplies. Friend Raquim has his duties, so why don't you join me?" He clapped the stout man on the shoulder. "What say, Mancil?"

"Someone needs to keep watch," Raquim said.

"How many more people do you think are out there?" Keelow asked.

"What's so important about a Village woman being out here with a Forester, anyhow?" Lovid asked. "Probably ran away with him. What's that to us?"

"Come on, Raquim," Mancil whined. "You know this is the first time we've ever caught anyone, and they weren't doing nothing. And apart from the girl's knife, they didn't have nothing worth taking." He looked over to the heap of things they had taken from Dovella and Zagoad. "What happened to it, anyhow?"

"Ancel took it," Keelow said, laughing. "Supposedly to show the priest, but I doubt he'll ever see it."

"Priest." Lovid's voice dripped with sarcasm. "Like most of them, he leaves the work to others."

"Careful," Keelow said sharply. "Havkad does his share. You just don't know what it is." He slapped Lovid's shoulder. "Anyway, I've got something that will compensate for the loss of the knife." He turned and gave Raquim an exaggerated bow. "If our 'leader' gives his permission, of course."

"All right," Raquim said, "just remember this: Ancel might not know if we don't keep a sentry posted, but he will know if you don't keep away from the prisoners."

The three men laughed. "We'll go over there on the other side," Mancil said, tugging at the waist of his breeches. "They'll be safe, 'less it hurts them to know we've got some quahila and they haven't."

A few minutes later they were sprawled on the ground, passing around a bottle and talking quietly. Now and then, one of them would laugh. Meanwhile, Raquim sat by the sick man, occasionally bathing his face.

As the night deepened, the three drinkers fell to snoring, the fire grew dimmer, and Dovella could see that Raquim was nodding off. She strained to listen. Nothing from the clearing except a low moan from the sick man, and nothing from the forest except the rustling of leaves and the occasional call of an owl. Now was the time to focus on getting free.

She twisted her arms, then stopped. There was a better way, and she'd almost forgotten it. Writhing around until she could reach her boots, she slipped free the weapon concealed there. It was difficult to grasp the knife in such a way that she could get to the bonds around her wrists, but finally she managed to turn it so that the blade was against the rope. Carefully she sawed, mindful that a slip would cause a nasty cut to her wrist.

She could hear the dull rasp of fibres giving way, then suddenly the knife slipped from her grip. Blast! She had to be more careful. Forcing herself to relax, she wiped her sweaty palms against her breeches, then ran her hands carefully through the leaves and twigs, feeling for the knife, taking care not to slice a finger on the blade. At last she found it, and began once more to saw at the rope.

Suddenly Raquim rose, and she froze. He took a turn around the fire, stretched, and looked toward her and Zagoad. A moan drew his attention away, and he squatted down to bathe his brother's face. When he'd finished he settled again, and Dovella resumed her efforts.

Finally, her bonds fell away. She looked around to see if anyone had noticed, then smiled. The only noise had been her sigh when she knew that her hands were free, and no one but Zagoad could have heard that.

"Take it easy," he said. "They've settled down now. If we can get close enough without drawing their attention, we might be able to loosen each other."

"No need for that," she said, trying to conceal the satisfaction she felt. "My arms are free. As soon as I have the rope off my ankles, I'll cut you loose."

Silence for a moment, then, "I thought they took your knife."

"They did. This one was in the boots Pandil gave me." She smiled at his grunt, then crawled over and quickly slashed the ropes binding him.

When he was free, he rubbed his arms, then whispered. "We'll have to go quietly. The three on the other side are no doubt out for a while, but Raquim is at least half alert. I'll get behind that tree, and you call him over."

And never a word of appreciation for what she'd done. Nothing she did was ever going to be good enough for him. Dovella watched until Zagoad disappeared into the shadows of the trees, then called out, "Are you going to let us die of thirst?"

Raquim jerked his head up, then stood and picked up a bucket of water. He came toward her slowly. As he passed the tree where the Forester was hiding, Zagoad moved out and threw his arm around the man's neck. "I don't want to kill you," he said, "but I will if you call out or struggle."

"I'm in no hurry to die," Raquim replied calmly.

"Good. Get some rope, Dovella," Zagoad said, sliding the man's knife from his belt.

She gathered up the pieces of rope that had been used to bind them, and Zagoad tied Raquim's arms together.

"At least leave me near the fire so I can watch my brother."

"Why should I?"

"I looked after you and the woman. If I hadn't, Keelow and Mancil would have been after her, no matter what Ancel said. My brother never hurt nobody."

"I'll leave you where you can tend your brother, but only

if you keep quiet. If you rouse the others, we'll have to kill them, and then ..."

"I'll be quiet."

Zagoad pulled Raquim over to the fire and pushed him down next to the ill man. Dovella knelt and bound his legs. Then they crept across to the sleeping men, and Zagoad stuffed a wad of grass into the first man's mouth while Dovella knelt beside the other two, holding Raquim's knife ready. Muddled by drink, the men didn't seem to realize what was happening, even while being bound. In a few minutes, Zagoad had all of them secured.

"We'll take their horses," Zagoad said softly. "I know a man nearby who will go after Ancel and send someone over here to collect these men. But we must go quickly."

"If Havkad traces my knife to Pandil, she'll be in danger," Dovella said as they gathered up their packs and weapons.

"I know," he said, "but we can't do everything."

"But she ..."

"I'll send word, but if we're to reach the source water in time, we must be on our way." He paused. "Unless you're willing to go through Hill country."

"No," she said quickly. "No, we'll go as planned." She wouldn't trust her life and her mission to those savages, no matter what others said.

Zagoad gathered up all the weapons he could find and put them in a saddle bag. "Take one, if you want it."

She needed a knife, now that hers was gone, but something in her recoiled at the thought of using anything that belonged to one of these men, whether they were really Raiders or not. Perhaps somewhere on the way they could find a blade that hadn't been contaminated; and yet, even as she considered the idea, she knew that after the knife Pandil had given her, nothing else would satisfy her. She would just have to rely on her staff and the small knife, though it would be of little use in a fight. Besides, Zagoad was there to protect her. She didn't like that, but she accepted it; he had his job and she had hers, and she had to be careful, lest in trying to take on both, she was able to do neither.

Zagoad boosted Dovella up onto a black horse with a white blaze, mounted a bay himself, and they led the other horses away with them through the forest. Dovella glanced back at Raquim. "Won't he warn somebody?"

"How? The other three will be useless for the next several hours, even if they manage to get loose. And Raquim won't leave his brother unattended. In any case, without their horses, they won't get far."

It was the first time Dovella had ever been on a horse, for she and Safir went afoot when they collected herbs. Despite the instructions Zagoad called out from time to time, she found herself sprawled forward, clinging to the horse's neck, her knees clenched against the saddle. They travelled at a good pace, but the horse went gently enough, and Dovella was soon sitting up and breathing almost normally. She reached out and ran her fingers through the mare's silky mane. I could learn to enjoy this, she thought. Still, it wasn't long before her legs were aching and she felt a dull thud in the nape of her neck.

The forest was thick around them, but the path was well maintained. As darkness waned toward morning, grey light filtered through the trees. Now that the frightening experience was behind them, she could admit to some exhilaration at escaping from their captors. And she had been the one to bring about their freedom. Though you wouldn't know it from Zagoad's behaviour. He hadn't even acknowledged her part in it. He might have said *something*, but no, he just went on and took charge as if he had been the one who had freed them. Her throat tightened.

Well, there was no point in dwelling on it. Zagoad was who he was, and she couldn't change that. He knew the way around the mountain, and she didn't, so she had to depend on him; but at least she had shown that she could look after herself, and if he ever said anything slighting to her again, she would remind him of this night. Dovella tossed her head. See how he liked that.

Zagoad halted his horse, and when she rode up beside him, she saw a young man standing in the path, his bow drawn.

Nine

"IS LAKON HERE? TELL HIM IT'S ZAGOAD."

The young man didn't move, nor did he shift his gaze, but Dovella saw another figure scurry away, and after a moment a short, wiry man limped quickly toward them. He said something to the archer, who lowered his bow and grinned self-consciously.

"Sorry about that," the older man said, hobbling closer. His thin brown hair hung limply around his ears, almost reaching his shoulders, and his smile revealed a row of crooked teeth.

"Nothing to be sorry about. He's a good man." Zagoad nodded toward the bowman, who ducked his head and blushed. Zagoad swung from his horse and grasped Lakon by the arm, and the man clapped him on the shoulder. His dark eyes flicked towards Dovella, but otherwise he showed no awareness of her presence.

Thighs aching, Dovella swung gingerly down from the black mare, winced and led her forward, trying to walk normally.

"We've had some trouble and I need your help," Zagoad said.

"Just tell me what you need."

"We've been up all night," Zagoad said. "Maybe you will share our breakfast and I can tell you about it."

Dovella glanced at him, then looked quickly away. He wanted to spare the man embarrassment, she realized. As with Coraine, the men who lived here probably had little enough for themselves, let alone visitors. Why couldn't he be as thoughtful with her?

Lakon nodded and turned toward a shack. "Look to the animals," he told one of the men who stood watching. The man stepped forward and accepted the reins of their mounts and the other three horses they had taken from the raider camp; as he led them away, Dovella and Zagoad followed Lakon to the shack. Dovella was so sore she could scarcely walk, but she couldn't spare the energy to heal herself.

Dovella sniffed the air as they passed several metal drums from which a small trickle of smoke ascended — smoked meat, her nose told her. Mouth watering, she followed the two men into the cabin.

It was not as well furnished as Coraine's house, but it was clean and orderly. Four bunk beds were lined up against one rough-hewn wall; a long table and an iron stove hugged the wall opposite. Dovella collapsed into a chair. She opened her pack and took out the food Coraine had given her, and Zagoad did the same. Lakon was at the stove, pouring tea from a large pot. She sniffed. Mint. Not her favourite, but anything would be good right now.

Lakon brought three steaming mugs of tea to the table; as he sat down, Zagoad pushed the bread and cheese in his direction.

"We were captured," Zagoad began between bites of food. Since they hadn't eaten the night before, Dovella was ravenous; Zagoad must have been as well. "Havkad's men, really, acting like Raiders. One of them will be off to the Village and we need you to stop him from getting there if you can. Name's Ancel. I can't go after him because we've got to get to the other side of the mountain as soon as possible."

Lakon bit hungrily into the bread and nodded. Again he glanced at Dovella, but asked nothing. Thank goodness Zagoad wasn't telling them about her business there. But that would be the way with these people, she realized. They kept their own counsel and allowed others to do the same. But when they needed help, they trusted each other to help.

She looked down at her bread, ashamed at the anger she'd felt earlier. She was too quick to judge, too easily angered. But Zagoad could trust her too, if only he would.

"You did well to escape. From what I hear, Ancel keeps tight reins."

"It was thanks to ... her that we got away," Zagoad said stiffly.

Dovella stared at him, then quickly turned her eyes away. She had been so sure he wouldn't acknowledge her part in the escape. It had not been easy for him, she thought. No, she realized, it wasn't telling Lakon about it that was hard; it was admitting to himself that he had needed her help. That must be new for him. And perhaps he, too, had realized that he hadn't acknowledged it before.

Lakon looked at her again, this time with respect in his eyes. He nodded. "Well done, miss."

Why can't Zagoad call me by name, Dovella wondered, frowning at her bread. Then it struck her: her name wasn't his to give out. Her business and her name alike were in his keeping, his trust; he wouldn't reveal them to Lakon. But if she was going to trust the man to help, she could at least trust him with her name. After all, she knew his, for Zagoad had used it in front of her.

"My name is Dovella."

Lakon looked at her gravely, then smiled. "Well met, Dovella. We'll find Ancel while you are about your business; may it succeed."

Zagoad relaxed then, and Dovella knew she had done the right thing. She bit into the rich, dark bread Coraine had given them, while Zagoad carried on with the story of what had happened at the camp.

"I know the woman, know of her, that is." Lakon quirked a smile and stood. "I don't expect Ancel will be getting an early start. Let me just send someone to see about him, and then we can finish up here and you two can get some rest."

Zagoad pushed back his chair. "We've lost too much time already."

Lakon motioned him to stay seated. "As to that, I might be able to help you. Anyway, sit for a minute and finish your food."

Zagoad glanced at Dovella, and then picked up his hunk of bread. They finished the meal in silence, which suited Dovella. She was too tired to quarrel, and she had nothing to say to him that wouldn't end that way.

A few minutes later, they heard hooves beating against the dirt path, and Lakon came back in, grinning. "Well, that's one thing seen to. Anything else, apart from your trip?"

"Two things," Zagoad said. "We need to get a message to Master Pandil, and we need to get rid of those horses."

"The horses are easy enough. I'll have someone take them north and sell them to Outlanders, except for one that we'll let loose. If it's found by any of Havkad's men, they'll think you went that way. As to Pandil, I was going in to the Village later this week, but I can go now."

"Tell her what happened, especially about them taking the knife."

"Done. Now, about your trip. I could let you take a couple of horses, and ..."

Zagoad shook his head. "Horses attract attention. Besides, now that the forest isn't safe, we're going to have to tackle more difficult terrain."

Despite her aching muscles, Dovella was sorry to give up the horse; it would have allowed her to reach the source more quickly. But she knew Zagoad was right.

"Just hear me out. You could take them up to the head of the river. You won't run into any Raiders or any of Havkad's men between here and there. Leave them with one of my lads who's got a house there, and take my raft downstream. I need to let him know what's happening anyway."

Zagoad frowned. "That takes us pretty far west." He glanced at Dovella, then shook his head. "Too close to Hill country."

"Well, I reckoned that Dovella might not be keen on going through Hill territory, her being a Villager; but taking the raft downriver will let you get back on track with less danger from Raiders, and you will still have time to get some rest. You know you can't afford to travel tired," he rushed on when Zagoad started to interrupt. "Not with the risk of running into more of Havkad's men."

He held Zagoad's eyes for a moment, then Zagoad sighed and nodded. "What do I do about your raft?"

"You can leave it at Brandle's place. He's not likely to be there, but you can still go in and rest a spell before you cross the high road. You'll need for sure to be alert there."

"Yes, we could have trouble there if we aren't careful."

"Good, now one more thing. Once you cross the high road, you'll have to keep pretty far away from the road itself. I don't know what's going on, but there's a lot of coming and going, and the men are well armed. We've got a track skirting the road and a few people posted who can help, but I'll need to give you a sketch of our trail."

He got up and limped over to one of the beds and pulled from under it a small case from which he took out a sheet of parchment and a pen. Sitting on the bed and resting the case on his knees, he began drawing, chewing on his lower lip as he drew. When he finished, he shoved the case back under the bed and returned to the table.

"Now, it's not drawn too good, but these are landmarks you'll recognize. You won't know most of the lads, but you know how to identify yourself, and they'll be ready to help."

Zagoad studied the drawing for a minute, then handed it to Dovella. "Study it," he said. "We can't take it with us."

She caught herself before asking why. Of course Lakon couldn't take the chance of anyone finding the diagram if anything happened to Dovella and Zagoad. She looked over the sketch, carefully committing the outposts to memory, then gave it back to Zagoad. "I'd like to look at it again before we go."

"We'll both look at it again," he said. "And now, Lakon, I think we'll accept your offer of a place to sleep."

"Right over here." Not looking at them, Lakon added, "I'll fix up one of my smoked rabbits for you to take along, to eat on the trail. I've got a fresh batch that's about ready."

Zagoad laughed and looked over at Dovella. "You are being honoured, Dovella. Not just anyone is presented with a gift of Lakon's smoked rabbit."

They left mid-morning, but there had been a shift in the wind, and the sun gave little warmth. Dovella pulled on her cloak before she mounted the horse Lakon had provided, a red mare with splashes of white on her face. She was more spirited than the black horse Dovella had ridden from the camp, but the riding was much easier, apart from the fact that her thighs still ached.

They began with a moderate climb along a brook that rushed over large grey stones, and then the path levelled out for a while, and moved away from the water. Tall trees flanked the trail, and unfamiliar bushes, though Dovella recognized blueberry bushes and an occasional goldkul.

A little past midday, Zagoad pulled up his horse. "We'll stop for some food," he said, dismounting.

Dovella nodded, trying hard not to show the pain she was feeling. Numbed by relief and weariness when they had stopped at Lakon's that morning, she hadn't realized how deep the pain went; but after the rest, the soreness from her earlier ride had intensified. She was determined, however, not to say anything to Zagoad.

She walked carefully to the grassy spot where Zagoad stooped, building a fire in a ring of stones. "We've time to make something hot to drink," he said. Then he looked up at her and smiled. "You don't have to pretend to be tough, Dovella. I know you must be feeling miserable. I'd forgotten that you had never ridden a horse." He grinned. "But I'll bet you're glad now I decided against trying to go by horse all the way."

She tried to return his smile. "I'm sure I could have managed, but right now, yes, I am glad." She flopped down on the grass and lay on her side.

"Don't you have anything you can take?"

"I don't like to use it for something like this. Besides, it would make me drowsy, and I think it's best to stay alert. I have some ointment I can put on when we stop to sleep."

"That will be this evening, when we reach Lakon's friends." He looked at her anxiously. "Can you manage that long?"

"We won't travel tonight?"

"It will be best to raft down the river by daylight. In fact, if all goes well, we'll be able to do most of our travel by daylight from now on." He glanced at her, then looked away. "Thanks to Lakon's trail."

She looked at him curiously, but he was studying the fire. He was still hoping to convince her to go through Hill country, she knew, and she could barely fight down the revulsion. Maybe the Hill Folk had been given cause to fight Villagers, but that didn't change the fact that they worshipped a false Goddess, and who knew what kinds of practices they followed. Practices much stranger than her healing gift.

Zagoad may have met some friendly Hill Folk, but meeting them was different from travelling through their territory. She couldn't understand his insistence; even Lakon had recognized that she had a reason to avoid the hills. Besides, she didn't see how it could possibly be quicker to cross over those mountains than it was to go around them.

"Here." Zagoad handed her a mug of steaming tea.

Dovella sipped it gratefully. She wasn't really hungry, but she knew she should eat something — who knew when Zagoad would stop again. She opened her pack, pulled out a slice of the smoked rabbit Lakon had given them and bit into it. The meat was juicy and tender. "Mmm. I wonder if he would teach me his secret," Dovella said. "Father loves smoked rabbit, but not the kind we can get in the Village."

"I'm sure Lakon would reveal even that secret for Safir."

Dovella stopped in mid-bite and looked at Zagoad. "He knows my father?" Her father had never mentioned Lakon. Usually Safir told her about the people he encountered.

"I doubt that he's ever met him, but most people have heard of Healer Safir. He's well loved by the woods folk."

"Yet you didn't tell Lakon who I was."

"Your business isn't mine to tell. Besides, I don't necessarily trust others in a camp just because the camp master does."

Dovella moistened her lips. "This business with Havkad — it isn't new, is it?"

"Havkad's involvement is relatively new, but the New School has been building up its strength for a while. They started in the outlying regions, where people are more isolated and generally more superstitious."

"Is that why they brought in that — whatever it is that Coraine fears?"

He glanced at her. "Coraine is not easily frightened, and she was very much afraid. I'm sure there is something roaming the woods, probably something tainted by sorcery." He paused as if expecting her to scoff. When she said nothing, he went on. "That kind of tactic wouldn't work in the Village. There Havkad and his people are more direct with their threats: and *that* directness wouldn't work in the outlying regions. The Outlanders and Foresters would fight back. Are fighting back. But Havkad has introduced a new terror — burning and looting. Lakon had a good trade in smoked meat before he was burned out."

She stiffened, expecting him to again suggest that they go through Hill country, but he just drank his tea and ate his rabbit and bread. When he finished, he began smothering the fire. "There's a stream just below," he said, "if you want to wash. When we reach the cabin, you can bathe in the river. I know you feel dirty, especially after last night. I'm sorry I haven't managed better."

"It wasn't your fault, but I do need a bath. It's not just that I'm used to being clean."

"I know that healers have to keep clean. I'll do the best I can." He looked up at the sky. "But for now, try to be quick. I want to get to the cabin in time to do some hunting before supper. We don't have a lot of food with us, and I don't want to go in and ask for food as well as shelter. I'd like to get enough for everyone there."

She packed up her things, then limped down to the stream to wash her face. She'd welcome a real bath later, even in a cold river.

As they rode on, climbing higher, the path grew rougher, the undergrowth thicker, until there was no path at all. Not that it mattered, Dovella thought; it had become so foggy she could only see a few yards ahead. She shivered as the fog crawled over her face.

"We'll rest soon," Zagoad said; "you must be aching badly." Then he stopped, sniffed the air.

Dovella did the same. Burning wood.

"A campfire," he said.

"But I see no smoke."

"The fog conceals it. Lakon said there wouldn't be any Raiders, but let me see who it is before we go further. If it *is* Raiders, ride back toward Lakon's camp as fast as you can."

Ten

ZAGOAD EASED DOWN FROM HIS HORSE AND HANDED THE reins to Dovella, then disappeared silently into the fog. After a few moments she heard a trill, like a bird alarmed by some intruder, then another that seemed to answer the first, but was a softer, reassuring sound. Zagoad reappeared and motioned her toward him.

"It's Brandle."

Turning her head to hide her wince of pain, Dovella managed to dismount. She flung her cloak across the saddle, and led her horse into the small clearing, where a man sat by a fire. He held one arm stiffly, and dried blood matted his sleeve. His bruised face was drawn with pain. He studied her for a moment; she saw no hostility, but no welcome either.

"Strange company for you, Zagoad."

"She's a healer, Brandle. I brought her out to look for herbs."

When she understood that Zagoad wasn't going to say more about their journey, Dovella relaxed. She wasn't sure why she had been willing to trust Lakon and not Brandle, but there was something about the hardness of his eyes — blue Hill Folk eyes, although he had the hair colouring of a Forester — that made her want to draw back.

"I could use a healer." It was a challenge.

Dovella walked over to him. "Let me see your arm." She tore away the blood-soaked sleeve, cleaned the wound and poured a drop of healing oil on it, then wrapped it with a clean cloth; that done, she placed her hands over the bandage. She could feel her energy draining as she absorbed the pain, and then the injured flesh began to knit. After a short time, sensing that Brandle's own body defences were ready to take over, she removed her hands and looked up.

The man's eyes were wide with amazement. "The pain is almost gone."

"It will come again, but the wound will heal. You must be careful with it, though. It was very deep."

Zagoad handed her a cup of warm bokra, and she accepted it gratefully. She would have preferred to sleep at once, but she wanted to find out what had happened to Brandle. While she sipped her bokra, she would focus on her energy stream, try to discharge the hurt she had taken into her body.

"How did you get that wound?" Zagoad asked.

Brandle shrugged. "Raiders — they destroyed the settle where my parents lived. After that, the householders moved to the woods in smaller groups, thinking they had a better chance to escape notice. My brother and I, along with two others, have been the links between the different groups of settlers, but somehow the Raiders are always able to follow. Two of the households have been slaughtered, and Varden and I barely escaped. We should have stayed," he said, the anger thickening his voice, "but the headman said we had to warn others. Varden went to see Lakon and I'm heading for the settles north of the high road."

He took a deep gulp of bokra, shuddered. "And the Village Council does nothing. They're willing enough to use us, to cheat us and tax us, but they do nothing to protect us."

Dovella leaned forward to protest, but before she could speak, Zagoad said, "It's the New Schoolers. They're terrorizing the Village as well. Last night we were caught by one of their groups. Leader named Ancel."

Brandle stared at him suspiciously. "How did you get away? Most folks don't escape Ancel's gang."

Zagoad nodded towards Dovella. "She got us loose. Had a knife they didn't find." He glanced over at her as if waiting for her to offer her name as she had done at Lakon's, but Dovella remained silent.

Brandle looked at her, his expression doubtful. He was unquestionably curious, but asked no questions. Dovella stared down into her cup. She had done Zagoad wrong to think he hadn't recognized her help. She would have felt better if he had admitted it directly to her, but at least he was acknowledging it to his friends.

Zagoad gazed at her a moment longer, as if puzzled by her silence, then he turned back to Brandle. "We stopped in at Lakon's, and he lent us the horses. We're to take his raft downriver and leave it at your place."

Brandle smiled. "A long way to go in search of herbs, especially in times like these; still, you know your business best. I may be back home by the time you arrive, but if I'm not, you're welcome to rest in my cabin."

"We'd be grateful," Zagoad said. "The New Schoolers have infested the forest."

Brandle laughed harshly. "Not so new, the New School. We've had their kind before. And there's talk of them attacking the Hill Folk again."

"Not the first time for that either," Zagoad said.

"Well, they may find it more difficult this time. The Outlanders — if any of us are left — will fight alongside the Hill Folk if they are attacked again." He laughed again, an ugly, bitter sound. "Maybe that's why they're trying to wipe us out first."

Dovella choked back her anger. How could he even consider taking the side of the Hill Folk? But before she could speak, Brandle pushed to his feet. "I thank you for your help," he told her.

"You should rest," she said. "I have something that will help you sleep."

"There's no time for that. I'll be as careful with it as I can, but I have to warn the other households, and our people near the trail need to know what's going on." He nodded to Zagoad. "Kavella guide your steps."

Kavella? Dovella searched her mind; she had heard that name. Surely it was the old Hill Goddess. Strange that he would call on that name instead of the gods; stranger still that he should speak it to Zagoad. And Zagoad accepted the blessing. That would bear thinking about.

Silently Dovella watched Brandle as he gathered his things and mounted his horse. Soon he had disappeared into the fog-blanketed forest.

"I knew Outlanders had little liking for Villagers, but I didn't know they were traitors." Her voice was thick with scorn.

"The way they're treated, they have little reason to feel loyalty to the Village. But remember, this war with the Hill Folk, if it takes place, is not the Council's doing. It's New School doing, even though Havkad will play on Village prejudice against the Hill Folk and inflame many Village men to take part."

"I know what he's doing in the Village, but if he's behind the Raiders and their attacks on Outlander settlements, why do people follow him?"

"Some for the new land he promises, others because they believe the lies told about the Hill Folk."

Dovella snapped her head up and glared at him. "What lies? They slaughtered our people." She fought tears. Why did he keep defending them?

"Do you know how many of their people Villagers slaughtered first?"

"First?" That was not the way she had learned it.

"Yes. The Hill Folk welcomed the first group of Villagers who came this way, helped them until they were established, joined in the taming of the source water —"

"What do you know about the source water?" Dovella broke in. Had she been right not to trust him after all?

"Very little, except that it's on the other side of the mountain. In the early days, there was a small settlement there where technicians tended the machine."

"I never knew that." How could Zagoad know so much when she, an apprentice engineer, had heard nothing of the source water until she learned of it in the Old Books?

"After the attacks led by the Schoolmen, they were expelled, though the Hill Folk were good enough to give them time to reset the machine so that it could be controlled from the Village. And they let a small group stay to look after it. Despite the massacres." He returned her glare. "Do you think Villagers would have been so generous?"

She wouldn't listen to his lies. "I don't believe the Founders would take part in massacres."

"This was long past the time of the Founders. Much of their teaching had already been forgotten. A group of religious fanatics decided that the Hill Folk had to worship the same gods as the Villagers. They defiled the Hill Folks' holy places, killed their priestesses and tore down their shrines. It wasn't enough to wipe out worship of Kavella in the Village; it had to be stamped out among the Hill Folk, as well."

Zagoad's voice, though low, was of an intensity Dovella had not heard him use before. "Only the Village gods were to be worshipped, they said; they called the Hill Folk idolaters —"

"They are!" Dovella broke in.

He looked at her with disgust, and continued. "They killed those who would not give up worship of the Goddess, and even turned on Village people who tried to stop them, made it seem that they were traitors. That's when most of the Hill Folk withdrew completely into the mountains."

Dovella was silent for a moment. None of these things were in the books of deeds she had studied, and while she wasn't sure she believed Zagoad, she was curious. "I thought they had always lived in the hills."

"Some did, but many lived in the foothills and plains, and tilled the soil. This land, including the land where the Village lies, was once their territory. They willingly gave part of it to the newcomers, but the Villagers took the rest, and moved in to farm it."

She hesitated, unsure of herself now. "None of the deedsrecords tell of such a thing."

"Perhaps it says something in their favour that they are ashamed of the acts."

She didn't want to believe Zagoad's story, yet she was

unable to discount it completely. "Did the Hill Folk not slaughter our people then?" If he denied it, she would trust nothing else he said, for she did not believe the deedsrecords lied about that.

"Oh, yes. And they were not always careful to attack only their enemies, but fell on any settle they could hope to destroy. Though Villagers started it, there was fault on both sides, no one denies that."

"And they still hate us," she said heatedly. "I can understand that better now, but it happened so long ago."

"There have been many battles since then, Dovella; more shrines desecrated, more land taken. And the Council has done nothing to bring peace. If we haven't forgotten the wars, why should they?"

They wouldn't, of course. Their anger would have grown over the years. And Zagoad wanted to deliver her into their hands. Perhaps he had a reason to guide her on this trip other than goodwill toward Safir, she thought, remembering how he'd accepted Brandle's mention of Kavella. She studied him carefully; she wished she had the gift of reading thoughts. Then she'd know if she could trust him. She buried her face in her hands.

He must have misread the gesture, for he leaned forward. "I'm sorry. I know you're aching, and helping Brandle weakened you. You need to rest."

Grateful for the change of topic, she said, "I'll get my cloak and lie down near the fire." She headed toward the horse where she had left her pack, but as she neared them, she saw that both horses had their ears pricked, their eyes were wide, and they were dancing about restlessly. "Zagoad," she said, "something is troubling the horses."

He was on his feet before she finished speaking, bow in hand. Dovella heard something crashing in the undergrowth, then a rumbling. She strained to see through the fog as she untethered the horses and led them closer to the fire.

Another rumble, and a roar that made her jump. The horses stamped nervously, yanking at the reins and snorting, eyes rolling in terror. Dovella struggled to hold them while she peered out into the haze, trying to calm her heart as well as the horses, but all she could think of was what Coraine had said: *Something is stalking about in the woods, something that shouldn't be.*

She glanced around, and there before her, a dark beast loomed in the mist. Dovella clung to the reins and stared.

The creature lumbered toward them, huge paws batting aimlessly at the tree branches. Its yellow face, almost bare of the thick, matted fur covering the rest of its body, was twisted into deep folds around a protruding snout. Its eyes, also yellow, were inflamed, and its bellow was one of loss and pain. As it lurched toward them, teeth snapping at the air, foam dripped from its mouth. Dovella shuddered, her eyes riveted on the beast's huge tusks.

Zagoad motioned for her to move back. He drew one of Coraine's white arrows from his quiver. Harving wood. It would kill any evil, Coraine had said. Dovella could only hope that was true.

Zagoad nocked the arrow, aimed and let fly. The arrow struck the monster in the breast; it howled piteously and faltered, but still reeled forward, raging at them, reaching out as if to sweep them into its powerful arms. Dovella needed all her strength to keep the horses from bolting, and herself from fleeing after them.

Another arrow. It too struck the creature in the breast. This time it must have pierced the heart — the animal stumbled, then collapsed, its howl fading to a moan.

Zagoad crept forward and knelt beside the fallen beast. When Dovella reached them, she saw a look of incredible sadness on his face. He looked as if he were about to cry. Drawing his knife, he slit the animal's throat. Staring at the blood covered knife, Dovella strangled a cry.

Zagoad looked up at her. "Poor creature might have suffered for the rest of the day. Harving wood gives a painful death."

Dovella crept closer. "It looks something like a tusked mountain bear, but I thought they stayed further north."

"They do; and in any case, they don't normally attack unless they are threatened."

"Is it ... what Coraine feared?"

"I expect it's been maddened somehow, maybe altered. That's a crime against nature. And anyone who would do that — such a man would do anything."

"But who? And what does he want?"

"To spread terror among the Outlanders, for a start. And sow further discord in the Village. What more, I don't know." His voice was cold with anger.

Dovella stepped back. She wouldn't like to be the person responsible when Zagoad caught up with him. And he would someday; without knowing how, she was sure of that.

He looked down at the fallen beast. "It is wrong to do such a thing to a fellow creature," Zagoad said. "We are all born of the same mother."

Although she had heard someone read the legend of the Great Mother almost every year at Festival, Dovella had never before known anyone who actually professed the belief. The priests had long since dismissed the story as being nothing more than an idolatrous tale — part of their reason for objecting to the Edlenal; and since the New Schoolers had become so powerful, even telling the tale could be dangerous. At the last Festival they had disrupted several of the storytellers.

"But ... how can you hunt, then?"

"It's permitted to kill for food or protection, but not wantonly. You may kill only what you can use, never for blood lust." He motioned to the animal lying at his feet. "There is no excuse for the man who did this. It was done only to cause terror."

He studied the creature, then shook his head. "I can't bury him; he's too large for me to move. We will have to leave him to the others."

"Others?" She looked around.

"Scavengers," he said. When Dovella wrinkled her nose, he shook his head. "They were made so for a reason; it's not for us to judge them as vile." He made some motions with his left hand, then dipped the end of one finger in the animal's blood and placed it against his forehead. He rested his hand for a moment on the beast's head.

Dovella was astonished at how gently he touched the animal. It was all out of keeping with how she perceived him. Had she misjudged him entirely? The thought made her uncomfortable, and she moved away.

He stood up and studied her for a moment, offering no explanation for his actions. "What about your rest?"

"I'll chew some macha. I don't want to sleep here."

Without further speech, they smothered the fire and gathered their things. Mounting the still frightened horses, they resumed their journey toward the head of the river.

Dovella began to notice small piles of crumbled stone. They had been statues of some sort, she thought. Then they came on a larger one, almost covered with vines. "What are those stones? I've seen quite a few of them."

"Shrines. When this was Hill country, they had many shrines to Kavella. The Villagers destroyed them. Or rather, their priests did."

"They were idols." She could hear the harshness in her voice and expected Zagoad to argue, but he just shrugged.

"And they did massacre people," she said, "whatever their excuse."

"They were fighting for their land," he said, "and their beliefs."

"The priests were trying to free them from idol worship. Trying to teach them the right way." Surely that was right, to teach people about the true gods.

"That's what Havkad claims to be doing — teaching the right way. There's little difference between him and the priests that destroyed these shrines."

To that Dovella had no reply. Knowing something about Havkad, she could believe that what Zagoad had told her of the earlier fanatics was possible. Certainly one of the things Havkad preached was the importance of following the true gods, and there was no tolerance for the worship of an alien Goddess.

She had always half believed that the stories about how the Villagers had wiped out idol worship and put unbelievers to the sword were mere tales, like the birth of the people of Edlena; and the part that she had believed, she had accepted as right. After all, only the gods of the Village were true gods.

But how would she have felt if the Hill Folk had tried to force their worship on her?

"I know you don't want to go through Hill country, Dovella, but it really would be safer. There would be no Raiders there."

"But there would be Hill Folk," she countered, "and they are just as bad."

"Hill Folk don't behave like the Raiders," he said hotly. "I've never had any trouble with them."

"Maybe not, but I'm a Villager."

She could see from the droop of his shoulders that he had given up hope of convincing her. He might not like it, but he would do it her way.

They rode on in silence, for the terrain was getting steeper and rockier as they picked their way down toward the river. But at least they had left the mist behind, and now the sun was bright and warm. Dovella felt her energy build as the sun warmed her back.

As they rode over the swell of a hill, Dovella saw thin wisps of smoke rising from the valley below.

"We're almost there," Zagoad called over his shoulder. "It's best that we make a reasonable amount of noise here so they don't think we're trying to sneak up on them." He laughed. "Though I expect they've had an eye on us for a while. It isn't too easy to sneak up on an Outlander."

"But Havkad's men have."

"They didn't have to sneak up. The Outlanders were just outnumbered."

But no one challenged them, and when Zagoad motioned for her to wait while he rode into the clearing, she pulled up her horse in time to hear him moan, "Oh, no."

Quickly, she rode up beside him, and looked down at the burnt-out house that stood in the clearing.

Eleven

A FEW CHARRED LOGS LAY TUMBLED AROUND THE STONE foundation of what had once been a small house, and the acrid smell of burning lingered in the air. Beside the ruins, a couple of makeshift tents stood among scattered household furnishings. Two men and a woman sat around a small campfire, while further beyond them, four dark-haired children played listlessly.

Dovella had heard about this kind of destruction, but she'd never seen a burnt-out homestead. She looked at Zagoad and whispered, "Raiders?"

Zagoad shook his head. "They would have killed the people." He kneed his horse forward, and Dovella followed him down the steep trail toward the house. The people by the fire watched as if stunned as Zagoad and Dovella rode up.

The men had the same sunlit Forester colouring as Zagoad, but the woman had jet black hair, and Dovella felt a stirring of anticipation. Clearly the woman was of Village blood, though it seemed strange that she would willingly live so near Hill country.

Zagoad dismounted first and walked up to the three people by the fire. "Lakon sent me," he said. He said a few words and showed them something he had tucked in his shirt, but Dovella couldn't hear what he said, nor see what he had shown them.

One of the men stood up, his grim, soot-streaked face softening. "Well met, Zagoad. I wish we could give you better welcome."

Dovella got down from her horse and stood rubbing its nose. "I thought Raiders didn't come here," she said, her voice tight.

"It wasn't Raiders," the man said. "'Least, I don't think it was."

"It was those godforsaken Hill Folk, and you know it." The woman's shrill voice was near breaking. "You just want to make excuses for them."

"Hill Folk!" Zagoad said. "Surely not."

The man cleared his throat and glanced at the woman, then looked at Zagoad. "Well, it did look like them."

"But there's never been trouble with them before," Zagoad said. He glanced at Dovella. "Unless Havkad's people have stirred them up."

"Then why don't they go after Havkad's people instead of us?"

"Leave it, Novise," The man's voice sounded weary, as if he had said it so often that the words came automatically. He turned back to Zagoad. "I'm Crade and this is my brother, Javon. If Lakon sent you, you are welcome to such assistance as we can give." He gestured at the clearing. "It will be little enough, I'm afraid."

"Mainly we need a place to sleep tonight. Lakon lent us the horses and said we could leave them here, and take his raft downriver. But now ..."

While they spoke, Dovella noticed the woman staring at her, and it was not a friendly look. Did she dislike Villagers, even though she, herself, was of Villager blood?

"Well, the raft is still here," Crade said, "and we can look after the horses, but as for the rest, all I can offer you is a piece of ground. I'm sorry it's not more."

"That's all we need. Is there anything we can help you with?"

"We're just trying to hold together till we get word from Lakon. My other brother probably passed you somewhere on the trail." Crade motioned with a hand. "Put your things wherever you like, and I'll see to the horses."

They handed him the reins of their horses, then Dovella followed Zagoad to the edge of the clearing. "We can sleep in the open," he said. "I don't think there's any danger from rain."

"What about from Hill Folk?" Dovella tried to hide the smugness she felt.

"If it really was Hill Folk," he said. He held up a hand when she started to speak. "They probably won't come back, whoever they were, but if they do, we're less likely to be surprised if we're out in the open."

They put their things down, and Dovella opened her pack. "I'll bathe now, and wash a few things as well. If I wait too long, they won't get dry."

"Good idea. We'll go down together."

They gathered their soiled clothing, some soaproot and fresh clothes, and walked down to the riverbank. It was all Dovella could do to keep herself from running. It would be so good to feel clean again, to wash off the remnants of her captivity in the camp of Havkad's men.

"Looks like there's an inlet around the bend," Zagoad said. "You can bathe there."

She followed his directions and found a cove surrounded

by blooming goldkul. Slipping out of her clothes, she stepped into the water, which was shallow enough for the sun to have taken off most of the chill. She loosened her braid, then submerged herself in the clear water. After cleansing herself, she rubbed her clothes with the soaproot and rinsed them, spread them out on a large white rock to dry, then returned to the water.

She lay back in the water, enjoying the sun's warmth and the gentle breeze that wafted over her. As she floated there, she reached down inside herself to focus on her energy. She would need a good night's rest, but already she could feel her strength returning.

This was the first chance she'd had to relax since her journey began, and she found her thoughts turning toward the Village. What had Pandil done with the information Zagoad had passed on? She smiled. At one time, she'd have wondered whether he had indeed passed on the information, but even though he angered her still, she was beginning understand her father's appreciation of the young Forester.

Then her thoughts turned to Jael, and she wondered whether she and Zagoad might be back in the Village before Festival. She drew a deep breath. No point in even thinking about that. She'd be fortunate to reach the source and do her work before that time. She had no time to think about the young security apprentice.

The cool water lapping gently against her body felt refreshing, and she was reluctant to leave, but she knew she needed to return to the camp soon. There must be something she could do to assist Novise.

She splashed to the rocky shore, dried off and put on fresh clothes. How invigorating to be clean again, and the bath had done wonders for her spirits. The sun was still shining on the rock, so she left her newly washed clothes spread out there and went in search of Zagoad.

"That felt good," Zagoad said when she rejoined him, "but I need to go back and get my bow if I'm to do any hunting. Why don't you stretch out in the sun and relax? You need the rest."

"I'll come back with you. I feel much better and I may be able to do something to help."

As they neared the camp, Dovella heard voices and stopped short.

"I don't want her here." The woman's voice was almost hysterical. "I want you to get that Hill woman away from here."

"Novise!"

"You heard me. I want her out."

Dovella went still. How dare the woman accuse her of being of Hill blood!

"Novise, get ahold of yourself," Crade said. "First of all, she's a guest; and she was sent here by Lakon. Besides, she's a Village woman, same as you."

"That's what they say, but how do we know?" Novise replied bitterly. "Anyway, Lakon didn't know when he sent her that the Hill Folk were attacking us."

"She's not a Hill woman. Anyone can see she's a Villager. Now, let it be."

Crade turned away and saw Dovella and Zagoad. He glanced at Novise, then came forward. "Sorry about that," he said. "She's just upset."

Behind Novise, Javon and the children huddled near the fire, as if for protection. They looked away when they caught

Dovella's glance. Were they afraid of her, too?

"I understand," Zagoad said. "You've been through a lot."

Dovella curled her hands into fists. You might know he would take the woman's side. Well, he might understand, but she didn't!

The woman came and stared at Dovella, her dark eyes bright. She turned on her husband. "Get rid of her," she said. "Isn't it enough that her people came and burned us out? Do we have to give her a place to sleep and feed her as well?"

"She's a Village woman," Zagoad said calmly.

"Look at her eyes," the woman said. "She may be able to do something with her hair to look like a Villager, but she can't disguise her eyes."

"That's enough!" Crade said. A vein in his temple bulged as if it were about to burst, and his face had gone red. "Mind your tongue. Now, it's time to see to dinner. It won't be much," he said to Zagoad, "but you are welcome. *Both* of you."

"I thought I'd do a little hunting," Zagoad said. "You'll let me add my catch."

"Gladly, and thanks," Crade said, but the woman just stood, arms folded across her breast.

Dovella turned and stormed away.

"Dovella," Zagoad called.

She walked on without responding, but he caught up and grabbed her arm. "Where are you going?"

"I'm going hunting." She didn't bother to lower her voice. "I won't eat her cursed food."

"Dovella, the woman is upset. Her home has just been burned down."

"Well, I didn't do it. And I'm *not* a Hill woman."

She pulled away from him and stalked into the woods while Zagoad went to fetch a bow and some arrows. She still had her sling attached to her belt; she didn't have to wait for him. Besides, she needed to be on her own for a while to sort out her feelings.

She understood the woman's anger and fear, but to have it directed at her was something she couldn't accept. Naturally the woman wouldn't like Hill Folk; Dovella both feared and hated them, even without seeing them burn her home. But to be accused of being one, just because of her eyes? Then she remembered how she had felt about Brandle. Clamping her lips together, she pressed on. She didn't want to think about that.

A rustle in the grass made Dovella pause and look around. After a moment, she spotted a rabbit a few feet away, crouched in the grass. Slowly she pulled out her sling and drew a small stone from her pouch. She took a calming breath and aimed, then released the stone. The rabbit fell. She ran forward and picked it up, quickly gutted it, and buried the entrails. Pleased with her catch, she turned to go back to the camp, then stopped. No, she would take another. She would also pay for her bit of ground.

It wasn't long before she had a second rabbit, but by then her rage had grown, prompting her to take a third. More than enough, but the fury and the killing seemed to feed on each other. To kill more than one could eat was wasteful and wrong, but she couldn't seem to stop. Again she sent forth a stone. Again and again. And then she saw a wild duck.

They were harder to kill than rabbits, and suddenly she felt the compulsion to prove herself against it. She smiled, thinking how they would look when she came into camp with a duck. It would need to hang for a while, and having to look at it day after day would add to Novise's shame. But she would have to keep it, prepare it and eat it; they could not afford to let food go to waste.

Dovella took aim. Just as the duck lifted its silvery wings and started to rise, she let fly the stone, and the bird plummeted to the ground, its feathers gleaming in the late afternoon sunlight. She rushed forward and grabbed it out of the grass where it had fallen, then strung the rabbits over her shoulder and started back to camp, unmindful of the branches lashing against her arms and face. She would show them.

When she arrived, the others were gathered around the fire. Zagoad rose as she walked up. She slammed the duck and four rabbits down on the grass, keeping the other two rabbits for herself. She would have one tonight, and take one with her tomorrow.

"There," she snapped, "that should pay for the bit of ground I use."

The woman blanched.

"That wasn't necessary, Dovella." Zagoad's voice was harsh.

"A lot of things aren't necessary." She struggled to keep back tears. "But you only object when it's something I do."

Clutching her rabbits, she stomped back into the woods where she sat on the grass and skinned them, letting the tears stream down her cheeks. Her anger evaporated as she worked, leaving her feeling all the shame she had wanted Novise to feel. Shame at using what should have been a free gift to humiliate her hostess. Shame at her senseless killing; her bloodlust.

Now that she had taken her stand, however, there was

nothing she could do. Besides, she thought as she rose, Novise had done her a wrong; she should apologize first.

Dovella carried the rabbits and the pelts back to the camp, but the others said nothing when she came in, so after a moment's hesitation she walked over to where she had dumped her things and cleared a space for a fire. She started a small fire with twigs collected from the forest, then used Zagoad's hatchet to cut enough wood to cook her meal and make tea afterwards, and to make a frame for smoking one of the rabbits overnight.

When she had finished her preparations and sat down to watch the rabbits cook, she once again felt the pain from the ride. Only by concentrating on that could she draw her mind away from the soft murmur of conversation at the other fire, and the reason she was sitting here alone.

Once the rabbit was done, she cut off a chunk and wrapped it in a piece of bread. It was juicy and flavourful, but as she ate, the food seemed to swell in her mouth, and she could barely swallow it. Bite by bite, she forced herself to finish the piece she had taken, then she sprinkled herbs on the rest and put it away.

Overcome by weariness, she added a few more pieces of wood to the fire and made some collitflower tea. Perhaps she should offer some to the others, she thought. No. They had not welcomed her company, so why should she offer them anything?

She drained her cup, then built a frame and piled some boughs on it so that the other rabbit could smoke slowly overnight. That completed, she spread out her sleeping roll and fell onto it. Pulling her cloak around her, she fell into a deep sleep.

Dovella awoke the next morning to the aroma of frying smoked meat. Though her legs ached, she felt refreshed — the bath and sleep were just what she had needed. She turned over and saw Novise squatting by the other campfire, and remembered where she was. She froze and closed her eyes, then turned over again. A moment later she felt a hand on her shoulder.

"Dovella." Zagoad's voice was gentle. "You had a restful sleep?"

"Yes." She was surprised that she had been able to sleep, but between her fatigue and the soothing collitflower tea, she had slept soundly.

"You needed it. But we have to be on our way soon. Novise has breakfast ready."

"I can't ..."

"You have to. She's trying to make up for her behaviour, the only way she knows how. But you were wrong, too; you have to meet her halfway."

She sat up, pressed her lips together and looked away, unable to meet his eyes. "I know. But I was ... I was so hurt that she would judge me like that when she didn't even know me."

Her eyes fell on the rabbit pelts she had strewn with herbs to keep fresh. She saw Zagoad looking at them too. "I saved them. I knew she could use them for the children." Again she turned her face away. "But I don't know how to give them to her."

"You'll find a way." She heard the smile in his voice. "Come on; they're waiting for us. I brought you some water to wash your face."

"Thank you." She rose and carried the basin over to

the edge of the woods to splash her face and rinse out her mouth.

Taking a deep breath, she walked over to the fire where the others were gathered, then stopped. Lakon sat with the settlers, with two of the children crawling over him. What was he doing here? He'd said he would be going to the Village today.

Lakon looked up and smiled at Dovella. "Well met. Come and have some of Novise's griddle bread. It's the best I've ever tasted. And I'll give you some smoked meat if these young rascals will get off my arm."

The little boys giggled and ran off to beg the two older girls to come down to the river and swim.

He must know, Dovella thought as she went over to him. They must have told him. But he was ignoring it, so she had to do the same. "Gladly. It smells wonderful."

Lakon patted the grass beside him, and Dovella sat down, then shifted her weight. Lakon grinned. "New to horseback riding? Well, I hope the raft will sit better."

Dovella dug into the food while everyone talked — everyone except Dovella and Novise. But Novise was moving around, filling mugs and refilling plates with food. When she reached Dovella she said nothing, but her eyes, rimmed with red, were no longer hostile.

After they finished eating, the men seemed suddenly to disappear, leaving Dovella and Novise alone by the fire. They avoided each other's glances.

Novise poured hot water into a pan and added a piece of soaproot, then began clearing up the remaining food. "I'm sorry," she said as she started washing the dishes. "I was upset, but that's no excuse for the way I behaved. I have shamed myself and my family."

Dovella picked up a cloth and began drying the dishes. "No more than I."

"You were tired, and frightened as well, no doubt. And you've no love for Hill Folk either, from what Zagoad said. That must have made it especially galling to be called one."

"I've less cause than you to hate Hill Folk." Dovella shook her head slowly. "I don't understand a lot of the things I've been told lately, don't even know if they're all true. But if they are, our people have done them a great wrong, and may be getting ready to do yet another. Did Zagoad tell you what has been happening in the Village?"

"A little. He thinks that the Hill men who attacked us are renegades, in Havkad's pay." She glanced shyly at Dovella, wiped her wet hands on her apron. "I don't know what your journey is about, but I'm certain it has its share of danger, and I've not made it easier for you."

Dovella knew she must acknowledge the justice of Novise's apology. To pretend that she had done no wrong would be to belittle Novise and her sense of a host's responsibility. But, thinking of her own behaviour, Dovella looked away in shame, wiping hard at a dish to cover her confusion.

"This is all we have left to do." Novise brought over the greasy iron pan. She pinched crushed herbs from a dish and scattered them over the pan. The grease foamed up, and she wiped it off with a handful of grass, then poured water over the pan.

"I've never seen anything like that before," Dovella said.

"Fenweed, we call it. Gets rid of grease. Even old oil that's gone hard. I also use it on skins to take off the last bits of fat."

After a moment, Dovella said, "I have a couple of skins I would like to offer you. If you will accept them."

Novise blinked hard, smiled. "Gladly."

And then the two women embraced. Laughing and crying, they pulled apart. "I'd better get my things together," Dovella said. "Zagoad wants to get an early start."

"I'll pack a nooning for you. I'm sure Zagoad will catch you something for supper, but he won't want to stop more than once."

Shaking her head, Dovella took hold of Novise's hand. "You will have need of your food. We can stop in time to hunt." Then she stopped, embarrassed, but Novise only smiled.

"I know you are a good hunter; even Zagoad was impressed. And I thank you for your offerings; we are more than glad of them. But Lakon also brought us some food, and we had some stored in the cellar. I would like to send something with you."

Dovella knew there could be no rejecting that offer. "Then you have my thanks."

Dovella packed hastily, knowing Zagoad would be anxious to get underway. Suddenly it struck her that someone had retrieved the clothes she'd left down on the rock and folded them neatly. She blinked back tears and went on with her packing. When she'd finished, Novise handed her a pack of griddle bread and smoked meat, which she put into the food pouch. Dovella added the remainder of the rabbit she had cooked the night before, but left the smoked rabbit with Novise.

"It's better for us to find food as we need it," she said, "and just carry a few supplies for emergencies. Our packs get too heavy otherwise."

"Take along some of the fenweed, anyway. You may not always have a good supply of water for washing your cook pot." She handed Dovella a small packet of the herb. "It won't take up much space."

"Thank you. It will make cleaning much easier." Dovella grinned. "That's always the part I disliked when my father and I went in search of herbs. We'd catch some nice fish for dinner, but then cleaning the pan was such an unpleasant chore." As Dovella put the packet in her pouch, she wondered if the herb might have some uses in healing. She'd have to think about that.

Dovella glanced around the clearing. Although she was eager to resume the journey, she wished she could talk further with Novise. Though Novise was now an Outlander, she was still of Village blood, and she had made Dovella feel, if only briefly, closer to home. Although Dovella would never have admitted it, she missed her parents.

"I wish we could stay longer. We could help you rebuild."

"I'm not sure I want to rebuild," Novise said. "One part of me does, of course; I've loved it here and I hate to give in, especially if it is the New Schoolers who are behind it." She let out a deep sigh. "I suppose there isn't any doubt, but it's hard to think your own people would do such a thing, especially in the name of religion. It's much easier to blame it on the Hill Folk."

"Have you had any trouble with them before?"

Novise hesitated, then shook her head slowly, as if reluctant to make the admission. "But I'm always aware that they're nearby, and I'm still afraid. I mean, it *was* Hill Folk who attacked us, no matter who was responsible for planning it."

Dovella nodded. And Zagoad was taking them ever closer to their territory. "I know what you mean," she said, resolving to continue her resistance against his prodding.

Novise accompanied Dovella down the ragged path to the riverbank where the raft was moored. Although she was less sore than she had been the day before, Dovella could still feel the stiffness tugging at her muscles. It would be good to lie on the raft and not have to ride a horse or trudge along rocky paths.

Zagoad was already at the raft together with Crade and Lakon, and his gear had been securely stowed in a box in the centre of the barge, together with some goods being sent downriver by Lakon. There was also cooking equipment, as well as a fishing pole and some bait, which left no room in the box for Dovella's pack.

Lakon dismissed her concern. "The river's pretty gentle along the stretch where you'll be travelling. Swift in a few places, but not rough. If it weren't for the need to steer, a person could sleep most of the way."

Novise hugged Dovella again, and Lakon patted her on the shoulder. "Blessings on your journey, Dovella." He stepped back and waved as Zagoad pushed away from the shore. "The Goddess steer you," he called as they moved away.

Dovella frowned. Perhaps she had been unwise in trusting Lakon. His calling on the Goddess sounded too much like Hill Folk idolatry. Just like Brandle.

There was nothing she could do now, however, except to watch Zagoad in the days ahead; if he betrayed her to the Hill Folk, she would find a way to make him pay.

Twelve

JAEL COULD FEEL MASTER PANDIL'S EXCITEMENT AS THEY rushed toward Havkad's house, accompanied by Maidel and Nesse, one of the newer apprentices. They slowed as they approached and walked up to the door as if they had been invited.

"Master Wraller has officially reported missing some scrolls that his apprentice gave Havkad without authorization. That gives me a legitimate reason for searching," Pandil said, "but I don't want a lot of talk among the neighbours. Someone might send for Havkad."

It didn't take long for Pandil to open the lock, and they entered the house, which had only one large room. It had a musty smell overlaid with a cloying incense. He had noticed the same smell clinging to Havkad's robes. Sensing Pandil's disappointment, he followed her gaze to the table in the middle of the room, bare except for an arrangement of three black candles surrounded by a handful of sickly green feathers that could only have come from the Karbus, a bird of ill omen.

He stopped short, sucked in his breath with a hiss and quickly made a warding sign with his fingers, which he then touched to his forehead. He felt himself flush when he realized that Pandil had noticed his gestures, and turned quickly to examine the rest of the room. What must Master Pandil have thought, seeing him make such signs? A familiarity with magic wasn't something you revealed to people of the Village. Despite their claims not to believe in magic, Villagers distrusted anyone who showed any sign that they might be using it. He grinned. They'd be dismayed to know that most of them, without even realizing it, used magic every day in the small rituals that they called routines.

"Here are the scrolls." Maidel's voice broke through his thoughts.

"Thank the gods for that," Pandil said. "It looks as if we will find nothing else."

Nesse squatted down to look into the bottom compartment of one of the cupboards. "There's nothing here but table linen and robes," he said, "and the others hold only candles. Were you looking for anything in particular?"

She paused, then shrugged. "I thought that if the scrolls were here, there might be something else."

As Jael wandered around the room, his eyes caught an irregularity in the floorboards. "There is. Look. The ends of every other board match along both sides of the room, but here in the centre they take on a different pattern. I almost missed it because of the way the chairs were placed. I think there may be a trap door under that table."

"Let's see," said Maidel

As he approached the table, Jael leapt to stop him. "Don't touch the table!"

Three pairs of eyes turned toward him and he felt himself flush again. He took a deep breath. "The grandmother of my grandmother was a Plains wise woman," he said. "We've — my family has passed on some of her knowledge. One thing she taught was that the Plains People laid traps for warding things of value. Some of them had very evil traps." Seeing the look on their faces, he rushed on. "Not all of them. I know the Plains People have a bad name, but not all were like that."

"No," Pandil said. "I know they weren't. But people came to fear them, and some of the fear lingers. I can understand why your family has been discreet. So what can you tell us about this trap?"

"It's very evil. It's dangerous even to be in its presence, let alone to touch it."

"And that's why you made a warding sign?" Maidel asked.

He nodded, swallowed hard and lowered his head.

"I thank you for protecting us," Pandil said. "Is there any way to break through the trap?"

He looked from one to the other, licked his lips. "I'll need a little time, and there shouldn't be anyone else here. In case it goes wrong."

Pandil nodded. "Maidel, perhaps you'd better take these scrolls to Master Wraller and let him know that it's all right to open Archives Hall. And have a good talk with his apprentices. See if you can find out why Havkad wanted them. Nesse, you can wait outside. If there is a problem, you are to go get Maidel."

"How will I know if there's a problem?"

"You'll know," Jael said grimly. He looked at Pandil. "You should also wait outside."

She shook her head. "I don't send one of my apprentices into danger alone. Besides," she added with a grin, "I know the odd trick. Not that I would have recognized or known how to deal with this trap, but I have a few ways to fight the old magic."

He gaped at her, but only for a moment; somehow, on reflection, he wasn't surprised. No doubt Master Pandil knew a great number of tricks.

After the others had gone, Jael approached the table and drew a calming breath. He had been taught how to dismantle evil wards, but he'd always been attended by others in his village. It was essential, the elders had said, to include the community in one's work, to let them know that their energy was important in such workings.

"But what if you are alone?" he had asked.

"Then," his teacher replied, "you must work with what you have. Make a community of whoever is present; make a community of the sunlight and air, or even the dust. Draw on the community in yourself. For when it comes to the working, it is really your mind that counts."

"What do you want me to do?" Pandil asked.

"I don't know. Just be here. Lend me ... whatever strength you can."

"It's yours," she said. "Take what you need."

Grateful for her trust, he nodded, then circled the table four times sunwise, chanting softly under his breath. From the neck of his tunic he drew out a small coiled shell; he put it to his lips and from it came sounds like raging wind and fire, and then rain, fierce and purifying. When he came to the front again, he stopped and stood silently, eyes closed, then he resumed chanting. After a few heartbeats that seemed like hours, he began weaving his fingers in a series of movements, his soft chanting becoming more insistent.

Then his knees folded. Pandil rushed to his side, but he

waved her way. "It's all right," he told her. "Only, I will need to rest for a few breaths."

"Shall I call Nesse?"

He paused. "I'd rather move the table first. Just to be sure."

After a moment, he made to rise and she helped him to his feet. Together they lifted the oak table and moved it to one side, taking care not to disturb the arrangement of candles. Then they pulled away the small carpet. Just as Jael had predicted, there was a trap door in the floor. It didn't take Pandil long to deal with this lock either, even though Jael insisted on monitoring every move she made. Gently he shifted her aside when it came time to lift the door. When he had decided that it was safe enough, he motioned her forward, and side by side they peered through the opening in the floor. It was impossible to see anything in the darkness below.

"Nesse said there were candles in the cupboard," Pandil reminded him.

But what kind of candles, Jael wondered. The ones in the first cupboard he rejected; they stank of evil. At last he found two white candles that satisfied him. He lit them and handed one to Pandil.

"Let me go first," he said.

Shaking her head, she stepped forward, then stopped, grimaced. "I don't like it, but clearly you're better prepared than I am to deal with whatever we find." She backed away, and let him take the lead.

Slowly he climbed down into the darkness, and moved around, holding his candle high. Once he deemed it safe, he waved to her and she descended the narrow stairs.

Pandil looked around the room and drew in a deep breath.

"If you think everything is all right, you'd better get Nesse. I think it will take all of us to go through this." He could hear a smile in her voice. "It wasn't what I'd hoped to find, but it's almost better."

Jael clambered back up the stairs and found Nesse waiting at the front door, closer than he should have been. Nesse reddened and shrugged. "I wanted to be able to hear if you called."

Grinning, Jael clapped him on the shoulder. "Come see what we found."

Box after box was filled with weapons, weapons Jael was sure would prove to have been stolen. There had been a rash of thefts reported over the past two years, increasing in frequency in the past half year. In all cases, however, there had been no sign of broken locks, which pointed the finger at someone who could convince a gullible locksmith to make a master key. And here were weapons, in Havkad's house.

Jael picked up one of the knives and examined it carefully. Osten, the knifesmith, had been robbed twice in the last half year, and this looked like his work.

"The knife that young foulhead was carrying yesterday looked very much like one of these," Pandil said, "and these markings indicate that this is one of Osten's knives." She frowned, as if she had thought of something that worried her, but whatever it was, she was not ready to share it.

"This should give you the evidence you need to tie the attack on Master Avella to the New School leaders," Jael said.

"Yes, and what's more, weapons similar to these have been found on Raiders who've been captured or killed by Outlanders. If I can tie the New School to Raider attacks,

I can bring Havkad down. Race back to Security Hall," she told Nesse, "and bring back a horse and wagon. Quickly."

While they waited for him to return, Jael and Pandil moved the weapons upstairs. Watched by curious neighbours, Jael, Pandil and Nesse loaded the wagon. As they led the horse away, Jael could see that this time, Pandil was happy to let the neighbours witness her work.

Thirteen

DOVELLA MADE A PILLOW FROM HER CLOAK AND PACK and curled up at the front of the raft to examine her surroundings. The dark water crinkled with the current as if covered by loose nets, the slight movement the only disturbance. Here and there, small green insects flitted just above the water, and occasionally a fish leapt up, a flash of silver.

She and Safir had often waded across shallow streams, but she had never travelled on a river like this, and it frightened her a little. Small trees hovered over bushes and flowers along the riverbanks, their fresh green leaves glittering in the sunlight. The rhythm and the gentle slap, slap of the water against the edge of the raft lulled her, and she almost nodded off, but jerked her head up and shook it vigorously. Tired as she was, she didn't want to sleep; there was too much to see here, too much she wanted to remember, to tell Avella and Safir. How he would have enjoyed this. Thinking of her parents, she felt a pang of longing.

Now the forest loomed on both sides, dark and forbidding despite the sun that brightened the water, and quiet except for the whooshing of leaves and the intermittent scolding of unseen birds troubled by the invaders. Here the river was clear and not too deep, and she could see the stones near the banks, gleaming through the radiant ripples of water.

Zagoad stood at the rear of the raft, gripping a crude rudder.

"Can I help?" she asked.

"Better let me tend to it, since you've never steered a raft before. Besides, if this is the first time you've been on a real river, you might as well enjoy it." He hesitated, then looked away, and so did she.

Much as Dovella loved the woods, she had found little pleasure in the journey so far, and she didn't expect to, not until she reached the source. And even then, there was apt to be little joy; but she didn't want to think that far ahead.

For a while, the river ran swiftly, then they came into a lazy section where the water was sluggish and turbid. The woods crowded thick at the edge of the river, and branches hung out over the water, sometimes almost grazing Zagoad's face. She let out a small sigh and realized that for the first time since she left Safir, she felt safe.

She shook her head. How naive she'd been when she volunteered for this task. So sure of herself. It was no wonder her father and Pandil had insisted that she bring Zagoad with her. True, it was she who had managed to free them from the raiders' bonds, but she'd never have escaped the camp on her own.

Nor would she reach the source without Zagoad. She thought again of his persistence in wanting to go though Hill country. After studying the map Lakon had sketched out for them, she saw the wisdom of that course. Yet the thought brought a knot to her throat. Reason told her that was foolish. Her father, Pandil, Coraine — all had spoken well of the Hill people.

It came to trust. Did she trust Zagoad? At one time she would have said no. Yet now she realized that it had never been lack of trust, but envy of her father's high regard for the young Forester, and resentment of his attitude toward Villager women. Or, to be honest, her perception of his attitude. Many Foresters did speak disparagingly of Villager women, but she'd never heard him speak so. She'd only assumed that he would. The differences they'd had on this journey had been due as much to her attitude as to his.

Still, could she bring herself to go through the hills?

She turned and glanced up at Zagoad, lost in his own thoughts. "How do you know the Hill Folk?"

He jerked his head toward her, and for a long moment said nothing. Just when she thought he was not going to reply, he said, "I've known them all my life. The forest is a huge place, with many small settlements. As a guide, I often take traders from one settlement to another, and I come across Hill Folk in the forest as we travel, and sometimes when I'm hunting."

"What are they like?"

He gave a little shrug. "Like folk everywhere. Some are kind and honest; some not. They have their fair share of foulheads, same as the Village. But there are many good people, too."

She could see that he wanted to say more, wanted to urge her once again to detour through the hills, but he didn't, and she valued him for that. She turned and looked at the river. So far from home, and so far to go. And she would need time when she got to the source. Taking a deep breath, she said, "I'll think about it, Zagoad. I can't promise more now."

After a time, Zagoad said, "There's a clearing a little way ahead. We can stop there and have something hot to eat."

"Do we have time?"

"We have to take time," he said. "Once we leave the raft, the going will be harder. And we've travelled more quickly than I had dared hope."

He steered the raft in to the bank, leapt out and tied it up. Soon thereafter he had a nice blaze going, and Dovella put on a pot of water to boil. Zagoad laid out his things as well, and sat cross-legged in front of the fire. Dovella prepared the tea and handed him a cup, and they dipped into the food pouch for Novise's griddle bread and cheese and smoked rabbit.

"Look," he said after a while, "we've got a long way to go, so we might as well get things clear between us. I didn't want to do this trip because I don't want to miss the chance to go on the expedition, and I will if I'm too late getting back. It's the kind of journey I've dreamed of all my life."

His voice was tight, and Dovella could see that the words didn't come easy. "I've not been fair to you, and you've every reason to be angry with me."

"Sometimes my tongue is too quick," she said, wanting to be just.

"As is mine. I'll try to do better." He smiled as he put down his cup, and she sensed that he was feeling more at ease. "I think we should overnight here and get an early start in the morning. We aren't far from Brandle's place, which is where we'll leave the raft."

Dovella wondered why he didn't want to stay at Brandle's house, but she was just as glad. She hadn't warmed to the surly Outlander.

"It's best that we keep the rest of the food Novise gave us for another day," he said, "and I'll hunt for this evening. Game may not be as plentiful later. Besides, it will be a courtesy to keep food to share with Lakon's men on the trail."

"I'll look for some greens and berries."

Dovella fetched a pan from the box on the raft and walked back to the congleberry tree she had spied just before they pulled into shore. The dark red berries were large and sweet, and despite the number she ate, she quickly filled her pan. Then she moved closer to the river where, as she had hoped, greens covered the banks. They were young enough that they wouldn't be bitter.

When she returned to camp, she remembered Lakon's fishing equipment. What a nice surprise it would be for Zagoad if she had fish ready when he returned. Not to prove that she could do it, not out of spite, as she had hunted the day before, but simply because it would be helpful. Then, whatever he caught could be prepared to take with them.

She climbed onto the raft and took out the pole. It took a minute for her to see how it worked, for it was collapsed into a short rod, but soon she had it open and a line dangling in the water. Lakon wouldn't mind her using some of his bait, she was sure, but she would have to ask Zagoad how she could replace it.

She felt a tug on the line and pulled it up. A golden flatfish dangled from the end of the line, just right for the pan. It danced about in the air, but finally she managed to get it within reach. It was slippery, and she almost dropped it, but she took a firmer grasp and eased out the hook. If she could catch two or three more, they would have a feast.

She sat on the riverbank, the sunlight warming her back. While she waited for another bite, she thought about the journey, trying to sort out what had happened thus far. She had learned a lot from Zagoad, and not just about woodcraft;

now she had to think about what she had learned, and make some decisions. Tomorrow, when they left the raft at Brandle's house, she would have to make up her mind whether she was going to follow Zagoad's judgement or her own.

By the time she reached that conclusion, Dovella had caught four meaty fish. She took them back to camp where she cleaned them, then buried the scales and entrails away from the clearing where they had set up camp. The fish were all ready to start cooking as soon as Zagoad returned. She put the greens in a pan to simmer gently, then gathered a few twigs and branches from the edge of the woods.

She lay back on the grass and looked up at the sky, clear blue, deep and pure. Today she should have been visiting the temple in the Village to purify herself for the Rites tomorrow. Somehow she felt that she should do something to signify the day, even if she would be missing the Rites, but there was nothing to do. She brushed a hand over her damp cheeks and got up to gather some more twigs.

When she saw Zagoad approaching through the woods, she put the pan on the fire, and the fish were sizzling by the time he reached camp.

"You've been busy," he said, laying down three rabbits.

"Yes, but lucky also. Looks like you did well, too."

"We'll smoke them. I think we should get to sleep early so we can start at first light. We've still got a lot of ground to cover."

"And river."

"That too," he said, and returned her smile.

He had a nice smile. If only he would use it more often. Dovella looked away and dished out the greens and fish, and they ate quietly.

"This is very good," he said, "but how did you get the fish?"

"I used the pole and bait in the box on the raft. And a pan and a bit of cooking fat. I didn't think Lakon would mind."

"Of course not. But how did you learn to fish? I thought, from what you said, you and Safir had never been on a river before."

"We haven't, but we've camped beside lakes. He showed me what to do."

He finished his fish, then licked his fingers and grinned. "Coraine would give me a clout for that, but it's too good to let any of it go to waste." He gathered up the dishes. "I'll clean up."

"Here." She handed him some of the fenweed Novise had given her. "Use this. I'll see about our pallets."

By the time they'd finished their chores, she had a pot of tea ready. She handed Zagoad a cup, and they sat down by the fire. "How do you know so much about the other people?" she asked. "The ones who went away?"

"Coraine. My sister and I lived with her most of our lives, and her mother's father was a deedsrecorder, as was his father, and his before him, on back to the beginning, I suppose. I grew up hearing the stories."

"Have you actually been into Hill country?"

"Only in the foothills, but I hope to travel farther in someday. What I've seen is very beautiful." He paused. "They don't welcome outsiders, but they don't attack those who mean them no harm."

That's what Safir had said when, so sure of herself, so sure she could manage on her own, she had suggested this journey. But even if that was true, she was still a Villager, and the Hill

Folk could not possibly welcome her presence any more than she would welcome the notion of being there. Still, if they would help, how could she refuse it?

After their tea, Zagoad suggested that Dovella sleep first, and then keep the second watch. "You can sleep on the raft tomorrow morning."

She returned his smile. During the afternoon, she'd come to be more at ease with him. For the first time, they'd had a chance to just sit and talk, get to know each other a little better. Perhaps that's all that was needed to get over suspicion: a chance to talk and get to know a bit about another person.

She wrapped herself in her frielskin cloak, still warm from the sun, and curled up close to the fire. Listening to the crackle of the flames, she found herself drifting, drifting …

Not into darkness, but into dreams. She remembered only traces of them when she awoke. Her father had been there, and they had been looking for the toutile plant to make healing oils. And when they crossed the river, they found fields of them, growing in profusion as far as she could see.

Later, as she sat watch, she pondered the dream. She didn't know what it meant, but she felt comforted somehow; and she felt more trust for Zagoad, for reasons she could not explain even to herself, though she spent most of the remaining hours of darkness trying to do just that.

In the clear night sky, silver Lucella and green Gaeltan, now half full, had been joined by golden Hari. All three would be full in just over a week, at Festival time. What was Havkad planning? And would Pandil be able to stop him? That was the question that pounded at her brain, and always the same answer: it depended on her. She had to get to the source; she had to restore water flow.

But what if she couldn't? Her heart raced, and she fought to regulate her breathing. Reaching out, she grasped Safir's staff as if that would protect her from whatever dangers she had to face. What was it Zagoad had said? When you let your fears race ahead, they will freeze your steps and make you stumble. She couldn't afford to let that to happen. Somehow she would have to pull her fears back beside her. Not so hard here in this quiet glade, with Zagoad sleeping peacefully nearby, but she knew this tranquility wouldn't last.

It was not quite daylight when Dovella and Zagoad set off on the raft again, not taking time to make a fire and eat breakfast. Instead Dovella made a cold herb infusion and they drank it as they travelled. Afterwards they ate some more of the provisions Novise had given them.

The morning was overcast and cool, but to Dovella it seemed a wonderful day. She clasped her arms around her shoulders, wanting only to continue in the feeling of euphoria that had enveloped her since she had finally let go her anger and bitterness. She knew that she and Zagoad were never likely to be good friends, but at least they had learned to respect each other, and now they could show that respect rather than hide it in the resentment that had been festering since the journey began.

Near mid-morning, Zagoad poled the raft into a sheltered inlet. "Brandle's place is just over the rise," he said as he secured the raft to a tree edging a small clearing.

They gathered their belongings and climbed up the embankment. Dovella was almost sad to leave the raft behind, for the trip downriver had been the only restful part of the journey.

"Try to be patient with Brandle," Zagoad said. "What you saw at Crade's place was nothing compared to what it's like to be burned out by Raiders. They blame the Villagers for not doing more, and you are the only Villager out here."

Yes, she thought; just as, to Novise, Dovella had appeared to be the only one of Hill blood. And just as Dovella herself had been suspicious of Brandle because of his blue eyes. She looked down, filled with shame. She'd been unfair with far less reason. With no reason but her fear.

With a great deal of trepidation, Dovella followed Zagoad up to the small cabin, but when he rapped at the heavy oak door and called out, there came no answer. Dovella was almost relieved that no one was home.

They went inside and made a quick meal, then gathered up their things and started off. It seemed strange, somehow, to be walking again, and yet they had spent only one day on horseback and one on the river. It was hard to believe this was only the fourth day of the journey. But even though much had happened already, much still lay ahead.

As they walked, she watched how Zagoad marked their way so that no one but he would see it, sometimes on the front of the tree, sometimes on the back; how he watched the sun and studied the shifts in the terrain; how he stopped every so often, cocked his head and listened. He had done that all along, but she hadn't thought too much about it before; she'd been too tied up with her own concerns. And her anger.

Now she started paying him more attention, tilting her head as he did when they stopped, even though she wasn't sure what she was listening for.

"Why do you mark so?" she asked. "If you can find your way forward, why could you not find your way back?"

He studied her for a moment, then shook his head. "I don't think you understand even now just what we are up against." His voice was uncommonly gentle. "Apart from Raiders, renegade Outlanders and wild beasts, the way itself can be dangerous. Sometimes the paths are narrow and rocky. What would you do if anything happened to me?"

Dovella felt as if he had slammed his fist into her stomach. She had never thought about anything happening to Zagoad. "I don't know," she whispered.

"Don't you?"

Now she understood. "The markings. I could follow the markings."

He smiled. "A little later today, I will let you take the lead, to see how much you have learned. I expect it's more than you realize. Now, let's make as much distance as we can." He hesitated, as if he wanted to say something more, then turned away.

The trees towered above them, but even though the branches blocked out the sun, the woods felt airy, perhaps because the limbs were so far above them. From deep within the foliage came the trill and chatter of birds. The air too was fresh, scented with honeyflower. Here and there Dovella spotted starbursts and bluebells as well as bloodheal and collitflower. Then there was a patch where nothing grew but a few scraggly weeds.

"This used to be thick with toutile," Zagoad said.

"I wonder what caused the blight. Everything else we saw was healthy enough."

"It happens sometimes, a strange sickness of just one plant. But this hit suddenly, and everywhere that toutile grew."

"Just toutile?" Dovella asked.

"A few other of the healing herbs here and there, but toutile everywhere."

Could it have been the New Schoolers? Dovella wondered. They were determined to destroy the ways of healing traditionally used by Villagers, and the toutile plant was central to many healing practices.

Zagoad motioned toward a rock just ahead. "We'll have to climb, but up there is a place where we can rest. After that, we'll go another stretch, and then stop again before nightfall." He paused and turned to Dovella, a question in his eyes. "By this time tomorrow, we'll reach the road to Vellaban."

Vellaban: the village of the Hill Folk.

Dovella tried to stifle a shiver. "Do you know someone who would lead us through? I'm not saying I'll do it, but if I do agree ..."

"I know a man called Lafhin. He patrols the road."

She took a deep breath. You fear what you don't understand, her father had said. And it was true that she didn't understand the Hill Folk, and that she was afraid. But her father had entrusted her to Zagoad, and she had come, if grudgingly, to trust Zagoad as well; if he thought this was the right thing to do, she would follow his counsel.

"All right." She took up her staff and pack. "If you know someone we can trust, we'll go through the hills."

She could sense his relief, although he said nothing, only nodded. After a little distance, he motioned for her take the lead, explaining how she should determine the direction by the sun. He watched as she made her marks, occasionally correcting her choice of direction, but most of the time when she looked back at him, he only smiled his approval.

Then, without warning, he grabbed her arm and yanked her back through some low bushes. The small branches lashed at her face, and she banged her knee when he pulled her down to the ground. She listened, but heard only her heart. It sounded like the beat of a drum. Then she realized that what she heard was the pounding of hooves. A band of Raiders flashed by on a path a short distance away.

When it was again quiet, Zagoad said, "That was close. Sorry if I hurt you."

Dovella shook her head. "Where did they come from?"

"It's one of the main byroads, but hard to see from here with all the grass and undergrowth, and possibly equally hard for them to see us; still, I couldn't take the chance." He rubbed his chin, and looked at her. "We need to cross the road, and soon, or we'll lose several hours. But we must be swift."

He explained that they would have to run along the road for a few yards, then dash across a meadow on the other side. "Beyond that there is another stretch of woods leading to a steep incline, and below that is the road to Vellaban."

Looking at the mountains that up till now she hadn't been able to see for the trees, Dovella trembled. She wasn't sure which frightened her more, meeting the Hill Folk or travelling up a mountain that seemed to be high enough to pierce the sky.

"Be very careful and quiet," Zagoad warned; "there could be a Raider camp in the meadow."

Again she nodded and rose painfully to her feet. They raced across the dusty road and onto the parched meadow. The scorched grass crunched under her boots, and the air was hot, but she felt a welcome breeze. They had almost reached the trees when a loud voice rang out behind them.

"Stop!"

She glanced over her shoulder and saw three riders charging towards them.

*f*ourteen

I N HEALER'S HALL, SAFIR SAT BY AVELLA'S BED WHILE Master
Healer Plais strode back and forth, occasionally stopping
to glance at her or fuss briefly with his packets of herbs and
bottles of tincture. "Master of Religion was in to see her,"
he said. "Came spouting his platitudes, hoping Avella would
soon be able to return to her 'valued' position." He grimaced
as he mimicked the voice.

Safir glanced at him in surprise, and Plais must have read
the expression, for he reddened. "You know I have always
supported Avella and Pandil. I have no quarrel with women
being in positions that befit them. But," he added, "I am
not a hypocrite. I still maintain there is no place for women
healers." When Safir didn't respond, he went on. "You know
what happened the last time we had a woman healer, a Master
Healer at that."

Safir knew the story, but not all of it. Others had also
objected to the woman, but he'd never been able to get an
explanation, only that she was 'not suited' to her position.
And Plais was the most vehement, and the most insistent
that this proved that women didn't belong in Healer's Hall.
Safir would dearly love to know what the woman had done
to anger Plais.

Safir didn't know what to say; he couldn't agree with the
Master Healer's position, but arguing with him was useless.

Plais came back to the bed and took Avella's hand. While he stood there, Pandil entered, her face drawn. "How is she?"

"She is stirring," Safir said. "I only pray she will regain consciousness soon. She needs nourishment."

"She needs more than that," Plais said. "She isn't responding as she should."

Pandil came to the bed and gazed down at Avella's pale form. "Is she going to live?"

"I don't know," Safir said heavily. For almost two full days now, she had been unconscious. "The coming night will be critical. If she doesn't regain consciousness by tomorrow ..." He shook his head. "It's beyond my understanding."

"And mine!" Plais' voice reflected his frustration. "Many times I've healed such injuries, and worse. Great as her injuries are, she still should have regained consciousness. So why in the name of all the gods is she not responding?"

The Master Healer walked over to the table and once again began rearranging his bottles and herb packets, occasionally picking one up and frowning at it before replacing it and selecting another.

"It's almost as if there is something holding her," Safir said, "something inside. And I've no experience with such as that."

"I hope none of us have." Plais' voice was cold.

Pandil looked at him sharply, then back at Avella. What does she know? Safir wondered, watching her.

"How about the others who were injured?" Pandil asked.

Plais turned and smiled. "The others, the gods be praised, were all sent home this morning."

"Thank the gods for that," she said.

"Thanks for something," Safir said. He couldn't hide his bitterness. He looked at Plais. "These New School foulheads are getting out of hand."

"Not all ..."

Safir held up a hand. "I didn't say all New Schoolers. I said the foulheads. And there are a lot of them. Egged on by irresponsible leaders."

"So, what are we going to do?" Plais asked.

Pandil looked at him, then back at Safir.

"Yes," Plais said with a grimace. "I still maintain that many of the New School teachings ought to be followed, but Safir and Elder Master Faris have convinced me that they are a danger to the Village. Not that I'll be all that much help. Havkad still has a majority of the Council on his side."

"A majority? Surely not," said Safir.

"I don't know which way Melkard will vote," Pandil said, "but I know the Master Trader is committed to the other side, though I'm at a loss to say why. So, unless Avella recovers ... well, you know there's no chance that Elder Master Quade will be re-elected to replace her. Not with the votes in Havkad's hands."

"That makes it all the more important that Avella regain consciousness," Safir said. "She has some influence with Melkard."

"Perhaps, though I doubt it will help. In any case, there is nothing more I can do."

Safir looked back at Avella. So many depended on her getting well, not just him. The Council needed her; the Village needed her.

The next morning, Jael hastened towards Master Pandil's

office, wondering why he'd been summoned. Did she have further instructions to do with the mission they had undertaken the other day?

After a cursory greeting, she revealed that she had other things on her mind. "Master Avella is still unconscious," she told him, "and the healers can't explain it. They say it's almost as if something is holding her. Could a sorcerer do that?"

Jael nodded, too ashamed to speak. Even if he would never do such a thing, even if the Plains blood he carried was far removed from that of the old sorcerers of his people, he still felt the burden of their evil.

"I don't know that it's the sorcerer who is keeping her unconscious," she went on, "but if it is, you may be able to detect him and release her."

He considered for a moment, remembering what he had seen the day before. "It's possible," he said at last, "but if so, it will be dangerous to try to break his hold."

"You did it yesterday."

"Yes, but that was different. He had set the trap in a place, and he wasn't guarding it. Besides, we both knew there were risks, and we could have tried to fight our way free. Master Avella is helpless." He paused. How could he explain? To enter a mind without the person's permission was a great evil, and there was no way for Master Avella to give permission. "If I make a mistake, it could kill her," he said quietly, "and she is in no position to agree to the risk."

Pandil nodded. "I could ask Safir," she said, "only I know him too well. He would trust my judgement and say go ahead, and then if it went wrong he would blame himself, not me. It's best that he not have to make that decision."

Still Jael hesitated.

"She's likely to die anyway," Pandil said gently. "But speak to Elder Master Faris first."

And so he left, his hands stuffed in his pockets, hoping Pandil would not see them trembling. Master Pandil had made it seem so easy, so natural, like the way he'd dismantled the sorcerer's trap the day before. He knew that she didn't underestimate the difficulty, nor the danger, in what he had done; rather, he feared that she overestimated his skill. But this — this was something else. Even with her blessing, he would be going against his teaching. And if he failed ... how could he ever bear that guilt?

And yet, Master Pandil had asked him to do it, and because he trusted her — trusted her enough to believe that if she judged him fit for the task, then he *was* fit — he would try.

Pandil had noted the trembling of his hands before Jael concealed them. She took a deep breath. What had she done? May the Goddess and all the gods be with you, she thought. But there was little time to worry about that now for she had to get to Archives Hall to see Wraller.

When she arrived, he looked up at her with bloodshot eyes.

"Have you been here all night? You are mad, Wraller. You've only now got up from your sick bed."

"Hush," he said gently. "Macil brought me a blanket and some food. And I've slept. Some."

"Very little, from the looks of you. I hope it's been worth it."

He shook his head. "I'm afraid there is little here that I can understand. We need someone who knows something of the old Plains lore."

She smiled. "I think I can help you there, though we'll have to keep it close." She told him about Jael. "He doesn't want one and all to know about it."

He met her eyes for a moment, then looked away. Sighed. "Can't say as I blame him. Only a few days ago, I'd have been as suspicious as anyone else. Well, send him over and we'll see what he can do."

If only others would let reason rule, she thought, perhaps they could rid themselves of some of the old prejudices. "I've just sent him to Healer's Hall to see Avella. Plais says something is interfering with her healing. I thought I'd see if he could detect the hand of that sorcerer. I'll bring him here later."

She hoped there would be a later, for even though Jael had not mentioned it, Pandil understood that not only Avella was endangered by her young apprentice's interference with the sorcerer.

When Jael arrived at Healer's Hall, he asked to be directed to Elder Master Faris. He thought it best not to mention Master Avella, best that no one associate him with her. As it turned out, Master Faris was on his way to see Avella and took Jael with him, taking care that no one saw them as they entered her room.

The room was scarcely big enough for the bed, with a chair on one side and room for two people to stand on the other side. Another person or two might squeeze in, but they would feel the warmth of each other's breath. The walls were painted a warm blue, and thin blue curtains hung over the single window on the far side of the bed.

Briefly Jael told the old healer what Pandil had asked him

to do, half expecting to be ordered out of the room. The old man nodded. "It may well be that she is right."

"But if I make a mistake ..."

Master Faris touched him on the shoulder. "A risk every healer takes each time he treats a patient. And we do make mistakes. But we can't let that paralyze us. Nor should you. Pandil would not have sent you if she hadn't good reason to trust your gift."

Jael felt himself flush. The old healer smiled. "It is a gift. Just as we healers have a gift, though not all of us are willing to admit it, even to ourselves. And, in the Village today, it is unsafe even for those who might be able to accept the truth to admit it openly." He shrugged as if to say, "There's no help for it."

"Now," he said, taking another look at Avella, "I will step outside and busy myself, and make sure you aren't disturbed. But call if you need me. I will be close enough to hear you." Again the healer touched him on the shoulder and smiled. And even though Faris made the movement of his fingers quickly, and possibly without even being aware that he had done so, Jael recognized the blessing sign and took comfort and courage from it.

He approached the bed and looked down at the sleeping woman. Petite and fair, very different from her daughter, people were wont to say. And yet he had seen a likeness in the focus and determination each brought to her work. Now he saw a greater likeness as he gazed on the planes of Avella's battered face.

He pulled out his small shell, put it to his lips, and softly played his purifying melody. Then he began a low chant, reaching out to run his hand through the air a short distance above her body. The air felt sticky, and a sudden stench made him gag. He swallowed hard and pushed his consciousness into Avella's still mind, felt the net that encased it. Yes, it had all the marks of the sorcerer whose trap he had dismantled. Carefully, slowly, he began loosening the threads that held the net fast.

Suddenly he felt as if he were staring into dark, malignant eyes. And something else. Greed and surprise ... and satisfaction.

The last threads of the net snapped. Master Avella was free. But it was the sorcerer who had let her go, not Jael himself who had freed her. He tried to pull back, but something held him. His throat tightened and he felt as if a bird were trying to burst out of his chest. He reached for the shell that hung about his neck to centre himself, then traced out a warding sign. In an instant, he was released.

With a rush of relief, he sank into the chair, spent. And afraid. What did it mean?

Heading back to Security Hall, Pandil passed Councillors Melkard and the Master Trader in deep discussion. Although they couldn't have failed to see her, they continued their conversation, but in much lowered voices.

As she walked by the door of the knife maker's shop, Osten rushed up to her waving his arms. "I've got a description of the thief."

For a moment she didn't know how to respond. Osten was normally the most placid person she knew, unless someone remarked that he was short for a Village man. Then his tongue proved as sharp as the keen blades he forged.

"I'm glad to hear it," she replied.

"A young Village woman," Osten rushed on, lowering his voice. "Traveling with a Forester. She had one of my knives, one of the special ones I make to show at the fairs. It was going to be my special piece at the Festival showing. It was described perfectly."

It had to be Dovella and the knife Pandil had given her. "Who described it?" she asked. "And why did they come to you?"

"Master Havkad. He knew that my shop had been broken into several times and came to tell me at once."

Havkad also knew that such a knife had not been stolen, thought Pandil; at least not by his people. But what had happened to Dovella that he should come by such a description?

"Go on," she encouraged.

"Well, he said one of his Outlander friends had been attacked by this woman. The man took the knife away from her, but then he lost it. He seemed very angry about that, I must say; angry that he couldn't return the knife to me." He smirked, and Pandil laughed. It felt good; she'd had little to laugh about of late.

So Havkad had wanted to know who bought the weapon, and to protect Pandil, the little knife maker had lied.

"Tell me, will your records support your claim that the knife carried by the Village girl was stolen?"

He smiled. "Never fear, Master Pandil. Every knife you've ever bought from me is listed as having been stolen. I know well you don't buy things to have them traced back to you." Then his face too turned serious. "But what about this young woman? If some of Havkad's men had her long enough to get that knife, she's bound to be in trouble, isn't she?"

"I'm afraid so, Osten."

And there wasn't a thing she could do about it. And what's more, she didn't know how she was ever going to tell Safir. And if Avella regained consciousness, telling her would be even harder.

She had just started to walk away when she saw Safir sprinting toward Healer's Hall.

Fifteen

"RUN!" ZAGOAD SHOUTED.

Eyes fastened on the thick forest beyond, Dovella sprinted across the seared meadow, the hammering hooves drawing ever closer. She glanced over her shoulder and saw the three men sweeping down on Zagoad. Her heart pounding faster than the horses' hooves, she sped on, then stopped herself abruptly. One, or even two, Zagoad might manage, but three were too many. Dropping her pack, she raced back.

One of the riders urged his horse toward her. Almost paralyzed by the sight of the drumming hooves, Dovella watched the man on the dappled mare bearing down on her. At the last moment she swung her staff toward the horse's muzzle and yelled, "Hi-ee!"

As she jerked the staff away, not wanting to hurt the horse, the startled mare shied and reared, dumping the rider to the ground. With a whinny the horse bolted into the woods. Dust whirled up to settle on the fallen man like a cloak. Dovella wiped her hands on her breeches and watched, trying to ignore the tightness in her throat. He was still for a moment, then fury kindled in his dark eyes, and he rose and lurched toward her, drawing a knife.

She stepped to the side, regretting that she had been so squeamish about taking a weapon from Ancel's camp. She swung Safir's staff again, catching her assailant just in the bend of the knee. His legs folded and he crumpled to the ground. Cursing, he rolled to his feet and charged her, his face mottled red, his eyes venomous.

Again she struck, and again — neck, face, hand, throat — all the time dancing beyond reach of his knife, assessing his moves. He was untrained in knife fighting, and rage was making him careless; she had only to await her moment.

Recoiling from her blows even as he tried to force his way toward her, he lost his footing and went down. As he tried to scramble to his knees, she hit him again. He collapsed forward, the knife twisting in his hand to plunge into his stomach. Dovella stared for a moment at his blood soaking into the dry ground, then turned away, her stomach heaving. Bile filled her mouth, and she retched.

She wiped the back of her grimy wrist across her mouth and looked around. Zagoad was holding off the other two, but blood soaked his tunic at the shoulder. Cursing again her lack of a blade, she dropped to her knees and turned the raider over to take his knife. She had never caused a death before, and at the sight of the knife, its handle slick with the Raider's blood, bile rose again in her throat.

Thrusting all compunction from her mind, she yanked the knife from the Raider's stomach and rushed forward, trying not to look at the blood glistening on the blade. One of the men attacking Zagoad moved toward her, an ugly grin twisting his lips. A better fighter than his companion, he came at her in a semi-crouch, watching her with flat, amber eyes.

She recognized the movements. This man, like Ancel, was no ordinary ragtag Raider. This man had been trained in the same school that had trained her.

Dovella countered his position and struck out at him with the knife. She saw surprise flicker in his eyes; he had not expected that. He parried, and his knife grazed her shoulder. She flinched and bit at her lower lip as blood throbbed from the wound and streamed down her arm.

She dared not shift her eyes for even a quick glance at Zagoad; she could only trust that, despite his wound, he would be able to hold off his opponent. She couldn't possibly manage both, not if the other were as well-trained as this one. She fought to ease the tightness in her chest.

Taking advantage of her momentary distraction, her adversary lunged toward her, and she stumbled, barely escaping another slash. She had to concentrate. The blood flowing down her arm mingled with dirt and sweat, making her skin itch. She swallowed hard, schooled herself to remember her training, to remember what Pandil had drilled into her. *Watch your opponent; be prepared for the unexpected.*

Drawing back, she focused on the man, trying to assess his weaknesses. He was left-handed, which made it more difficult to block his thrusts; but he had the same disadvantage, and it gave her a weak spot to aim for, if she was quick enough. She'd also noticed him turning his shoulder slightly when he was ready to raise his arm.

She shifted her weight, feinted a blow. His shoulder twitched. She stepped to one side, sprang, and slashed under the raised arm into his stomach. Gasping with relief and revitalized energy, she began to crowd him. *Steady*, she thought, confident now that she could take him. *This one we'll keep alive.* Her strike had gone deep enough to give him trouble, but he was strong and skilful. Then his eyes widened, his lips compressed, and he moved back.

"You could have killed him already," Zagoad said from her side. "What are you playing at?"

She saw him circling the other way from the corner of her eye. "He may have information we can use."

She caught his quick nod and understood that he'd do it her way; but from the set of his lips, she knew he would argue later.

The man's amber eyes flickered back and forth between them. He licked his lips, took another step away from them, and in a quick movement, turned the knife toward himself. Dovella sprang and kicked his left hand. He dropped the knife and, cursing, grabbed at her. Blocking the movement with a swing of her arm, she whirled and kicked the back of his knees. He hit the ground rolling and was almost on his feet when Zagoad lunged forward, pulling the man down under him.

After they bound him, Zagoad rocked back on his heels with a groan. "I don't care for slaughter either," he said, "but these men were trying to kill us. We can't leave him, so why did you insist on sparing him?"

"As I said before, he may have some useful information. He's a Village man."

He jerked his head around to look at the man. "Are you sure?"

"Only someone trained in the Village would fight the way he did. Another of Havkad's jackals, no doubt."

Zagoad nodded. His face was white with pain. "I expect that's why he was prepared to die rather than be taken. If Havkad got hold of him, death would look good. Still, he's a problem. If you couldn't bring yourself to kill him, you should have let him kill himself."

"Let me tend your wounds," Dovella said, "then we'll talk about him."

"What about you?" He nodded toward her arm, caked with blood and dirt.

"It's not as bad as it looks." She opened her water canister and moistened a soft cloth and bathed his cuts, then took her salves and healing oil from the medicine belt and smoothed them gently over the slashed flesh. After wrapping the wounds, she placed her fingers over the bandages and felt herself absorb the injury, felt the fibres of flesh begin to knit themselves together.

He needed to sleep, if only for a few minutes. It would be dangerous, for she was drained from the fight and the healing, and also badly in need of rest. She would be on her own if Zagoad slept, and he would be unable to defend even himself; but rest was essential for his complete healing.

"What is this?" he asked when she handed him a draught.

"A cleanser for the blood," she replied, knowing he would refuse it if she told the truth. He gazed at her for a moment, then raised the vial and drank. After a few moments, his eyes glazed over and he began to sway. She rolled up her cape for a pillow and eased him down onto the ground, then turned her attention to the attackers.

There was nothing she could do for two of them, but the bound man, though still bleeding, was not seriously hurt. He watched her with eyes full of hatred as she cut his clothing away from the wound. Hatred turned to puzzlement as she began cleaning the gash. "First you try to kill me, now you want to heal me."

"I didn't try to kill you; I only defended Zagoad and

myself. But now I'll do what I can for you."

"And what then?"

"Why did you attack us?" she countered.

He laughed, an ugly, raucous sound. "Since when do Raiders need a reason? But if you must have one, we wanted to rob you."

"That won't do. I'm well aware that you're a Village man."

"And no doubt you've ways of getting the truth."

"No, but Pandil does."

He blanched. "She'll have to kill me first."

"I doubt that." Dovella finished dressing his wound, laid on her healing touch and poured a draught.

He glanced at the sleeping Zagoad. "For my blood?" he sneered.

"You need a brief sleep," she said, "even as he did."

A mocking smile swept across his face, but when she held the vial to his lips, he swallowed the medicine without a struggle. While he slept, she tended her own wound. She was almost exhausted, but she couldn't stop yet. She wished she had some jubana to restore her, but had to be satisfied with chewing some macha leaves.

After putting her things in order, she turned to the Raider's pack. In it she found a small shield, stamped with the symbol of a gold book under which was a scrawled H. That was how Havkad always signed his orders to apprentices. She also found a map and drawings of the machine and the water source. Scribbles on the margins of the smudged parchment gave instructions for closing off the flow of water.

So, just as she had thought, the problem was at the source. What she hadn't considered was that Havkad was behind the problem. It made sense, of course. Having located the water source, Havkad had sent these men to sabotage it, planning to close it down completely. He must have taken the volume missing from the library. But why were these men returning to the Village? Was it too late already?

She looked down at the instructions. No, according to this schedule, the date for stopping the water completely was Festival day, so there was yet time. But she needed to get this information back to Pandil so she would have evidence that Havkad was behind the problem with the water flow. Only there was no one to send but Zagoad, and without him to gain the aid of the Hill Folk, she would have to go around their territory. Even with no more difficulties, she would barely have enough time to get to the source before Festival.

She retrieved the packs of the other two raiders. The man she had fought first had a familiar look about him, and yet she knew she had not seen him before. Opening his pack, the first thing she saw was the knife with the curved blackwood handle that Pandil had given her.

She shook her head, baffled but relieved. There was no point in trying to guess how this man got it, nor why he hadn't used it. At least it hadn't fallen into Havkad's hands. She took it out, fingered lightly through the rest of the pack, but found nothing else of interest.

Dovella strapped the knife onto her belt and went back to bathe Zagoad's face with lotion to bring him out of his sleep. He looked around quickly, saw the sleeping raider, then turned his blue eyes on her again. "For my blood, was it?"

"That too." Before Zagoad could speak, she explained who the man was. "We can't leave him and we can't take him with us, so you'll have to take him back to the Village."

"Are you mad?"

"This will give Pandil proof of what Havkad is up to, proof she can take to the Council. The damage at the source has gone much further than I thought. We can't risk not getting back to her with this. Especially if I'm unable to repair the damage."

"What about you?"

"I've taken his pass. It's signed by Havkad. I can show it if I get stopped."

He frowned and rubbed his hand over his stubbled chin. "I had hoped to get passage through the hills. Going around will take you at least five more days. Surely you know by now it's too dangerous for you to try to go alone."

She felt the familiar tightness in her chest at the thought of the Hill Folk, but she knew it had to be done this way. "It's even more dangerous not to get him back to the Village and let Pandil know what is happening. This will give her the proof she needs to hold off Havkad."

He looked at the sleeping man and his face hardened. "We can get word back to the Village somehow and simply leave him here with the others," he said. "He won't last long."

Dovella kept her eyes averted from the two bodies. Had a healer ever killed before? She remembered with a jolt: today she would have gone through the Rites. How could she tell her father what she had done, and on the very day when she should have taken her vows? "I can't do that," she said, "and even if I could, it wouldn't solve the problem. Pandil and my ... the Master Engineer have to know what is happening so they can go to the Council before it's too late. They *must* know, Zagoad."

She could see that Zagoad agreed, but that he didn't want

to leave her on her own. "Perhaps we can find someone at one of Lakon's outposts who could take him to the Village."

"We still have to get to the outpost," she pointed out, "and we can't just leave him here alone. No matter what we do, it will mean separating."

"There's got to be another way."

"There isn't. You know there isn't."

"No doubt you're right, but I don't like it," he said. Then he stopped, listened.

Dovella held her breath. More Raiders? A whistle came from the woods at the edge of the meadow; Zagoad replied.

A figure on horseback emerged from the darkness of the forest, holding the reins of the horse that had almost run down Dovella. She recognized Brandle as he came closer.

"Are you all right?" he asked, swinging down from his horse.

"Barely," Zagoad said, "but we're better now. What are you doing here?"

"Warning Lakon's men to be on the lookout." Brandle nodded toward the men on the ground. "What's going on?"

Quickly Zagoad explained what had happened. "Maybe you can help us. If you could get this man back to the edge of the Village and get in touch with Pandil, I could go on with Dovella."

Brandle nodded, then stopped. "Where did you get that?" he asked, pointing to Dovella's knife.

"It's mine," she said. "Ancel took it when we were captured. One of the men had it in his pack."

But Brandle was already walking over to look at the two dead men. "Varden!" he cried, and fell on his knees beside one of them. He looked back, his eyes filled with tears. "Who killed my brother?"

Dovella and Zagoad glanced at each other, then back at the kneeling man. "He was with them," Zagoad said.

"With them? Why would you kill a prisoner?"

"He wasn't a prisoner," Zagoad said gently. "He was fighting with them."

Brandle stared at him as if he couldn't understand the words, then he looked back at his dead brother. "He was left to guard Ancel when Lakon's men caught him. Both of them disappeared, and we thought Ancel's men had freed him and taken my brother hostage." He got up and walked toward them, then turned back to look at his brother's body. "We ought to have known better. Raiders don't take hostages."

He kicked the toe of his boot in the dust. "That's how they knew," he said, his voice wrenched with pain. "That's how the Raiders always knew where we had moved after they attacked a settle. Time after time, they turned up at our new hiding places. I trusted him! May all the gods damn him, I wish I could kill him myself." He looked back at the sleeping Raider and drew his knife.

"No," Zagoad said, grabbing his arm.

"Why are you protecting him?"

"I'm not protecting him, but we have to get him back to the Council alive, force him to tell them what Havkad has planned."

Brandle's eyes flared, then went blank. "You're right," he said, sheathing his knife. "Yes, I'll take him if you want me to."

"I think you'd better do it, Zagoad," Dovella said.

"Don't you trust me?" Brandle's hand fell to his knife and he took a step toward her.

"Should I?"

He dropped his hand, looked away. "I need to warn my people anyway," he said. "There are more of these vermin, and thanks to my ... to Varden," he almost spat the name, "all the settles in the forest are in danger." He turned back to Dovella. "I wish I could help," he said, "but you're right — you couldn't trust me not to kill him."

With that he turned and strode back to his horse, mounted and rode into the woods, taking the dappled mare with him, but leaving his brother's body and scattered belongings lying in the dust.

Zagoad gazed down at the sleeping raider, ran a hand across his face and scowled. "If I sling him over a horse and take the clothes and badge of one of the others, I shouldn't have any trouble on the road."

"How will you get him into the Village?" Dovella asked.

"With luck and hard riding, I'll get there by tomorrow night. I can tie him up and leave him near the tunnel while I go get Pandil. She'll know how best to proceed."

Dovella reached into her belt for some of the sleeping potion and filled a small vial. "Put this in his water before you leave him and he'll sleep until you get back. His wound is not so clean as yours, so he'll need it in any case. There's enough for you to be able to get some sleep too on the way without worrying about him. And let me get you some macha leaves to chew when you get tired."

She handed him the vial and laid out two small packets of the leaves. Then she filled another vial. "Bathe his face with this if you want to rouse him quickly. My father should look at his wound, too."

She averted her eyes as Zagoad stripped the two bodies.

It was just as well she hadn't gone through the Rites, she thought, brushing a knuckle across her eyes. Best, perhaps, that she never could.

"Before you go," she said, "will you review Lakon's route with me?" She stopped, suddenly anxious. "I will be able to use the track, won't I?"

"Of course," he said, "although —" He stopped. Motioning her over to a patch of dust, he said, "Sketch out what you remember."

She took a stick and drew the track and the various outposts. He nodded. "That's the way I remember it too. You should take my hatchet, and a bow and some arrows."

"I've got my sling," she said.

"That's fine for hunting rabbits, but you may need something more powerful."

"I'm not very good with a bow," she said, surprised at how little it hurt to admit that.

"If it's big enough, you'll hit it. Just remember, don't let ..."

"... my fears race ahead of me." She smiled weakly. "I'll try."

Zagoad, clad in Raider's rags, readied the horses while Dovella bathed their prisoner's face. He came to with a start, then glared at her. "And did I tell you what you wanted to know?" he snarled.

"I've asked you nothing. I'll leave that to Pandil."

Sweat beaded on his forehead. "Why don't you just kill me?"

"Pandil won't kill you."

"She might as well. My life won't be worth dross when she's finished with me."

Zagoad gagged him, and together they slung him on one of the horses and tied him securely. Then Zagoad took Dovella's arm and led her a little way away. He hesitated for a moment. "Look, you might just think about trying Hill country anyway. I know they would help you. My friend, Lafhin, will be on patrol tomorrow morning. Show him this." Zagoad took a medal from around his neck and gave it to Dovella. It was a small gold coin embossed with a woman's face. That of the Hill Goddess, Kavella.

Her hand trembled as she took it. Today she should have received the Healer's medallion, a large sunburst on a red ribbon, hanging from a chain of smaller medals. "What is it?"

Zagoad hesitated. "Just something he will recognize, and when you tell him that I sent you, he'll trust you. His shelter will be at the side of the road into Vellaban." He stopped. "I wish there were some other way. I don't like to send you on alone."

"I don't like it either, but I really think it's our only chance. Pandil needs to know what's going on."

"I know." He smiled ruefully. "But I expect when Pandil gets through with our friend there, she'll skin me as well."

Sixteen

Safir raced into Avella's room, knelt by her bed and pressed her pale hand to his lips. At the head of the bed sat a smiling Elder Master Faris, his wan face drawn with fatigue.

Avella's blue eyes were open, although she hadn't yet spoken. But her breathing was easier than it had been before.

Pandil ran through the door after him, and Master Healer Plais puffed in on her heels.

"The gods be praised," he said. "She's awake."

"Is she going to be all right?" Pandil asked.

Safir tried to speak, then swallowed and nodded as he stroked Avella's brow.

"She'll gain strength now that she's conscious," said Elder Master Faris.

Plais looked around. "How did it happen?"

"As you said," Faris put in quickly, "the gods be praised. They brought her back to us. Perhaps she needed the rest."

"As you do," Safir said, turning his attention to the old man. "You've sat with her a long time, for which I thank you. But I don't want to see you occupying a bed in here."

"I'm well enough," the old healer said, "but you're right. I need to go home." He looked up at Pandil. "Perhaps you would walk with me."

"I'll be glad to," Pandil said. "I'm on my way to see Master Wraller at Archives Hall, so it's on my way." She bent over and squeezed Avella's hand. "I'm glad to have you back with us, my friend. Rest now, and I'll be in to see you later."

Avella smiled as Elder Master Faris stroked her forehead, then she closed her eyes. But this time, it was in natural sleep.

As the others left the room, Master Healer Plais took the seat vacated by Faris. His craggy face had a gentleness to it Safir had never seen before, and his eyes were moist. But that sorrow, real though Safir believed it to be, only made him angrier.

It's not over, Safir thought. The attack on Avella had changed him as well. Much as Safir had distrusted Havkad, he had been prepared to believe that most of the New Schoolers were sincere in their faith. But no more. They might claim that such violence was not their way, but they had done nothing to curb Havkad and his followers. They had let it happen. And others, others like Plais, had excused them; they, too, were responsible.

Perhaps Plais felt the weight of the unspoken accusation, for he looked over at Safir and said, "I truly never believed that New Schoolers would do anything like this. But that's no excuse, is it?"

Safir just looked at him. Afraid to let himself speak, he got up and walked from the room before he said words he would later regret. But his walk through the Village fanned his anger rather than cooling it. As it chanced, he found himself near the Council Chamber when he came upon Melkard in the middle of a heated discussion with Master Staver.

The two men broke off their debate as he drew near, and

Melkard smiled. "I heard Avella has regained consciousness. I'm glad she's out of danger."

"Is she out of danger?" Safir snapped. "If your friends gain power, what do you think will happen to her? What will happen to my daughter, and others like them? Have you thought about that, or don't you care?"

Melkard stepped back as if Safir had hit him. And that's what he felt like doing; he felt like smashing the face of anyone associated with the New School, of doing to them what they had done to Avella.

"Look," Melkard said, "I don't blame you for being upset, but it isn't the New School way to attack people like that. We can't be held responsible for foulheads."

"You can be held responsible for the teaching that makes them think violence is the way to win what they want," Safir shouted. "You can be responsible for not finding the ones who did this and punishing them."

"But we don't know who did it," Melkard said.

"Someone knows," Safir said, his voice quieter now but tight with anger. "Someone knows, and you could find out if you tried."

Melkard's face turned stony and he pressed his lips together. He looked as if he would respond, but he only turned his back and strode away.

Safir started to go after him, but Councillor Staver grabbed his sleeve. "You have every right to be angry, Safir, but don't let them cause you to be less than you are."

But what am I? Safir wondered. I let it happen, too. By not recognizing them for what they are, and stopping them, we are all guilty.

He had always been a peaceable man, but now there was

no peace left in his heart. The cowardly New School attack on Avella and the Engineering Building had brought the struggle to his door. He had no intention of turning it away.

Resting upstairs in the home of Elder Master Faris, Jael heard the door open and a voice call, "You can come downstairs now, young Jael. Master Pandil is here."

As Jael came down the stairs, he heard Master Faris say, "I've never seen anything like it, not in all my days."

Jael smiled. Weary as he felt, what he had achieved filled him with wonder.

"Here he is," Faris said as Jael joined them. "Before you question him, I'd like to make some collitflower tea, so don't start until I return."

When she nodded her agreement, he scuttled away toward the kitchen.

Jael started to speak, but Pandil motioned him to silence. "I promised the Elder Master that we would wait for him. Tell me only this: did you take any harm?"

The wave of concern he felt coming from her surprised and warmed him. "Not to my knowledge. And the Elder Master said he thought not, though he wants to monitor me."

Faris returned shortly carrying a tray, and Jael jumped up and went to take it from him. When Jael had poured the tea and passed around the cups, Pandil said, "Now, take your time, Jael, and tell us."

Master Faris laughed. "Only not too much time, or Master Pandil will burst, and I have no remedy for that."

Jael sputtered in his tea. It was hard to imagine anyone teasing Master Pandil in such an easy manner. He wiped his mouth and took another swallow. "It was very strange," he said. He told them what had happened.

"But you managed to wrest her away from him," Pandil said.

Jael spread out his hands as he searched for an explanation. "I had almost freed her when he discovered me, but then he didn't try to keep her. He seemed almost pleased that someone was trying to take her."

"That is strange indeed," said Pandil.

"I got the feeling that he was more interested in me than her."

She went very still. "How so?"

"It was like he was trying to see me in some way. And he seemed ... pleased about something." He paused, shivered. "There was something familiar ..."

"I don't like the sound of that," Pandil said. She leaned forward. "Are you sure he didn't hurt you?"

"I think he just wanted to identify me."

Faris smiled at Jael. "No doubt he was surprised to find a shagine in the Village."

Jael stared at him for a moment, then shook his head. "I'm not a shagine," he said. "There are only four shagines left in our village, and two of them are very frail. I had hoped to finish my training during my summer leave, but now ..."

"Your training is important," Faris said. "Maybe you could go earlier."

Jael looked toward Pandil. It would be good to get back to his outsettle to continue his studies, but could she spare him now, of all times?

"I think that's a good idea," she said, "but I'll need him here for a while yet. I'm hoping he can help Wraller."

"Then you'd best be off to Archives Hall," Faris said. "But

despite what the young man says, he needs some strengthening, for what he did was something he's never tried before. Next time, he'll be better prepared; it won't be so difficult."

"Next time?" Jael asked, suddenly afraid. He didn't want to see those eyes again.

Faris looked at him, his eyes sad. "Yes, my young friend, next time. If not for retrieving someone's mind, then for something else. Now that the sorcerer knows a shagine exists — and he will consider you a shagine whether you call yourself that or not — he will be looking for you. And for others like you."

And that made Jael even more afraid.

A little later, in Archives Hall, Jael studied Councillor Wraller as Pandil explained what she wanted them to do. He knew the Master Archivist from attending Council meetings, but he had never dealt with him personally.

After Pandil left, Wraller turned to Jael. "Well, let's see what we can find, shall we? I've looked through the scrolls Havkad had, and I can't see what help they would have given him, but maybe you'll find something I missed."

But after spending a full night going through the scrolls, Jael knew no more than when he'd started. "The only reason I can think of for Havkad wanting these scrolls is to learn more about the old Plains People."

"Maybe he was hoping to find some way to control his sorcerer."

Jael snorted. "No doubt he'd like that, but he wouldn't have found it in these scrolls."

"Can a sorcerer be controlled?" Wraller sagged with weariness. Clearly, the night had been hard on him.

Jael shrugged. "Perhaps, but I don't think Havkad would be able to do it, not unless he knows a lot more than I think he does. And in that case, why would he need the sorcerer? Is there anything else in the Archives about the Plains People?"

"Not a lot. Much of what we had was destroyed by the old Schoolmen long ago. Along with a lot of other material we could ill afford to lose."

"Why?" Jael couldn't grasp that anyone would willingly destroy so much knowledge.

"Didn't want the people to know the truth about our past, perhaps, or to eliminate all but the material that would support their point of view. They destroyed a lot of what we had left from the Founders as well." He shrugged. "Perhaps because that way no one could disprove their claims about what the Founders taught."

Just like the New Schoolers are doing now, Jael thought.

"No doubt they wanted to keep that knowledge to themselves," Wraller said. He paused. "I know only a little about what went on before the Schoolmen, but I suspect it was to control the magic that they tried to stamp out worship of the Goddess Kavella and began their campaign against the Hill Folk. They wanted to keep that power for themselves, as well."

"Havkad has no idea what he is dealing with," Jael said.

Wraller studied Jael for a moment, then opened his desk and handed him a piece of parchment. After only a glance, Jael dropped it onto the desk as if it had burned him. Heart racing, he glared at Wraller. "How did you come by such a curse?"

Wraller nodded, his eyes filled with anger. "I thought that's what it might be. Pandil found it the first time she entered

Havkad's house. She memorized it and copied it down for me."

"The first time?"

"She had learned that Havkad was having secret meetings there with a stranger," Wraller told him, "so she went to investigate. She saw the scrolls, which gave her a legitimate reason to go back with her team. She also found this."

Jael looked at the parchment and shuddered. This curse should have rebounded on anyone who came into contact with it, regardless of whom it was meant for. "Master Pandil must have some powerful protection, to have stayed long enough to memorize this."

"I expect Master Pandil has a lot of protection … and other knowledge that we don't know about," Wraller said, showing less surprise than Jael would have expected. "What can you tell me about this?"

"Only that it's evil. And very powerful. Our shagines would know more." He remembered what his mentor had said about mind power being enough if there was no community to draw on, and for helping Master Avella it had been, but even if he had enough power to nullify this kind of curse, he didn't know how. "I could try to send word to our shagines. One of them might be able to come and help."

When Pandil arrived at her office later that afternoon, she found Lakon waiting for her, several sacks at his feet.

"By Kavella, you haven't been burned out again, I hope."

"No, just bringing in a few things. Smoked rabbits for the butcher shop." He picked up one sack. "And a brace for Healer Safir. I understand he has a fondness for them."

Pandil jerked up her head. "You've seen Dovella."

He smiled broadly. "I have indeed, and she was doing splendidly."

She felt an easing in her heart. "She escaped, then?"

"You know about her capture?"

"Someone has been making inquiries about a knife taken from a young Village woman. I assumed someone had caught her."

"They were captured, and the knife taken, but seems she had another knife hidden in a boot and she got them free of their ropes. I expect Zagoad wasn't best pleased that it was she who freed them, but he managed to chew the bitter lump. And swallow it, too."

And a bitter lump it would be, Pandil thought wryly, but she had little concern for Zagoad's vanity. "What about the men who captured them?"

"The head man was called Ancel. Village man in Havkad's pay. We caught him, but somehow he got away. One of our men was guarding him, but ..." He shrugged. "Don't know what happened, but they're both missing, so I guess some of Ancel's men freed him and they took our man with them. We still have the others, but they don't seem to know much. Just that Ancel was working for a priest. Has to be Havkad."

She nodded, ever more relieved. "Well, Havkad managed to describe the knife well enough, but the knife maker has his wits about him. What more can you tell me of Zagoad and Dovella?"

"I sent them on to the river, suggested they take my raft down to Brandle's place and go on from there. Zagoad was hoping to convince Dovella to go through Hill country, but I doubt he succeeded, especially since Crade's place was burned out by Hill Folk."

She stared at him, felt her stomach clench. "I can't believe that."

He shrugged. "Renegades, I've no doubt, probably in with Raiders, or maybe paid by Havkad. Or maybe disgruntled Outlanders who look enough like Hill Folk to pass. Doesn't matter; the Hill Folk still get the blame."

Pandil let out a deep sigh. This was ill news, even though she felt sure it was renegades who'd burned out the homesteaders. "I had hoped Zagoad could convince her to ask passage of the Hill Folk. It would save them a lot of time."

"I've given them directions through the woods along the high road. They should be safe enough as long as they stick to that."

"I'm relieved to know they're safe." She told him of the attack on Avella. "I've not said anything about Dovella's capture, so I'm glad now I can report that she's well."

"And deliver the rabbits I promised."

She smiled. "That too, though I'm sorely tempted to keep them for myself. What else do you have in those sacks?"

"The weapons taken from the men who were with Ancel. They are too good for the likes of them. You might find out who bought them."

"Or who they were stolen from," she said. "We found a whole cache in Havkad's 'sacred' house."

Lakon snorted. "Sacred, indeed. When are you going to put an end to him?"

"As soon as I get enough ammunition to make it hold. It will be a lot easier if only Dovella ... " She stopped, wondering how much she should confide. As with Drase, she had complete confidence in Lakon's trustworthiness, but there was something in her that didn't like to spread information.

A weakness, perhaps, but in the past her caution had served her well.

"Well, I don't know, and don't *need* to know what she's up to," Lakon said, "but there's lots of activity around there, some rough people, too. And if she doesn't go through Hill country, it's going to take a lot longer for her to reach the other side, even with all the help my people can give her. Your time may be running out."

"I know," she said. "Believe me, I do know."

"Still, you know she has good reason to be afraid of going through Hill country," he said. "They have their share of foulheads, same as Villagers. If she ran into a band of them without Zagoad, who knows what might happen to her."

"Surely the Kaftil wouldn't permit that."

He snorted and leaned forward to rub his leg. "Could you prevent Villagers from attacking someone from Hill country?" he asked, glancing up at her. "I'm sure the Kaftil would punish them if she came to harm, but it would be too late for her. And even if they only took her in, well, the Kaftil has no great love for Villagers and in all fairness, he has little cause to. She'd still have to convince him of her reasons for being there, and he doesn't convince easily." He shook his head. "I'm just glad she has someone like Zagoad to intercede for her."

"The question is, can he persuade her to let him?"

Lakon shrugged. Neither could answer that.

He was reaching for his sacks when Nesse rushed in, shouting, "Another disturbance at the Engineering Building, Master Pandil!" He dashed away.

They jumped up and ran after him, Pandil pausing only long enough to sound the alarm for the volunteer forces to gather.

Seventeen

OVELLA MUSTERED UP A SMILE OF CONFIDENCE AND waved as Zagoad rode away with the prisoner, but her palms felt clammy. How foolish she had been when she set out; how arrogant to have thought she needed no help. She longed to call for Zagoad to take her, too. She clamped her mouth shut, as if crushing the words would also crush the wish. Her parents and Pandil were relying on her to complete her task. Having the prisoner would help Pandil confront Havkad, but there was still the danger at the water source, for surely some men had been left there to carry out the destruction on schedule. She had to stop them — on her own.

But could she? Would she even get there in time? Zagoad had brought them in dangerous proximity to Hill country, and now he was leaving her. A surge of anger warmed her cheeks. What had he been thinking? Her nails bit into her palms as she fought back tears.

No, she was being unfair. She was the one who had sent him away, had insisted that he go. Dovella shook her head vigorously as if to shake loose the blame. Zagoad was not at fault; only the New Schoolers who tyrannized both Villager and Outlander. She had learned much from observing Zagoad; now she must put that learning to use. Shouldering her pack, she raced across the withered field toward the forest beyond. There she would rest and refresh herself, and prepare for the remainder of the journey.

The air shimmered with midday heat, and even in the shaded forest it was sweltering. Sweat dripped down her legs and back, and she squirmed her shoulders, trying to relieve the itch. How she longed for a brook where she could drink her fill of sweet water and bathe her face and legs. And she needed rest badly, but as yet she had found no place that felt safe.

She stopped for a moment, glanced around at the lay of the land, then veered to the right. If she had guessed correctly, in that direction the forest would be thicker and rockier, and according to Lakon's drawing, she should find a stream. She pushed on through the undergrowth, occasionally hacking her way with the hatchet, and at last she spied an outcropping of rock similar to the one where she and Zagoad had sheltered earlier in the journey. Behind that, perhaps, she would find a concealed spot in which to rest.

She climbed up the outcropping, and sure enough, found at the top a sheltered dip in the rock. She slipped down into it, looked around, and sighed, elated that she had recognized the possibilities. Zagoad would be pleased with her. That thought filled her with more pleasure than she could have imagined; she had come to value the Forester, just as her father did. Here she could not be seen except by someone who had also climbed up the rock, and there were enough branches and dry leaves at the base of the outcropping that anyone trying to climb would make enough noise to waken her, as long as she didn't take any of her sleeping draught. She needed it badly, but she dared not take the risk.

Hunger clawed at her stomach, but she was too tired even to contemplate eating. She curled up in her cloak. Please, gods, she thought, let Zagoad reach the Village safely. And then she fell into an exhausted sleep.

When she awoke, she drew some smoked rabbit and bread from her pack and ate greedily; then, more slowly, she chewed on some macha leaves as she resumed her journey.

Picking her way through the woods, it seemed natural to follow Zagoad's methods, cutting the slight markings where only she would find them, stopping to listen and note the sun's passage, making sure no sound reached anyone who might be on the road nearby.

When she came upon a small brook, she sighed with relief. She knelt and drank, filled her water bag and looked around. It seemed secluded enough. She removed her boots and tunic and pushed up the legs of her breeches, then waded in to wash as well as she could. When she had finished, she returned to the edge and sat for a few minutes with her feet resting on a cool blue stone. The bracing water trickled across her feet. Here the air was fresh, and there were few signs of the drought that plagued the Village and its outlying areas. How she wished she could undress and bathe, put on fresh clothing. The clothes she wore, caked with blood and dust, reminded her too vividly of the fight, and of the men who had died. Although she had not actually slain them, she had been part of the fight. And on a day when she should have been going through the Rites of the Healer.

She pushed aside that thought, and leaned forward to once again bathe her face and throat. At least it was cooler, now that the sun had disappeared behind the mountains, though it was still muggy and, she noticed, slapping at her bare arm, insects were beginning to swarm.

Tomorrow would likely be another scorching day. She

dreaded the thought of more trudging through the heat, perhaps several more days of it, if she pursued Lakon's track. She pulled out the medal that Zagoad had given her and thought about his friend Lafhin, then shook her head. Regardless of his assurances, without Zagoad, she dared not take the road through the hills. She had to make her way through the woods as well as she could, trusting that Lakon's men would help her, perhaps lend her a horse to hasten her journey.

She dried her feet, put on her boots and gathered her things. Carrying the bow and hatchet had been awkward at first, but she'd adjusted her pace, and now she was used to it. As she picked her way through the forest, she thought of how much she missed Zagoad. Not just for the additional safety he afforded or his knowledge of the woods, but for the companionship. Zagoad would be proud of me, she thought, for finding such a perfect place to rest, and for following the terrain to search out water.

By morning's first glow, she saw far below her the thin ribbon of the road to Vellaban, the village of the Hill Folk. Beyond, the mountains thrust up toward the sky. She stopped and gazed in awe. A bird squawked, startling her and pulling her back to the present problem. If she climbed down and crossed the road now, she could still travel a few more hours before her midday rest; but if she went farther, to where passage down to the road would be easier, she would be closer to the sentries, and might have to wait until nightfall before crossing over. Then she would have to seek Lakon's trail in the dark.

She stopped, and again drew out the medal that Zagoad had given her. The Hill Goddess. Why would Zagoad have such a thing? Even though Lakon had invoked the Goddess's protection over them, Dovella had seen no sign that Zagoad was one of her worshippers.

She ought to wait, give it more thought before deciding, but time pressed. Despite what Zagoad had told her, her distrust of the Hill Folk was so deep that even the thought of going through Vellaban on her own made her stomach knot. Which would determine her path — her fear of the Hill Folk, or her fear of what the New Schoolers were planning, were already doing?

She dropped the medal back inside the neck of her tunic, and drew a deep breath. *You are afraid of what you don't know*, Safir had said. Frightened or not, she had to look for Lafhin, and ask his assistance; she had to face the Hill Folk.

Her decision made, Dovella stepped forward. The ground shifted and she found herself skidding down the steep escarpment. The thick brush kept her from tumbling headfirst, but jutting branches caught at her pack, throwing her sideways, while brambles snagged her shirt and tore at the skin of her hands, and rocks dug into her flesh. At last she thudded onto the road and lay there a moment, mentally probing her injuries. The scratches burned and she felt bruised, but otherwise she was intact. She got to her feet and began brushing the dirt from her breeches, then stopped, hand in mid-air. A soundless protest rose in her throat.

Bodies were strewn along the edge of the road, their gaping wounds crusted with dried blood, their unseeing eyes staring as if in wonder. Like the scattered corpses, she stared too, unable to move. Did Raiders dare come so near Hill country?

Dovella crept closer. These were Hill Folk — at least,

some of them were. That made no sense; the Raiders were dangerous, but even they must stand in awe of the Hill Folk. Unless Havkad's men were already starting their war on the Hill Folk? Slowly she approached one of the bodies.

She heard a groan. Somewhere amongst all these, one still lived. Her heart pounded and she felt a spasm in her stomach as she walked from one to the other. All past help.

Again the faint moan. There. The one half-buried beneath the body of another young man. She peered closer, then stepped back, startled. A woman! Dovella reached for her medicine belt, then shook her head. Staying to tend the woman would put Dovella herself in danger, for the Hill Folk would surely come looking for these people soon. They mustn't find her here. This changed everything. Now she had to circle the hills, for even if she could find Lafhin, even if he was not one of the men lying here, he would not help her, not after witnessing this slaughter.

Remembering the stories she had heard of the Hill Folk, of massacres, kidnappings, idol worship and bestiality, Dovella shuddered. No matter what Zagoad said, she couldn't trust them, especially not now, for just as Novise had blamed Dovella for the burning of her home, the Hill Folk would surely blame her for this butchery.

But she was a healer. Already she had caused a death; she could not leave this injured woman without aid. Even the Raider she had taken time to tend; she could not do less for this woman, even if she was of the Hill Folk.

No. She had to go on, she had to save her own people. She looked up toward the hills; beyond them, the mountains loomed dark and frightening and perilous. Turning her back on the carnage, she raced across the road to the forest beyond, closing her ears to the woman's moans. But even after she was far enough from the injured woman that the weak moan could not reach her, it still burned in her mind.

She was a healer.

But her village depended on her.

Still the voice nagged. Only yesterday she might have gone through the Rites of the healer. But instead of life, she had brought death. You make a mockery of it, she thought. You cannot leave her.

"You cannot" strove with "you must" until, scarcely aware of what she was doing, Dovella turned and raced back to the road, praying that she was not too late, half-hoping she would be.

The young woman, her fair skin drained white as winterfruit blossoms, still breathed, though with difficulty. Dovella struggled to tug off the hefty body of the warrior who had tried to defend the woman, then knelt to minister to her wounds. They were deeper than she had thought. The sun climbed higher as she worked, and sweat dripped from her brow and ran down her neck. At last she settled back and placed her fingers over the cleansed wounds, felt her body absorb the injury, felt the drain on her energy as the rebuilding of the woman's body began.

The woman responded to her touch and, as always when she used her healing power, Dovella felt joy bud then slowly unfold into flower. With care, the woman would live, but Dovella could not tend her here on the road. Apart from the danger of Raiders, the hot sun would kill the woman, weakened as she was from loss of blood. Like it or not, Dovella would have to take her to the Hill village. She would have to go into Vellaban, and without Lafhin's aid.

She wiped a hand across her mouth. Go into the hills? Alone? Dovella's throat tightened. No. She would leave the woman in the shade at the edge of the woods. The Hill Folk would surely come soon; they would find her. But what if they didn't? She groaned her frustration. There was no other way. She could not leave her work half done, she could not desert her charge.

Dovella searched the brush nearby until she found a long, stout branch to pair with Safir's staff. She tied her extra shirt and cape around them, and strapped the woman onto the makeshift litter. It would be a rough and bumpy journey, but surely the Hill Folk would have lookouts posted; when they saw her, they would send someone to help. The question was, would they allow her to go on her way?

Her ears strained for the sound of footsteps as she dragged her burden as gently as she could along the road, but all she heard was her own rasping breath. What would they do to her? Again she was tempted to leave the woman; but she pushed herself on, dragging her burden as gently as she could up the road to the village. Sweat soaked her clothing, right down to the liners in her boots, making walking even more difficult. She staggered, nearly exhausted from the energy drain that attended healing. Still she trudged on.

It was slow progress, trying to keep the makeshift litter from jostling the injured woman, and she hadn't gone far when a troop of fair-haired men loomed up ahead, spears at the ready. At the sight of them, Dovella froze like a rabbit caught in a varlag's gaze. The yellow braids and ruddy faces would have proclaimed the men to be Hill Folk even if they had not been here on the road to Vellaban. Dovella's heart beat faster, but she willed herself to show calm. If she tried to run away, they were sure to attack. Their weathered faces were hard, and two of them raised their bows as they drew near, while two others came forward to grab her by the arms, their fingers pinching into her flesh.

One of the men bent to look at the injured woman and began shouting at Dovella.

"I found her on the road," she said, too frightened to struggle. She tried to moisten her lips, but her mouth was too dry. "The others were dead."

They stared at her blood-caked clothes. She shook her head. "No. I was attacked earlier on the way." Dovella held out her arm to show the torn sleeve of her tunic and her bandaged arm. "I didn't kill them!"

She had caused the death of another man, though, and that guilt ripped through her.

They conversed heatedly among themselves for a few chaotic moments, then one of the men came up to her. "What have you done to her?"

"I gave her a potion," Dovella said. "I'm a healer."

"What kind of potion?"

"To purify the blood and give her rest. I can bring her out of it, but it is too soon." How could she explain so the man would understand? "She is still in shock. She must rest."

The men pressed forward around the litter and Dovella almost wept in frustration. Their suspicions were going to undo all that she had done.

Four of the men lifted the litter and carried it, while Dovella followed, her arms still gripped firmly by the two warriors, though they were kind enough to avoid her wound. The one who had spoken to her walked beside the injured woman as they made their way toward the Hill village. Every now and then, he reached out to touch the woman's cheek. Though he said nothing, his eyes were filled with tears.

One man had already raced ahead. Two others sped back along the way Dovella had come, toward the spot where the bodies lay scattered. Watching them go, she shuddered, remembering the horror of that sight.

The climb took only a short time, but it seemed like days to Dovella, itching to be on her way; she had work to do. But even if they let her go, which was unlikely, she would never make it to the source in time now. Her impatience hid a deeper fear. Clearly there was no goodwill toward Villagers here, though they hadn't exactly attacked her. Still, she could see from the way they scowled at her that they would like to, that only the need to discover what she had done to the wounded woman restrained them.

They came to a small building, a watchman's tower from the look of it, where the men gently placed the injured woman in a cart. They gave Dovella a mount, and she considered escape, but for only a moment; even if she could stay astride a galloping horse, the men rode too close for her to bolt away.

On they rode, ever deeper into Hill country, farther and farther away from where she should be, the danger to her own people increasing. There was nothing she could do but go along and hope she would have a chance to explain, hope someone would listen.

Here the woods were airier, but she recognized most of the trees: oak, blackwood, greenalls and thorns. And there, growing among plants she had never seen before, were bloodheal and maywhites and little blue gillyflowers, all the things she would find in the woods around the Village. At that thought she had to smile. Had she really believed that even the familiar vegetation would be afraid to grow here?

As they rode out of the woods into a clearing, Dovella clutched the reins and looked around in wonder. She wasn't sure what she had expected, but certainly not this village of sturdy stone houses with well-tended gardens, clean streets of stone and people with a look of health and well-being. Though they stared at her with open curiosity, she saw no hostility in their piercing blue eyes. Eyes like Avella's, like Dovella's own. And yet she felt no such kinship to them as she had to Novise, with her copper skin and jet-black hair.

On through the streets they rode, the horses' hooves tapping against the stone. They passed a park where the chatter and whooping of small children filled the air as they raced with dogs, jumped hurdles, wrestled, or balanced on bars, watched over by both women and men tending smaller children. Several of the children stopped and waved shyly, until a young man spoke harshly to them and herded them away.

A bit farther along, she saw a small market stocked with cages of fowl and rabbits, and bins of glowing fruits and vegetables. Clearly there was no shortage of water here, Dovella thought with some bitterness.

When they reached a large square, two guards pulled Dovella from her horse, their blue eyes cold and full of hatred, and prodded her into a building set a little way back from the square. Although she was not chained, as she had expected to be, the men shoved her roughly into a small chamber, muttering words that, although indistinct, she knew contained threats. They shut the door firmly behind her, and she heard the thump of a sliding bolt.

Eighteen

As Pandil raced into the Engineering Building, she saw Elder Master Quade, Carpace, Narlos and the two security apprentices who'd been stationed there desperately trying to hold off intruders armed with knives, swords and axes.

Narlos's knife hand was a mass of shredded flesh, but his opponent's arm gaped open. Blood soaked the left shoulder of Carpace's tunic and she hugged her left arm close to her body as she fought to intercept a man who yelled, "Do you want this to split your head, old man?" while shoving his way toward Elder Master Quade.

On his knees, one of the security apprentices pounded his opponent in the face, while the other slashed at a tall, stocky man wielding a knife.

Nesse and Jael, who had reached the building seconds ahead of the others, had already taken on two other men. The remaining attackers, unchallenged, bashed at everything in sight, shattering windows and shredding tapestries. Furniture lay smashed on the floor. Pandil stared appalled at the vandalism. It served no purpose, but it was just like such fanatics to wreak destruction for its own sake.

While Maidel went after one of the vandals, Pandil rushed to Master Quade's rescue. She grabbed the big man who appeared to be the leader. Swinging him around, she kneed him in the groin, then twisted his arm until he screamed. He was no weakling though, and he knew how to get out of an arm hold. Face contorted in pain, he jerked around and swung at her. She sidestepped his swing and danced around to come in on him from behind, jabbing him behind the knee with her boot. When she threw him against the wall, he slid to his knees and fell over, senseless.

She paused for breath, and saw Jael subdue one of the rioters while Maidel deftly tied the wrists of a man sprawled on the floor. Blood ran down the side of Maidel's face. Lakon, meanwhile, had gone after the young man fighting Carpace. Pandil had been vaguely aware of his sack of rabbits flying across the room. The youth's knife, which had flown from his hand as he tried to protect his face, had skidded over toward Lakon. Now it protruded from the young man's chest, and before his screams had died down, Lakon started after a man smashing windows.

By then the volunteer forces, led by Osten the knife maker, were swooping into the building armed with bludgeons and knives, stout ropes tied to their belts. As before, Councillor Blaint was there, as was old Councillor Staver, brandishing his stick, though his face was still mottled purple and yellow with bruises from the last fight. Those invaders who hadn't been disabled turned to flee, but it was too late; two or three strong Villagers surrounded each.

Once the attackers were securely bound, Pandil thanked the volunteers and sent them off, smiling and cuffing each other lightly on the arm. The healers arrived and set to work on the injured. Cradling his mangled hand against his chest, Narlos stood stoically as they examined the cuts on his arms and shoulder. Carpace, stretched out on the floor, stifled a moan when a healer started tending her arm and shoulder.

"She's taken some deep cuts," the healer said.

"What about Master Quade?"

"Bruised and shaken, but otherwise well."

Elder Master Quade limped over, smiling through tears. "My young apprentices fought valiantly for me."

"They did, indeed." Pandil touched his arm. "Thank the gods." She felt guilty about putting him in danger, and was relieved that he'd come to no greater harm.

Stepping carefully around broken glass, she went to check on her two security apprentices who had taken minor wounds, then walked over to see how the attackers had fared. All had cuts and bruises, but two were lying on the floor, including the one she'd bashed against the wall.

"They'll live," said Safir, who had just arrived, "but it will be some time before they're on their feet again."

"Well, I wish no man ill," said Master Quade, "but I can't say they don't deserve it, seeing what they did to Carpace and Narlos."

Carpace struggled to her feet, staring at one of the men in custody. Tears streaked her face. "My father," she said, pointing to a tall man still struggling against the ropes binding him. "My own father attacked me." She closed her eyes and leaned against the wall.

Lakon swore, but Pandil said nothing.

Carpace wiped her eyes with her good hand, then moistened her lips. "I joined the New School. I did everything they asked of me."

"You're a disobedient child," her father retorted. "If you'd let us pass, no one would have been hurt. You're responsible for this."

From the look on her face, she'd take the blame, too, Pandil thought. She started to intervene, but Carpace straightened her shoulders and replied, "I couldn't let you damage the machine. Everyone would suffer from that. Besides, it's my duty to protect the machine. I swore an oath in the name of the gods."

The man Pandil had fought leaned forward and snarled, "The gods are against the people who run the machine."

"Then let the gods destroy the machine, if it offends them," Carpace said.

"We are meant to carry out the work of the gods," her father said quietly. "You'll be punished for this."

"No doubt I will," she said, "but you are the one who will punish me, not the gods. They are not so weak that they need people like you, or work such as this."

"You'll have no more part in our family," said one of the young attackers.

She turned, raised her chin. "I've never had much part in it, brother. I thought that might change if I did what Havkad asked, but I know now that he was just using me. You were all just using me."

"Let's get these foulheads to Security," Pandil said.

Pandil had scarcely locked up the six men who were well enough to be taken prisoner, when Havkad came marching into her office.

"I'm running out of patience," he said. "When are you going to let me and my people resume worship in our sacred house?"

Pandil leaned back in her chair and studied him. "There has

been another New School attack at the Engineering Building," she said. "This time they tried to destroy the machine. This will put an end to your support in the Village."

"Do you think I'd be stupid enough to countenance something like that?" He glared at her, then smiled. "Your work, no doubt; now you'll try to blame it on my people. It won't work, Pandil. No one will believe you."

"It was Carpace's father and brother, among others. You'll never convince anyone you didn't send them to do it."

His face went white and an artery bulged in his neck; Pandil wondered idly if it might burst. "I'll have their hides," he growled. "Did they damage the machine?"

"No."

He raised his hands and looked toward the ceiling. "The gods be praised!"

"Actually, it's Carpace and Narlos along with my apprentices and the volunteer forces who should be praised. Without them, I expect your gods would have allowed it to happen."

"You'll stop your blasphemy when —" He stopped. "Did you say Carpace?"

"Her arm was broken and she took several deep cuts on her shoulder trying to protect Elder Master Quade."

He clenched his fleshy hand. "The fools." Then he tightened his lips and glared at her. "Still, it's time the Village learned to abide by New School teaching."

"Most Villagers don't want New School rule, and you know it." Like talking to a stone wall, she thought, watching him.

"I don't care what the people want. I intend to carry out the will of the gods."

"The will of the gods or the will of the New School leaders?"

"It comes to the same thing. We are spokesmen for the gods, and I intend to bring it about now. I'm using councillor's prerogative to convene an emergency meeting of the Council for tomorrow morning."

She felt as if the walls were closing in on her. By the Goddess, she couldn't face him so soon. She had to find out what was going on with that Plains sorcerer. That was the only thing that would be likely to turn Havkad's people against him. Even if Dovella repaired the problem at the source, Havkad would only claim that power had been restored in answer to his prayer. No, she had to find a way to tie him to the sorcerer.

"You can't," she said. "Notice has to be given. A full day plus three hours."

"Then it will convene at three hours from this time tomorrow," he said, and stalked out, almost knocking Maidel off his feet.

Dear Goddess, Pandil thought, what am I to do? If he put it to a vote tomorrow, he would win. None of her evidence would matter because he controlled over half the council. "By the Goddess and all the gods, I'll never be ready by tomorrow night."

Maidel sank into a chair. "But you have all those weapons taken from his house, and the weapon pulled against you by that foulhead who attacked Master Avella — surely that can be traced to one of Havkad's supporters. And then this brawl today."

She paced. "He'll be able to convince the few decent people who follow the New School that we planted the weapons, and the others won't care. I need something to prove that he is in league with that Plains sorcerer. Otherwise he'll find a way to justify to his followers even the charges I can prove, and other Villagers are afraid to speak out against him, afraid they'll be called on by people like those men we caught today. And we can't protect everyone."

"Well, what about those men today?" Maidel's handsome face reflected weariness and pain, for he'd taken a glancing blow from an axe, as well as the cut on his face. Not enough to merit a stay at Healer's Hall, but enough to make him favour one leg. "He can hardly deny that Carpace's father is one of his chief supporters."

"We have another worry. What are we going to do with all of them? This place wasn't intended to hold so many prisoners."

"We could open up the old cells," Maidel said.

"What do you know of the old cells?"

"In the dungeon."

"Old men's tales, Maidel," she said. "Told to frighten children."

He shook his head. "The Archives were one of my special studies. I almost apprenticed with Master Wraller, remember."

"Yes, I remember." She grinned. "He wasn't very happy about my getting his best student, although he agreed you were too restless to sit in Archives Hall."

He returned her grin. "I remember. Anyway, I studied a lot about security practices over the centuries. The cells down there were walled up when the Schoolmen were defeated."

"If they were Schoolmen cells, I'd hate to be the one to reopen them."

"If you don't, Havkad's people will. You can be sure they know about them."

"Then do it."

Pandil sank into her chair when Maidel left. At times like this, she was used to seeking Avella's advice. Though the Master Engineer stuck to her duties with the machine and stayed out of political intrigues, Avella often provided sensible advice. How Pandil wished she could go to her now.

Well, why couldn't she? Indeed, she must, to give her the news of Dovella's safety. But she would have to keep quiet about Havkad's threat.

By the time she reached Healer's Hall, however, Havkad had seen to it that the news was spreading, and it had already reached Avella. She was sitting up in bed when Pandil arrived, sipping a cup of tea.

"What are you going to do?" she asked.

Pandil smiled. "I might have known I couldn't keep it from you."

"You shouldn't even try. So I repeat: what are you going to do?"

"I have a certain amount of ammunition in reserve. But you need to be recovering, not troubling yourself about that. Here, I've got news to make you happy. I've just talked to an Outlander who saw Dovella and Zagoad a few days ago." She wouldn't tell Avella about the ills that had befallen her daughter. They were over now, and Dovella was safe. No need in worrying the girl's mother.

Although Avella smiled, she refused to be diverted. "You know that your news makes my heart rest easier, my friend, but you should also know that I haven't forgotten my question."

Pandil dropped into the chair by Avella's bed and buried her face in her hands. She wasn't used to feeling so helpless. "I don't know, and I can hardly bear to think about it." The harm the New Schoolers would do could never be undone. The Village still carried scars from the work of the old Schoolmen.

Before she could voice her fears, Elder Master Faris came in supporting Carpace. "I hope you feel well enough for company, Avella," Faris said.

"Certainly, Elder Master," Avella replied. "Perhaps Carpace and I can think of something that will help safeguard the machine."

Carpace looked at her and began to cry. "You are much too generous, Master Avella. I have betrayed your trust. Please believe that I would not have let them hurt the machine. I believed that the gods would help us restore power if the New School controlled the Village. I've been taught from childhood that we were chosen by the gods to bring the Village to rightful worship."

"I believe you," Avella said. "You proved your loyalty today." She looked back at Pandil, still waiting for an answer.

"All right, to get back to your question, Avella, there is nothing I can do. Havkad has a right to call the assembly. And I fear he has a majority."

"Perhaps not." Avella put her cup down and leaned forward. "With Plais on our side, all we need do is convince Melkard. If you show him what you have, we may be able to convince him."

"We?"

Avella pushed a strand of blonde hair behind her ear, a gesture Pandil knew well. "Oh, I'll be there."

Pandil smiled. How like Avella to be ready to wade into the fray, especially when a friend was threatened. "I know you're in a fighting mood, but you're far too weak yet."

"I'll be there," Avella repeated. "Even if I have to crawl."

"And if Master Avella can make it, so can I," Carpace said.

"I can't allow that," Faris said.

"Why not? Master Healer Plais is a councillor, so he will be on hand if either of us needs assistance." Everyone stared at her for a moment, and she reddened. "I know you doubt that you can trust me, but you know that I take the true New School teachings seriously. So I swear by our gods that I will not deceive you. And to prove my goodwill, I'll tell you all I know about what Havkad is doing."

"All right," Pandil said. There was no harm in listening to the girl, who had certainly fought well to defend Elder Master Quade. Besides, she'd learn as much by what Carpace kept hidden as by what she told.

"I understand now," Carpace said, "that the only reason Havkad paid me so much attention was because of my position as Master Avella's apprentice."

"Did he ever ask you to damage the machine?"

"Never! That's why I was so surprised today when my father and those others burst in the way they did. I've no doubt Havkad was behind the attack on Master Avella, no matter how much everyone denies it, but I can't believe he'd want to harm the machine. After all, he has promised to restore the flow of water." She shook her head. "I don't know how he thinks he can do it when Master Avella has failed, but even if the gods are with him, he'll need the machine undamaged. And a lot of New School followers will turn against him if he can't keep his promise. They would see him as a false prophet."

"Do you have any idea how he plans to restore power?" Pandil sat back. This would prove whether the girl was to be trusted or not.

"I'm not sure." Carpace wrinkled her brow. "Havkad is very secretive." She looked from one to the other as if weighing whether or not she should go on. "But he ... he's using sorcery."

"What?" Avella's blue eyes blazed. "Havkad is a fool if he thinks he can use a sorcerer."

"I hadn't realized you were so trusted," Pandil said to Carpace.

"Trusted?" Carpace laughed. "I wasn't. But I am an apprentice to Master Avella, and I'm young so I guess they thought they could control me. I'm not sure, but —"

"Did they hurt you?" Elder Master Faris leaned forward.

"No, they —"

"What do you know about the weapons stored underground at Havkad's 'sacred house,' as he calls it?" Pandil broke in.

Carpace looked at her blankly. "Weapons?"

"There were several crates filled with weapons — most, if not all of them, stolen."

"Oh, no, that's nothing to do with Havkad! He said that he could turn the Village to rightful worship by peaceful means. He swore that he was against violence."

Although Pandil was still not sure she wanted to trust the girl, she'd studied with Drase long enough to know truth when she heard it. But then, she could hardly be surprised that Havkad had kept the girl ignorant of his true purpose and methods.

"And if Carpace finds it hard to believe, other people will need even more convincing," Avella said. "I have to be at that meeting, Pandil."

"I can't keep you away, Avella, nor do I truly want to. But both Plais and Wraller have talked with Melkard, and I'm convinced that he cannot be swayed."

"Perhaps not, but even if we fail, I am determined to have my voice heard. And to look Havkad and his toadies in the eye."

Jael wasn't sure which pounded loudest, the thud of his boots on the cobblestone road or the thump of his heart. Gasping for breath, he fell against Pandil's door frame and pulled the doorbell. He didn't know what was going on, but just beyond the Village wall, when he'd been on his way to visit the friend he had hoped might take a message to his outsettle, he'd run into Zagoad. The Forester had insisted that Jael get Pandil and bring her out to where he would be waiting with a prisoner. "And tell her Dovella is safe," he'd added.

Jael had wanted to ask what *that* meant, but he'd seen that Zagoad was nearly exhausted. His own concerns about Dovella would have to wait until he got back with Pandil. Now he understood why he hadn't seen Dovella lately; she'd been off with Zagoad. But where? And why wouldn't she be safe? He'd been so relieved that she hadn't been caught up in the riot at the Engineering Building, and now it looked as if she'd been in even greater danger.

The door jerked open and he faced Pandil, still half asleep. She gaped when she saw him, but he gave her no time to speak. "I ran into Zagoad outside the Village. He wants you to meet him there."

"Zagoad! Alone?" She sagged against the door.

"No, he has a prisoner and he needs to see you at once. He said tell you Dovella was safe ... whatever that means." He'd hoped she might tell him, but she had already dashed back into the house to get dressed.

A thousand questions ran through his mind as he waited, but he knew she wouldn't answer, not yet, so there was no point asking.

They set off, waiting until they reached the park before breaking into a run. If there was anyone about in New Village to wonder about their rush, they'd be more likely to hide than to follow. "I trusted him to look after Dovella," Pandil stormed as she ran. "If he's let something happen to her, by the Goddess, I'll have his hide."

And she would too. Jael admired and trusted Pandil, but he would not have wanted her anger directed at him.

When they reached Zagoad, he didn't give her time to berate him. "This prisoner is Havkad's man," he said urgently. "I can imagine all the things you want to say, but given what Dovella and I have gone through to get this foulhead here, let's get him to Security House before day breaks. Then, you can strip off all the skin you want."

Thanks to the light of the moons, Jael could see the limp figure draped over one of the horses, but the man's face was hidden from view.

"Dead men can't tell much," Pandil snapped.

"He's not dead," Zagoad said. His voice was heavy and Jael saw it was taking great effort for him to talk. "I used some of Dovella's sleeping draught to keep him quiet, and I have here something to bring him out of it. But we'd best have him somewhere safe before I use it and he starts making a ruckus."

Pandil looked as if she wanted to lay into him then and there, but it was clear that Zagoad had the right of it. "All right," she agreed, her voice tense, "but if you didn't make arrangements for someone reliable to guide her, I *will* have your skin."

And I'll help, Jael thought. He took the reins of the horse with the prisoner and, as quietly as possible, followed Pandil through the Village, Zagoad behind him. From the looks of him, Zagoad needed to ride, but he stumbled alongside the other horse, leaning heavily against it. Jael knew better than to offer help.

When they reached Security House, Zagoad and Jael hauled the prisoner from the horse, and Pandil called Maidel to help carry him to one of the deep cells they had been opening up. Jael looked around in wonder. He'd had no idea these cells existed.

When the three men returned to Pandil's office, she turned on Zagoad, her eyes hard. "First thing," she said, "I want to know why you left Dovella."

"Because she insisted," he sputtered, "and by the Goddess, that girl's as hard-headed as you are." He glared at her. "Do you have any idea what you saddled me with?"

At the look on his face, Jael had to laugh. If Dovella had managed to get the best of Zagoad, good for her. Jael liked the Forester, trusted him, but he knew Zagoad didn't like his instructions to be questioned. Jael could imagine how frustrating the trip must have been, for that reason if no other.

Then Pandil laughed too, and it looked as if all her anger

had dissolved in that laugh. She dropped into her chair, still smiling, and toyed with a dark stone on her desk. "She is strong-willed, yes. Just tell me what happened."

Half sitting on the side of her desk, Zagoad related how they'd been attacked, and why Dovella had insisted that he return with the prisoner. Jael squirmed. He'd have liked to ask more about that fight, but he knew he had to let the Forester finish.

Zagoad handed Pandil the papers they'd taken from the prisoner. "Dovella said these were vital. That's why she insisted that I leave her." Jael saw that he was still unhappy about that, but whether it was leaving her or having to admit she was right that upset him most wasn't clear.

Pandil thumbed through the documents, starting at Havkad's instructions on the drawings and examining the map. "So, Dovella guessed aright about the problem being at the source. Still, no one suspected anything like this." She got up and began to pace around the small room, then glanced back at the incriminating papers on her desk. "Yes, this is vital. It may be just what we need. But even so, it worries me that you had to leave her."

"The Hill Folk will help her."

Jael was eased by that thought but Pandil ran her fingers across her eyes and sighed. "Maybe. But, don't forget, some of the Hill Folk hate Villagers. With good reason, I'll grant you; nonetheless, if Dovella runs into one of them, she could be in grave danger."

"She won't be going in as a stranger, Pandil." He steadied himself against the desk. His face was pale and drawn.

Pandil rushed toward him. "I'm sorry, Zagoad. You must be exhausted."

"Well, I am," he admitted, "and I've a wound that needs attending."

"You should have said so." She stopped. "Why didn't Dovella help you?"

"She did, or I would never have made it. But she needed to go on, and I had to get that skrev here. I'll see Safir later."

"I should have noticed. I'm sorry. But I'm worried about Dovella."

"I gave her my medal. Once she shows it to Lafhin, he'll treat her as he would one of us. I expect she's in Vellaban now, and they're already making plans to help her." He smiled. "She has a sharp tongue when she's crossed, I'll give you that, but she's resourceful. She'll convince them."

"I hope you're right. If anything happens to her ..." Pandil sighed and rubbed the back of her neck.

You're near to exhaustion yourself, Jael thought. And, if anything happened to Dovella, Pandil would hold herself responsible, no matter how much she railed at Zagoad.

"Well, it can't be helped," Pandil said at last. "As you say, after all you've both gone through to get this man here, I'd best hear his story."

As they walked down the cold hallway leading to the cell, Pandil strode ahead of them, clenching her hands. Jael knew her well enough to understand that part of her anger at Zagoad was due to the dread of facing this man. If he was one of Havkad's minions, he wasn't likely to talk willingly, and she might be forced to live up to her reputation.

Jael knew that Pandil had never before broken into a man's mind in order to wring information from him, had never wanted to, for all her fierce reputation. But if that's what it took to find out what was behind this map and the cryptic marks on it, then she would do it. And she'd suffer for it too, for though such questioning was painless for the person being questioned, it left the interrogator feeling exhausted ... and tainted.

Before they reached the cell, Maidel strode ahead of Jael and Zagoad and caught up with her. "Why don't you let me question him?"

Pandil laid a hand on his arm. "I thank you for trying to spare me, Maidel, but you should know by now that I would never let you do something I'm not prepared to do myself."

And she wouldn't. That's part of why they were all willing to follow her without question. So Jael wasn't surprised that Maidel had made the offer, only that his fellow officer had the skills that would be needed. But he shouldn't have been surprised about that either, he told himself. Master Pandil chose her apprentices carefully, and made sure they got the training they needed.

When they reached the cell, the prisoner lay stretched out on a small cot. Pandil drew in her breath sharply. "Konell!"

"You know him?" Maidel pulled the cell door closed.

"Yes. And to my regret, I had the training of him. It was a few years back, while you were studying with Drase. But he was a little too fond of hurting people. I knew I could never take him to apprentice."

She watched as Zagoad bathed the man's face. When Konell opened his eyes, he shuddered. "I told them they might as well kill me, because I won't tell you anything."

Pandil grinned. "Finally met your match did you?"

"There were two of them against me."

"Why don't you start from the beginning?" Zagoad asked, steadying himself against the wall. "Tell how there were three of you on horseback against two of us afoot, and Dovella with no weapon until she got one off your fellow skrev. And why don't you tell how Dovella held you off on her own long enough to give you those wounds? And how I was already badly wounded when I joined her."

Jael smiled picturing Dovella trouncing her attackers, a smile that faded when he considered how easily she might have been killed.

Konell cursed, but he made no attempt to get off the cot.

"Who were the men with you?" Pandil asked.

He smirked. "Since when do Raiders give the names of their companions?"

"Probably doesn't know," Zagoad said with a sneer. "I expect he was just one of Havkad's lackeys, sent to guard the higher-ups. I doubt he ever knew what they were even there for." He turned and walked toward the door. Pandil made as if to follow.

Konell jerked himself upright and swung his feet to the floor. "That's all you know." He leaned forward and poked his chest. "*I* was the one who carried the map wasn't I? It was the other two that were lackeys."

Maidel laughed. "Sure you were," he taunted, and turned to follow the others. "As if Havkad would trust trash like you with something this important."

"I was in charge. Do you think anyone would trust?..." He stopped, glared at Maidel and let out a string of curses.

The job wasn't finished, Jael thought, but having brought him to admit to so much, perhaps Pandil could get the rest out of him without ransacking his mind.

But Konell had recognized the trick, and refused to say anything more. Pandil sighed, nodded at Maidel. "You three had best leave," she said. "I'd rather do this alone."

"No!" Konell pleaded.

Jael hesitated for a moment, then nodded as he followed Maidel and Zagoad from the room. "You need to see the healers," he told Zagoad. "Maidel, why don't you go to Healer's Hall with him? It wouldn't hurt for them to tend your wounds again."

Maidel glanced down the hall.

"I'll wait for her," Jael said.

While he waited, Jael pondered recent events, wondering how it would all end. Remembering the look in the sorcerer's eyes, he shivered. He didn't ever want to look into those eyes again, but he knew that Pandil was right. Eventually he'd have to face the man, he or someone from his village. Maybe all the shagines would be needed, for where there was one such man, there might well be several more.

When Pandil returned to the office, the sun was high. Jael saw that she was exhausted, as much from grief at what she had done as from the effort of doing it. The invasion he'd made into Avella's mind, though it had been done to help her, had left him feeling that he'd besmirched his gift. He could imagine that after prying into Konell's mind Pandil felt dirtier than she'd ever felt. Though she wasn't one to take time for self-flagellation, not when there was work to be done, it would come later; he was sure it would come later.

"I'm going to ... clean myself," she said and went into her inner office. When she returned, Jael held out a cup of freshly brewed macha. "If you're going to go on like this with no rest," he said, "you need something to strengthen you."

"You've been going as long as I have," she said, "and you

had that long run in from outside the Village."

"Yes, but I've already had two cups of macha, and Maidel brought me some breakfast, while you've taken neither food nor drink."

"Well, and so I haven't. I forgot. But you're right and I thank you." She took a sip of macha and sank into her chair. "I need to speak to Plais and Wraller, but after that, I'll rest." She put down the cup and stared at him for a moment. "We should send you home to complete your training earlier than we had planned. Maybe today."

Jael nodded. He was eager to resume his studies, but he didn't want to leave the Village right now. "Only … maybe you'll need help with Havkad."

Pandil's eyes widened as if his words had startled her. After a short pause, she said, "Yes, maybe I will. But after the Council meets, I want you on your way."

He glanced down at his hands which, to his surprise, lay clenched in his lap. If Pandil lost the vote in Council, would completing his studies be of any help to her or the Village?

At Healer's Hall, Pandil told the Master Healer and Wraller what she had learned about Havkad's actions, though not how she'd gained the information. She showed them the documents they had captured.

"This is outrageous!" Plais stood, his cheeks afire. "We should call in Havkad right now."

"I'd rather keep it quiet until Council meets," Pandil said. Relieved as she was to have Plais on her side, she worried about whether the healer would listen to her. "I don't want him to have time to work up a defence."

"Will it make any difference?" Wraller asked.

"What do you mean?" the Master Healer asked. "Surely the other councillors will feel the same way I do."

"The ones who already oppose Havkad will be as enraged as you are, Plais. But Havkad's supporters? They probably already know, and even if they don't, I'm not sure they will care as long as they win control."

"But surely we will have at least half the votes," Plais insisted.

"I doubt it," Pandil said. "Even with Avella here, we still need Melkard."

Wraller sighed. "And he's even more stubborn than you are, Plais. If he's given his pledge to Havkad there'll be no swaying him. We have to find a way to draw someone else from the other side."

That was one of the things Pandil liked about Wraller, his certainty that there was always a way. It helped offset her own pessimism. But this morning she felt only the cold hand of defeat.

"If we can't persuade Melkard, who can we persuade?" She shook her head. "No one."

"Then we are in for trouble," Wraller said, "because once Havkad has rid the Council of you, Pandil, he will turn on Avella, and then on each of us in turn."

"I've no doubt he will," said Plais, fidgeting with the belt of his robe, "but it's the Guilds who elect councillors. If they re-elect Pandil and Avella, Havkad will have to accept it."

"But will they re-elect Avella and me?" Pandil shook her head. "Havkad has influential people in all the Guilds. He'll make sure they speak lies about why the Council expelled us."

"Then we'll have to do something about that, too."

Wraller's face lit up. "And I think I know how. All that study I went through will bear some fruit after all." He sat back and smiled, rubbing his hands together as if getting ready to sit down to a feast. "Sweet fruit, indeed."

Nineteen

D OVELLA PACED THE WINDOWLESS CELL, TRYING VAINLY
to find some means of escape. Light streamed through
narrow slits in the thick walls, and it was dry and clean, but it
was clearly meant to hold a prisoner for a while, for there was
also a bed, and a table and chair. At least the bed was made
with clean linens, and the room smelled fresh.

She was exhausted from her healing, not only of the injured
woman today, but of Zagoad and the Raider and herself
the day before, so she threw herself on the bed, tempted to
sleep, to leave all this in the hands of the gods. The bed was
comfortable, but she was too agitated to sleep, and she still
dared not take any of her draught. She sat up and tried to
concentrate on restoring her energy, but all of her training
seemed to have deserted her.

A few minutes later, she heard the bolt slide and pulled
herself to her feet. An old woman, dressed in a leather skirt
and red blouse and accompanied by three armed men,
stood in the doorway. The woman gestured to the guards,
who withdrew, weapons still at the ready, and she walked in
alone.

Her blonde hair was faded and her skin coarse and deeply
lined, but her blue eyes were clear and penetrating. They met
Dovella's, then widened briefly. "Tell me what you did to
Tavel."

Dovella explained how she had found the slaughtered Hill Folk, how she had done what she could to heal the injured woman. "But her injuries go deep," she said. "I need to … touch her again."

The old woman studied her for a moment. "You are in need of healing yourself.

"I've seen to my wounds," Dovella told her. "I only need rest, and to be clean."

The woman nodded and turned towards the men. Some signal must have passed for after she left with two of them, the third came forward. Dovella recognized him as the one who had spoken to her on the road.

"Come with me." His eyes were like a stormy sky, but his voice was friendly enough. "I am sorry if we have treated you badly, but there has been much trouble from your people lately. And Tavel is my betrothed."

Saying no more, he led Dovella across the square to a house, and took her to a chamber upstairs. "Refresh yourself," he said, "and I will have some food sent. The Kaftil will see you later."

The Kaftil, chief of the Hill Folk. Dovella had heard from her teachers of his cunning and cruelty; she knew she would have to be alert to defend herself. Perhaps the woman would help her, she thought.

She glanced around the room, saw that all her things had been brought here already; they rested on a narrow bed and a table beside it. Her cloak, washed and neatly pressed, was draped across the back of a beautifully carved wooden chair. The chamber was pleasant, light and airy, its open windows curtained with a gauzy, white material that billowed gently in the breeze. She found a large blue tub in a smaller room on one side of the chamber. Surprised, and a bit envious when she discovered the hot running water that flowed so freely here, she filled the tub, added some fragrant oil she found on a low table under the window and stepped in, sighing with pleasure. At least she would be able to restore herself to some degree before she went to face the Kaftil.

She had almost fallen asleep when a noise from the adjoining room jerked her back to an awareness of her surroundings. A young, fair-skinned woman entered hesitantly, carrying a tray that held a small plate of plantuff, hot and aromatic, a jug with a glass, and a small carafe. She drew up the low table next to the tub and put down the tray.

"When you have refreshed yourself, please come down." The woman spoke in a controlled voice, but her movements were wary and she wouldn't meet Dovella's eyes. It was almost if she were afraid. Why would she be afraid of me? Dovella wondered. Looking down at her hands, the young woman continued. "I have left clean clothes in the other room and will see to repairs to your own." She hesitated, moistened her lips and stammered, "The Kaftil is waiting."

And no doubt he wasn't accustomed to being kept waiting. Dovella nodded, not daring to speak, and the young woman left. Sitting up, Dovella looked at the tray. Hunger and thirst tore at her, but she wondered if she dared eat. She lifted the carafe and sniffed. Jubana juice. She recognized the aroma even though she had tasted it only twice before.

On the first occasion, she had overtired herself at fight practice, determined to prove worthy, even though she had just come from a healing; the second time, she had exhausted herself almost to death trying to save a woman whose injuries were too severe.

"You are not a god," Safir had said as he lifted the glass of jubana juice to her lips, "only a human healer. Even the most skilled among us cannot work miracles."

"But I couldn't just give up," she had cried, lying back on her pillow. Saving someone was the only way she could assure herself that her gift was good.

"Sometimes, you have to." Safir had stroked her brow, his eyes even darker with understanding of her grief. "With time you will be able to feel the difference, and when you sense that further effort will only drain your own life, then you must withdraw. You misuse your gift if you kill yourself."

"How can you bear to let them go?" she'd burst out, feeling the tightness in her eyes that threatened to give way to tears.

"Oh, my child," he said, his voice hoarse with pain, "you *can't* bear it. There is a great joy in being able to heal, but with it comes also the great anguish of knowing that you will not always be able to do so. It is part of the burden of the gift. In nothing can you hope to experience joy without being prepared to accept the pain that accompanies it."

Now she poured a glassful and drank greedily. Whatever they were planning for her, it had been a kindness to send this. She felt the jubana juice rejuvenating her, felt her muscles relax and strengthen, felt the rhythm of her heart slow, felt her mind throw off the fatigue.

Hungrily, she reached for a plantuff, and poured a glass of cold water from the jug. The plantuff were filled with a savoury mushroom mixture, much like one that Avella sometimes made. A welcome change from smoked rabbit, however good that had been. Soon she'd finished the plantuff and drained the jug.

Feeling restored, she got up and stepped from the tub, dried herself and rubbed some lotion on her body. Dressed in the clean, soft leather clothing she found on the bed, her medicine belt secured around her waist, she made her way down the stairs into the hallway where the young man who had guided her before stood waiting. Without speaking, he motioned her to follow and led her into a spacious chamber filled with Hill Folk. The murmurs that greeted her arrival sounded like the roar of a turbulent river.

In her soft boots, she padded across the polished floor to stand before a powerfully built man who sat watching from a wooden chair on a low platform. His braided hair was as fair as Avella's but his skin was ruddy from sun and wind. His blue eyes blazed with anger, but he remained silent. He wore the same tan skin breeches and embroidered tunic as the warriors she had met on the road, yet there was something in his bearing that commanded attention.

Since childhood, Dovella had heard tales of the Kaftil's brutality, and seeing his stern face, she could believe those tales were true. His mouth was set in a thin line, and his jaw was hard. She straightened her shoulders, determined not to show her fear, and forced her eyes to meet his briefly then pass on, as if she were moved by nothing but curiosity.

A giant stood beside the Kaftil, one hand resting on the back of his leader's chair, the other hovering near his sword. His eyes brushed Dovella as if she were only a gnissling, but she was sure that no movement on her part would go unnoticed. He was fair also, but his hair was almost silver, though he was a young man. She froze for a moment, remembering yet another legend of a race of silver-haired giants that had once inhabited Edlena. Woods tales, everyone said. Quickly she turned her eyes away, reluctant to catch his gaze, should he glance back at her.

She looked at the Kaftil again, but he was leaning back, almost at ease, almost as if he had forgotten her. Clearly he was waiting for someone else, and Dovella was not to be questioned until that person arrived. Now she could study him more carefully.

His long fingers moved idly along the sides of his chair, which was carved with intertwined leaves and fruits, much like the carvings on the chest in her father's room, the ones she had traced with her fingers as a child. She noticed deep wrinkles around his eyes. She looked away quickly when they caught hers.

Trying to quieten her fear, she turned her attention to the room. It was octagonal, with arched windows in five of the walls. A crystal chandelier hung from the ceiling right above the Kaftil's chair, but it was unlit, there being plenty of sunlight flowing through the undraped windows. She could see the surrounding forest through them. How different, she thought, from the Council Chamber back in the Village, where nothing could be seen through the windows.

A stir ran through those gathered, drawing her attention away from the windows, and she turned to see the old woman come in. Four men accompanied her, carrying a litter that they placed on a stand in the middle of the room, near Dovella. On the litter lay the injured woman.

"No," Dovella cried. "She needs rest." She turned angrily toward the Kaftil. "Why are you bringing her here? Her injuries are grave."

"We appreciate your concern," he said, his voice hard. "However, it must be so. The people *must* see Tavel."

Dovella turned to the old woman, who was standing beside the litter. Her face was gentler now as she motioned for Dovella to join her. Dovella lifted her head and walked over.

"Do what you need to do to continue your healing of our Tavel," the woman said.

Dovella pulled her thoughts back to Tavel, lifting the young woman's hand to study the fingertips. They were pink now. She touched the pulse in her neck, then eased her hand under the back of her head. The room and those in it faded from her consciousness as she focused on her healing.

Again Dovella felt the surge of joy that always flowed through her body when her healing power was fruitful. Tavel would heal, she knew it. She pulled a vial from her belt, and from the corner of her eye saw a warrior start forward. A gesture from the old woman stopped him.

Moistening her fingers from the vial, Dovella touched Tavel's brow and throat, and soon the injured woman began to stir.

The old woman took Tavel's hand and rubbed it gently. "You are at home," she whispered, "you are safe."

Tavel's eyelids fluttered, then she open her eyes. She turned her head on the pillow, and when she caught sight of Dovella, she shuddered.

"Who attacked you?" The Kaftil's voice cut through the room.

"Village men." Tavel's voice was almost too weak to be heard.

"No," Dovella protested. "Village men would not do that."

"It was," Tavel insisted.

Dovella shook her head vigorously, then stopped. Much

as she hated to admit to these people what was going on, they had to know. "Men of the New School," she said, turning toward the Kaftil. "They would. But not the rest of us."

An angry grumble ran through the crowd. The people drew nearer to the injured woman, pressing closer and closer. Dovella could only stand there, stunned with fear, and await her fate.

Twenty

Acknowledge your fear, Zagoad had said. Remembering this, Dovella tried to control her breathing, tried to see only what was happening now. And for now she was safe, for the Kaftil held up his hand, and the room fell silent.

"What is this New School?"

"A group of fanatics who have perverted their religion." As Dovella explained to him what was happening in the Village and why she had undertaken the journey, he listened attentively, but she could see he was not fully satisfied.

"The Council would not send a young woman on such a mission alone."

"The Council doesn't know. Only my parents and Security Master Pandil. And I didn't leave alone." She told him how she and Zagoad had been attacked. "He had hoped to beg passage through the hills."

"Zagoad? I know that name." The Kaftil looked up at the giant, who inclined his head slightly.

"It was necessary to get our prisoner back to Pandil," Dovella rushed on. "Zagoad would be in less danger than I in taking him back, and in any case, he wouldn't know what to do at the water source." She tried to crush the uncertainty that rose as she spoke the words. Would *she* know what to do?

"And you were making your way down the road, seeking a way around the hills, when you came on our Tavel?"

Dovella nodded. She wondered if she should show them Zagoad's medal. They would likely ask why she was looking for a way around the hills, if she had that. She had no wish to explain to the Kaftil how she feared his people.

"Why did you stop for Tavel if your errand is so urgent?"

"I'm a healer! I couldn't leave her wounds unattended." And yet she had tried. The Kaftil stared at her and she wondered if he could read her heart.

"They send a healer to see to the water source?" His voice was gentler, but he still didn't sound convinced.

"I follow my mother as engineer, but my father is Safir, the healer." Again a low murmur filled the room. Even to her, the story sounded unlikely, but she had to convince him. "I have studied the workings of the machine in the Old Books; besides, being only an apprentice, I could leave without being missed. Zagoad alone came with me so we could travel quickly and unnoticed." Why wouldn't he believe her?

"A good plan, yes." Then he leaned forward, as if about to rise from his chair and come out to her. "Yet, I ask again, if your mission is so urgent, why did you stop?" His eyes held hers.

"I am a healer," she said again. She stopped. She had to be honest with this man. "I wanted to go on," she said in a soft voice, and looked down, unable to meet his gaze. "I *tried* to go on, but I couldn't leave her." She look up and blinked, determined not to show tears. "I couldn't."

He nodded and sat back as if that was an answer he could understand. "You have gone through the Rites?"

"I was to have gone through yesterday, but we couldn't

afford to delay my journey."

The Kaftil wiped a broad hand across his chin and raised his eyebrows. "You gave up your chance to go through the Rites in order to rush your journey, yet you tarried for Tavel?"

Dovella felt herself wither. She could see he didn't believe her, yet she had no answer other than the one she had already given. Repeating it would not convince him. She lifted her head. She would meet her destiny with the dignity befitting a daughter of Safir and Avella, but first she would try to make them see the dangers. She stepped forward, but the Kaftil held up his hand.

"There are new Village men at the lake over the mountain," he said. "And the lesser lake has been filled almost to the top. Should that overflow, our valley will be flooded, our crops destroyed. That is why we sent Tavel, my sister's child, to ask your Council why they wish to break the peace."

"It's the New School people. They want to take over the Council. They sent the men to tamper with the machine. Once the New School has control of the Village, they plan to restore the water flow and convince the people that it is a sign from the gods." She stopped, thinking of what Brandle had said, wondering if she should, if she dared, pass on the warning. "And I think they would like to weaken your people as well," she said. "I have heard that they plan an attack."

"Yes," he said, showing no surprise. "No doubt they will invade the hills as soon as they are strong enough."

"We have to stop them," Dovella said. "You can't imagine what they are like."

"I think we can," the Kaftil said. "Our people have met their kind before. But what can *you* do?"

Dovella hesitated, full of doubt. But she couldn't show it.

"They expect no trouble at the source camp," she said boldly, "so the night watch will surely be light. If I can get by them, I can try to restore the flow. If power is restored, it will support Zagoad's report of what we learned." Yet even as she spoke, she feared she would fail.

"We can get you in," the Kaftil said. His eyes had gone hard again, and one large hand was clenched. "I and some of my people will come with you, and I will send a message to the Council. And this time I will be sure that the envoys are well armed."

Dovella felt herself relax. She was going to reach the source, and in good time.

The old woman came up and placed her hand on Dovella's shoulder. "Our guest must have rest before she takes on more burdens. She has travelled hard. And she has healed our Tavel."

The Kaftil smiled and the wrinkles around his eyes deepened. "Yes," he said. "Let her rest while we make our preparations." He motioned to the young warrior who had accompanied Dovella to and from the chamber where she had refreshed herself. "Daneel," he said, "go with our sister back to her chamber and see to it that she has everything she needs for our journey."

Our sister. He'd called her "our sister."

The young man took Dovella's arm, his fingers gentle now. "Come," he said. "Come and rest."

"I'm not sure I can," Dovella confessed. And yet, without sleep, she would be unfit for the journey.

"Once you are in bed, sleep will come," Daneel said. They walked up the stairs in silence, and then Daneel asked, "How fares Zagoad?"

"You know him?"

"He was a friend of Lafhin. My brother."

"Was Lafhin?..."

His face showed no emotion, but his voice became harder. "Yes, he was among those killed. And I almost lost Tavel as well." Then, more gently, "I thank you for stopping to give her aid."

She bowed her head. "I'm sorry about Lafhin. Zagoad trusted him." She reached into the neck of her blouse and pulled out the medal. "Zagoad gave me this and told me I should show it to him. I was trying to decide when I came upon them. On the road."

Daneel looked at her with a puzzled frown. "Do you know what that is?"

"No, only that Zagoad said Lafhin would recognize it."

"Anyone in Vellaban would recognize it, as would many of your people, though it might not be so well received by all of them. He must trust you greatly to give you that."

"What is it?"

"It is the medal of the Goddess."

"The Goddess?" She stopped and stared, unbelieving. Surely Zagoad was not an infidel. "Is he a believer in the Hill Goddess?" She could hardly whisper the words.

Daneel shrugged. "Who knows? People who earn that medal do it with deeds, not beliefs. The Goddess demands work from those who serve her. She doesn't exist only because people believe, nor cease to exist if they do not."

What kind of deeds, Dovella wondered. She found it difficult to reconcile these people with what she had been taught about the Hill Folk, but it was as hard to let go of her fear as it had been for her to face it.

"Zagoad received that when he saved my brother's life. Lafhin was trapped under a fallen tree during a dangerous fire in the woods, and Zagoad managed to dig him out and carry him to a nearby settlement for treatment, though Lafhin was not a small man."

She felt Daneel looking at her, and turned toward him, waiting for him to continue.

"Zagoad is a friend to us, Dovella, but he is not a traitor to your people. He is one of many, both among your people and ours, who think it is time that Hill Folk and Villagers put aside ancient feuds and become friends again."

"That won't be possible if the New School wins."

His blue eyes suddenly went cold. "It won't be so easy this time."

"What happened before?" she asked. Not that she could believe him, she told herself. Naturally he would tell only what he had been taught. Still, she wanted to know what he would say.

"They razed our shrines," he said, "killed those who would not deny the Goddess and worship their gods. Took our lands."

Dovella nodded, remembering the ruins she and Zagoad had seen in the forest.

"But they do not know our hills," he went on. "Here they will not fare so well. For now, however, we must concentrate on your work at the source."

Dovella began to tremble. "What if I can't do it?"

"Time enough to think of that when we get there." He rested his hand on her shoulder as they arrived at her chamber door. "For now, however, you must think only of yourself — rest, sister; rest."

Dovella went into the chamber, undressed and fell into the bed. It looked now as if she would at least reach the source in time, so now she had to face the question: what was she going to do when she got there?

And, even more frightening, what would happen to the Village if she failed?

Twenty-One

A TAP AT THE DOOR WOKE DOVELLA, WHO SAT UP QUICKLY and looked around, her heart racing as she surveyed the unfamiliar surroundings. The young woman who had served her earlier came in. She ducked her head in greeting and smiled, but Dovella could tell by the way she kept her distance that the young woman was still not at ease. Dovella felt a surge of sympathy, tinged with vexation. *She* had done nothing to frighten anyone. And yet, if their positions were reversed, how would she behave? Dovella brushed that uncomfortable question aside and threw back the covers.

She glanced through the open window, saw faint tinges of pink in the sky. "I've slept through the entire night."

"The Lady knew you would be very tired after your journey and the healing, so the Kaftil gave orders that you were not to be disturbed before morning."

"The Lady?" She must mean Tavel, Dovella thought, or possibly the old woman, though she hadn't behaved like anyone of great importance.

Still, that someone had arranged for her to rest was considerate, especially since they wouldn't understand how a healer could be drained. But then, the Hill Folk she'd met had shown themselves in everything to be more thoughtful than she could have ever imagined. Even her short confinement had been comfortable, apart from her fear. How else had she misjudged them?

"What is your name?" Dovella asked.

"Lucella." Her voice was little more than a whisper. Lucella. The great silver moon. No one in the Village would have dared name a child after her.

Lucella carried the tray over to the table near the open window and set it down. "The Kaftil asks that you eat, and then prepare yourself for the journey."

Dovella nodded and slid out of bed. Even though she'd eaten nothing since her meal of jubana juice and plantuff yesterday, she was far too nervous to think about food. But the Kaftil had been thoughtful, and Lucella was being gracious despite her fear. Dovella smiled. If only Lucella knew that Dovella herself was equally frightened of the Hill Folk.

"Thank you. I will be ready." Even as she spoke, Dovella dreaded what lay ahead. She felt utterly unprepared. No wonder Pandil and Avella had stared at her as if she were a stupid child when she'd volunteered for the journey. Still, "She is a resourceful young woman," Pandil had said, and Avella had shown confidence in her abilities. Pray the gods it was so!

She sat down at the table, knowing she had to eat, sure she could not, but the fresh air and the aroma of the food soon made her mouth water. There was a bowl of porridge, fragrant with spices and filled with a small red fruit that was foreign to Dovella but tasted both tart and sweet; a small loaf of nut bread, still warm, with butter; and a pitcher of milk. Perhaps she would try just a little, she thought. As she ate, she realized just how hungry she was, and made a hearty meal.

When she was done she sat back, suddenly homesick. The

porridge, of course; that was what Avella had prepared for her the morning she left. If she were at home — Dovella shook her head and frowned. She hadn't time to indulge in regrets. She pushed back the chair and started her preparations for the last leg of her journey.

The sun had just risen when they started out. The Kaftil and his giant companion Bofast led the way, mounted on sturdy horses; Dovella, accompanied by Daneel, rode after them, and several other warriors followed. Of medium height and solidly built, Daneel reminded her a little of Jael in the quick yet graceful way he moved, the way his darting eyes took in everything. He caught her glance and gave a smile of encouragement, which heartened her, to her surprise. "Tavel is much improved," he said. "We owe you our thanks."

She bowed her head, pleased at his words, yet shamed; had it not been for Villagers, the young woman would never have been injured.

They soon left Vellaban behind and climbed rapidly along a rocky trail that narrowed until they had to ride single file. Looking at the mountain that rose before them, Dovella asked herself again how crossing it could be quicker than going around. Surely it would take days to cross that gargantuan height, even on horseback.

She had been given a gentle grey mare, sure of foot, as she needed to be on the steep, narrow path with its eroded shoulders and loose rocks. Dovella patted the horse on the neck, more to comfort herself than to encourage her mount. The mare's coat was warm and sleek. She nickered with pleasure, then continued placidly along, occasionally tossing her head.

Dovella shifted her weight and grimaced. She had barely

recovered from her last bout of horseback riding, and now she was going to have to live with those aching muscles again. Still, at least this time she could feel safe from Raider attack, if not from rock slides.

As they ascended, she was tempted to close her eyes, for the sides of the canyon were almost too steep to be seen from above, except for the occasional jagged ledge; below, she was sure, rested the polished bones of many who had been foolish enough to trek along this treacherous trail. The snow-covered peaks above looked equally daunting. When the trail widened, Daneel rode up beside her. She found his presence reassuring.

Occasionally she saw a well-tended shrine nestled within flowers and vines beside the trail; in each, a niche held a statue of a woman clad in breeches and tunic, holding a sheaf of wheat in one hand and a bunch of grapes in the other. A child and a woodcat were carved at her feet on a base adorned with carvings of intertwined leaves and fruit. As she studied them, Dovella realized that these were the first shrines she had seen, apart from the fragments that she and Zagoad had passed in the woods. She turned to Daneel. "Why are there no shrines in your village? Is it only the —" She stopped, uncertain. "What do you call the Hill Folk who live outside your village?"

He smiled. "Hill Folk. Same as us. What do you call such people in the Village?"

"Outlanders," she said, suddenly ashamed. She turned her face away.

"There are shrines in the village," he said quickly. Dovella was grateful to him for helping to cover her embarrassment. "At least, of a sort. They are in the temple. These shrines are a place for us to go when there is no temple. In some ways that makes them even more sacred, because the people visiting them have no other holy place to go to, and in this kind of country, their need may be great, with no help available but that of the Goddess."

Idol worship, something in her said; and yet it wasn't for her to scorn his beliefs. But she would like to know why the Hill Folk worshipped the Goddess when her own people worshipped the gods.

"I have heard that the archives here are more complete than ours, that they tell about the first people. And the others."

"Others?"

"Aren't there other people besides Villagers and Hill Folk?"

"Oh, yes, but they live far from us."

"You know about them?"

He laughed. "We all have to study the great books, of course, but my father is an archivist, so I probably hear more than most. Sometimes more than I want to hear."

"Do you think I could see the books?" She felt shy about asking, but her curiousity won out.

"Anyone can see them. But there are a lot of them. Rooms full."

She gaped, unable to hide her surprise. "Even the holy books are available?"

"I'm not sure what you mean by 'holy books,'" he said. "We have books written by the Founders, of course, as well as those of our holy sages. We believe the Goddess still speaks to us, so we are always adding books to the archives. That's part of the archivists' work, to keep all the books in order."

"But how can you know them all?"

"You can't — not even an archivist can know them all. We study selections, but all of them are open for anyone who wants to study them."

Dovella sat back. Now that was something to think about: an archive full of writings, open to all. With additions made regularly. No one would presume to add anything to the Old Books back in the Village. Except, perhaps, the New Schoolers. But they would pretend that the writings had been there all along. Nor would she herself have accepted that anything should be added, until now. But what Daneel said made sense, for why would the gods suddenly stop speaking to their people? Perhaps it was the people who stopped listening.

Ahead, the mountain loomed, cold and menacing. "How will the horses ever be able to climb up there?" she asked. She shivered, as much from the thought of the climb as from the chill of the rising wind.

"They won't." He must have seen her shiver. "There's an extra blanket in your saddlebag if you get cold."

She shook her head, and he reached out to touch her arm. "There's no weakness in being cold, Dovella. We are used to this weather, but you have never been in the mountains before. No one will think less of you."

She shook her head again, for Daneel's words had almost made her forget the cold. If the horses would not climb the mountains, that meant the party would go on by foot. Frightened as she had been on the narrow path, she trusted the mare's sure feet far more than her own. How would she manage to scale the mountain on such narrow, rocky trails?

After a few hours, they stopped and Bofast built a fire. She watched how the giant moved, quickly and silently. He was dressed like the others in skin breeches and an embroidered tunic, only he wore a band of silver disks around his upper arm. His dagger was as large as a short sword, and he also carried a coil of some type of thin rope attached to his belt.

"I've never heard him speak," Dovella said. "Is he mute?"

Daneel shook his head, but his eyes held a glint of laughter. "Bofast can speak well enough when he chooses, but he's not one for chatter, as he calls it. That's why he usually looks after the meals — it lets him escape talking."

"He looks different. I mean, besides being so big."

"He is different."

"You mean there really are giants?"

He nodded. "Not many, of course. Most of them were hit by a disease, imported no doubt by the Founders; others were killed for land or out of jealousy."

"Jealousy?"

"Jealousy of their magic, which the settlers couldn't master."

At one time she would have scoffed, but after seeing that tormented beast in the forest with Zagoad, she couldn't deny that something existed beyond her understanding. And then there was her own gift ... No, she thought firmly; the two were totally different. But maybe that was why she had to hide her gift — because Villagers saw anything beyond their understanding as evil.

Bofast poured some liquid into a pot and set it on a stone near the fire to heat. They gathered around to share the bread and cheese and smoked meat that had been prepared for them. The bread, chewy and moist, was unlike any Dovella had tasted before, and the meat was tender and juicy. Father would like this, she thought. "What is this meat?"

"Vesson," Daneel said.

She lifted her eyebrows in surprise. Vesson was a large, antlered hill animal, something she had seen in books, but she had never heard of anyone eating it. It was delicious, though. She glanced around at her companions, all chewing silently. Appreciating the food, she wondered, or were they quiet because they were as frightened as she about having to climb the mountain? The bread suddenly felt like a stone in her stomach.

After a while, Bofast ladled the steaming liquid from the pot into cups. Dovella accepted a cup and returned to sit beside Daneel. She took a sip. Slightly bitter, but it was good. The Kaftil moved among the men as they ate, his comments greeted with soft laughter. Dovella was astonished at how easy his men seemed to be with their great chief. He looked over at her and smiled. Strange how he no longer seemed so fearsome.

She turned to Daneel. "Will the trails be as narrow and rocky up there?" She gestured toward the mountain without looking at it.

"What?" Daneel glanced up, shrugged. "Oh, I suppose they are, but you needn't worry about that. We won't be going up there."

A wave of relief washed over her, immediately replaced by another worry. "Then how will we get across?"

"The old road. Back when the Villagers were still our friends, they helped us build a road through the mountain."

"Through? We are going through the mountain?"

Daneel laughed. "It's quite safe, Dovella. Don't worry."

He was right, of course; if they were used to travelling the road, it was safe — it must be safe. It was absurd to be frightened. It seemed she was frightened of everything since leaving the Village, she who had always been so sure of herself.

Bofast killed the fire, and soon they were on their way again. After a while, they came to a black hole in the face of the mountain. Fear gripped her, but the grey mare marched steadily onward into the black corridor, and Dovella braced herself against the darkness. She would trust herself to the gentle horse, just as she had on the treacherous paths before. Nevertheless, the hollow, echoing clatter of the horses' hooves on the stone floor made Dovella's throat tighten, and she clutched the reins until her fingers were numb.

Bofast and a few others lit torches. In the flickering light, Dovella could make out Daneel's face. He seemed at ease, but that brought little comfort. She pulled her cape closer and sniffed the air. Though it was colder here, there was no dampness or mustiness. But Dovella still felt as though the blackness was smothering her, as surely as if it were a pillow pressed over her face. Her mouth was dry and she struggled for breath.

Again she felt Daneel's hand on her arm and knew that the darkness was not to be feared. She swallowed hard and forced herself to breathe, reminding herself once again of Zagoad's advice about dealing with fear. And here, beside her, was Daneel, not danger.

When it seemed that she would be unable to go on any longer, Dovella saw a prick of light in the blackness ahead. She wanted to urge the mare toward it, but instead she forced herself to relax her grip on the reins.

When they rode out of the tunnel, she stopped the mare and gazed below, her lips parted in wonder. The source. Larger than she had thought any lake could be, and beautiful.

So beautiful. The water, broken here and there by ripples of white, reflected the soft colours of twilight. Trees circled its shore, their foliage deep red and gold interspersed with green. A broad river meandered away from it. The image blurred and Dovella blinked, ashamed to let anyone see her wiping her eyes.

Daneel stopped beside her. "The water runs through the mountain too." He pointed to a large stone structure that seemed to block off part of the river. "It was diverted long ago to give water and power to your village, and ours."

The Kaftil joined them as Daneel pointed to a second lake. "It's called a reservoir," he said. "Twice a year the water rises, then gradually falls. But now, you see, it's near to overflowing and the water is still rising. If it continues, if there is a breach ..."

It's almost time for harvest, Dovella thought. They will lose everything.

"We don't know anything about the controls," the Kaftil said, "and we soon realized that the new men would do nothing to stop it, were probably even making it worse. And they would tell us nothing. That's why Tavel was going to your village."

"You've mentioned 'new' men," Dovella said. "Were there other men here before?"

The Kaftil stared at her for a moment. "You don't know?"

She shook her head, feeling foolish.

"The keepers, we called them," he said. "During the Schoolmen war, they sided with the Hill Folk, so when it was over, they were left here, never relieved. There was nothing for them to do but go on doing what they'd been taught, even though they had no contact with the Village. I suppose they

· 253 ·

hoped that eventually the Schoolmen would be overthrown, but it didn't happen in their lifetimes. After that, well, I suppose the Village forgot they existed. My people helped them as much as we could, for the source provides water and power for our village, too. And there was a certain amount of intermarriage with the farming families around the reservoir. Over time, they became more like our people than Villagers, even though they kept pretty much to themselves."

"What happened to them?"

He shrugged. "These new men came and took over; that's all I know. No one knows what happened to the others. Had they still been here, they would have fixed the problem."

"Dovella will know what to do," Daneel said, and smiled at her.

Dovella went cold. She had read the Old Books, yes, and she had studied the drawings taken from the man who had attacked her and Zagoad, but she was only vaguely aware of what they meant. She had to be truthful with them. "I am only an apprentice; I don't really understand how it works. No one in the Village understands the machine anymore. I will have to go cautiously."

"But quickly," the Kaftil said. "The reservoir will overflow at any time."

"Yes," she agreed. "Let's go on."

"We must wait for darkness, or we will have no chance to surprise them," he said. "We'll go when the moons are high."

The moons. Dovella looked up. It was not dark yet, but already she could see faint outlines of the three moons. If all went well, Festival would take place in peace. And even more important, there would be a reconciliation between Villagers and Hill Folk.

She dismounted and tethered her mare beside the other horses, then went to join the Hill men. There would be no fire, but Bofast was passing out strips of dried meat, hunks of bread and clumps of grapes. There was also a jug of some beverage that Dovella couldn't recognize. Probably has macha in it, she thought, or something similar. In any case, when she had finished eating, she felt revitalized. The others were more talkative now, though they spoke in whispers that blended in with the susurration of the leaves above them.

When the moons were high, the Kaftil got up and looked around. "It is time," he said, and the others pushed themselves to their feet. He turned to Dovella. "Daneel and Bofast will attend you," he said, "while the rest of us deal with the men."

The Kaftil had brought only ten men besides Bofast and Daneel. Although the Hill Folk were known to be brave warriors, the slaughter on the road showed that the New School people were well-armed and skilful in the use of their weapons.

"Don't worry," Daneel said, reading her expression. "We've been watching them for some time; the Kaftil will manage."

Dovella nodded, then closed her eyes and pictured the drawing. "There," she said, pointing to a structure beside the river. "The controls to the gate should be in there."

Doubt snagged at her like the brambles on the hillside as she remounted the grey mare and followed Daneel. She hadn't the training to do this job, but she mustn't let Daneel know how afraid she was. She could only hope that, when faced with the controls, her meager understanding would suffice.

Ahead of her, Daneel reined in his horse. "From here we go on foot. Let's wait for Bofast."

"I thought he was the Kaftil's bodyguard."

Daneel smiled. "The Kaftil has no need of a bodyguard, but Bofast has been his nearest companion from the time they were boys. He taught all of us our fighting skills. Had the party going to your village been permitted by the Kaftil to carry more weapons, there would have been fewer Hill Folk among the dead. As it was, our six dead took ten with them." Mixed with his anger was pride that his people had fought well.

When the giant joined them, they crept through the woods, stopping at the edge of a clearing. "No fence?" Dovella asked.

"There was no need," Daneel explained. "When this was built, our people were friends." They crouched at the clearing's edge for a few minutes, then Dovella heard a soft whistle, like the call of a nightbird. "They've dealt with the guards on this side," Daneel said. "We can go now."

There was no sign of anyone outside the squat building. They raced across the open yard, reaching the door without interference. Daneel patted her arm. She smiled at his reassurance, but anxiety still gripped her. If she failed, the Hill Folk, the Villagers ... all would be lost. Havkad and his New School would have no opposition.

Bofast led the way, moving up the stairs with a silence that astonished Dovella. They stole after him, if not as silently, still quietly enough not to alert anyone who might be in the room above. They stopped at a closed door at the top of the stairs. Bofast reached for the handle. Slowly, silently, he pushed the door open.

A man standing before a wheel whirled toward them, reaching for his knife. Before he could draw it, Bofast had crossed the room and pulled him down; they grappled on the floor.

When the man uttered a strangled cry, Dovella looked at Daneel in alarm. He stood at the door, listening. Bofast and the man struggled a few moments more, then the man slumped, unconscious. Bofast bound him tightly with his rope.

Dovella's breath caught as she looked around. So many dials and controls! It was as if the room had been painted with them. Trying to hide her fear, she walked to the window and gazed at the reservoir; the water had risen. In the moonlight, it looked beautiful, but there would be little beauty in flooded fields.

Sensing Daneel's impatience, she walked over to the wheel where the man had been working. She remembered this from the drawing. "This controls the water flow to the Village." Dovella grasped the wheel and tried to turn it, but it wouldn't budge. She shook her head.

"Bofast is strong," Daneel said as the giant stepped up beside her. "He can turn it."

"But if he breaks it," she said, "we are worse off than ever." She looked closely at the wheel. "Look. The metal is tight here because it's been a long time since this wheel was last turned. In trying to force it beyond the point where it was meant to move, they jammed it. Now it won't move in either direction. And they've put something sticky on it that makes it worse. We need to clean it first, then oil it properly."

"Do we have time?" Daneel asked.

"We have no other choice."

Frantically, they searched the room for oil and rags. Bofast triumphantly held up a can, and Dovella smiled her relief. He pried it open and held it out, but it contained only sludge. She shook her head.

"That's probably what the new men used," she said.

And that must have been the reason Havkad's men were returning to the Village. They, too, must have been looking for something to ease the turning of the wheel.

Her stomach knotted up. How could she have been foolish enough to think she knew enough to repair the machine? And yet, something pulsed in her mind, something called to her. If only she knew what it was trying to say.

"Maybe it would help if we cleaned off that old oil," Bofast suggested.

"But how?" Daneel asked, poking at it with a finger. "It's so sticky it's impossible to scrape off."

And then a picture sprang into Dovella's mind, a picture of Novise cleaning her greasy pan. She reached into her pouch and took out the packet of fenweed Novise had given her. "We'll use this."

Quickly she poured some of the herb onto the mechanism. Nothing happened. She let out a groan of disappointment. "I was sure it would work."

"Wait," Daneel said. "Look!"

Peering closely, she saw tiny bubbles forming, and then a thin trail of liquid ran down the shaft as the heavy grease dissolved. She rubbed at it with the hem of her tunic until all traces of the sticky mess were gone. But still the wheel would not turn.

"It needs fresh oil," Bofast said.

She paced around the room, asking herself what she should do. Suddenly she stopped. Biting her lip, she crossed her arms and hugged them against her stomach. Against her medicine belt.

She had oil.

Twenty-Two

D OVELLA HESITATED. THIS WAS THE LAST OF HER FATHER'S precious oil, and it was dedicated to healing. To pour it on a machine would be sacrilege. Yet, if the Hill Folks' crops were destroyed, there would be starvation. Surely preventing that was also a kind of healing.

Dovella hugged her arms tighter, trying to keep from crying. She couldn't use the healing oils on the machine; she couldn't add that offence to the ones she had already committed. And yet, if she didn't, she would never be able to turn the wheel. And that doomed both the Hill Folk and her own people.

"What's wrong?" Daneel asked.

Slowly Dovella drew the vial from her belt. "I have oil," she said, trying to keep her voice steady.

He looked at her. "That is the healing oil," he said, his voice level. He could have taken it from her, even without Bofast's aid, but he made no move to do so, neither did he try to persuade her.

"It's all we have."

Daneel said nothing more. Bofast walked over to look out the window.

Dovella took a deep breath and gently poured a drop of the oil onto the mechanism. She felt Daneel move a step away. Another drop, then another. Her chest tightened with each bead of oil. After using the last of Safir's precious healing oil on a machine, she could never face her father. Nor had she any right to call herself a healer.

She ran her tongue across her lips and swallowed as she rubbed the oil around the shaft, then poured another drop. She felt the shaft become smoother. Putting the cap on the vial, she tried to turn the wheel. It moved slightly. Then it stuck again.

"It's going to work," she said, releasing her pent up breath. "It will be slow, but I'm afraid to open the gates too fast in any case."

Bofast stayed looking out the window; she could tell from the tension in his shoulders that the reservoir was still rising. She would never stop it in time. Her stomach knotted. She frantically waved Daneel over. "Here, keep rubbing oil around the wheel's shaft; I'll see if I can make any sense of these other gauges."

Daneel drew back.

"It's only oil now," she said. "There's no harm."

He hesitated, then took the vial and began applying oil, drop by drop, rubbing it in as Dovella had done. She watched for a moment, then move intently around the room, resisting the pounding voice in her mind that urged *hurry, hurry, hurry!* There must be a safety valve somewhere, some way to control the level of the reservoir other than by the gates; for if there were a flood, the flow of water would be too great for the mountain tunnel to handle. Surely the Founders would have thought of that.

One by one she studied the gauges, shaking her head. Only the ones on this one wall seemed to be functioning. Perhaps that was so one person alone could operate the machine from here. Think! she told herself. Do any of the gauges correspond to the ones in the Village, or in the Old Books? The missing volume! She'd almost forgotten. Perhaps it had been brought here to help the men. "Bofast, help me look for a book."

They clawed through drawers, cupboards and piles of debris left by the men, slinging rejected material aside in their haste. Dovella's heart thudded ever more rapidly as she shuffled through the mess. Nothing!

Her eyes fell on a table in a corner of the room, half-hidden in darkness. On it lay a book! She ran over and opened it. Page after page of pictures of dials! But useless, she realized, after the machine had been altered to be controlled from the Village. Perhaps that's why the men had tossed it aside. Why they had to return to the Village.

Or, was it useless? Thumbing through, Dovella found the section that dealt with the reservoir.

She could feel Daneel's impatience reaching out from across the room, but she forced herself to ignore him as she continued to read.

"The reservoir is starting to overflow," he said urgently. "I see it spilling over the near right corner."

"Bofast," she called. "You can help me with this." The giant was at her side almost before she finished speaking, Daneel close behind.

"Look," she said, showing them the drawing. "This is what we need to find. There is a safety tunnel that leads back into the river. Help me find the control for it."

The wall was full of gauges, but they each took a section to study, looking for something that matched the drawing. Glancing through the window, she saw that the gates were open wider than before, but it was a slow procedure and the reservoir gauge was still rising. She knew that, given enough time, she would be able to restore water and power to the Village, and stop the threat of the New School, but would she be able to stop the overflow from causing a breach? If not — she dared not think what would follow.

"Here!" Bofast's voice sliced through her fear.

She raced to his side. Yes, that was it. Below it was a small wheel, also stuck fast. Daneel handed her the vial of oil, already half empty. This wheel must now take precedence. There was no way she would be able to open the other gates quickly enough to prevent the overflow of the reservoir. Thankfully, this one had not been jammed, so it should move more easily.

Something seemed to be reaching for her, the same way she was called to a person in pain. The machine, she thought. Feel the machine. She could do it in the Village, so she should be able to do it here.

And then she remembered what her mother had said about the routine. Perhaps these gauges needed to be oiled in a particular pattern. Taking a deep breath, she placed her hand on the wall, felt a pattern form in her mind.

Yes!

Following the pattern, she touched oil to the dials, though there was little left. She felt the machine respond. "Check the reservoir gauge," she said.

Daneel ran to the gate wheel. "It's still at the point of overflow," he reported, his voice tight. "We're too late."

She ran her hands over the gauges again in the now familiar pattern. She held her breath and watched as the needle began slowly to fall. But in her ears, Daneel's words kept ringing: *too late.*

Footsteps pounded up the stairs. Bofast drew his knife, but when the door flew open, it was the Kaftil who rushed in. He was bleeding from the shoulder and his face was grim.

Dovella blanched. "I couldn't stop it," she said, her voice ragged and thin. She was unable to look at him; her people had done the Hill Folk too much harm. "I'm sorry, but I was too late. I shouldn't have taken time to sleep."

"You did well, sister," he said. "The overflow has ceased, and there is no evidence of a breach; I believe the damage to our crops will be minor."

Dovella sank to the floor and buried her face in her hands. "Thanks be to the gods." She fell back against the wall, relief rushing through her like the water through the riverbed.

The Kaftil came over to her. "Are you all right?"

"I'm just glad it's over." She caught her breath. "At least, here."

"Ease yourself," the Kaftil replied. "If you can teach Daneel what to do here until you are able to send someone or come back yourself, Bofast and I will take you to the Village."

She sensed that the surprise of her companions equalled her own. At no time in recent memory had a Kaftil visited the Village.

The Kaftil looked around at all the dials, his eyes wide, then wandered around the room. "How did you make it work?" he asked, his voice hushed.

"It was her magic," said Daneel, his voice full of awe.

She jerked her head around. "No, it was the oil. I just had to use the proper routine."

The Kaftil touched the wheel, then rubbed his fingers together. He lifted them to his nose and sniffed gently.

She swallowed hard and met his gaze. "It was all I had," she said.

He squeezed her shoulder. "We are ever in your debt," he said. From around his neck, the Kaftil lifted a medal, a small gold coin imprinted with the head of the Goddess, just like the one Zagoad had given her. "For your services to our people, I give you this medal of the Goddess. May she bless and preserve you in all your undertakings. It will give you passage through any of our lands and the aid of any of our people."

Dovella couldn't speak, but the Kaftil appeared not to notice. He dropped the gold chain over her head. She gazed down at the medal.

"There are others among your people who bear this medal," the Kaftil went on, "and you will do well to wear it, as they do, concealed beneath clothing. One day, we hope, you can wear it openly, proudly, just as we do."

"Some day soon, I hope," Dovella whispered. "You do me a great honour. When our people learn how you have helped me, I'm sure we can begin working toward restoring peace."

"May the Goddess make it so," the Kaftil said.

Gazing at the small medal, Dovella remembered how Pandil had touched something hidden beneath her tunic, and wondered if she, too, had such a medal. She ran her fingers over it. It was not the same as the medallion of the healer, but it was something she would treasure always. She could not regret helping the Hill Folk, even though that help had required her to desecrate the sacred healing oil.

"I know that you used your oil for our sake," the Kaftil said, "and though it hardly repays our debt, I will replenish your vial before you go."

Dovella stared at him. With the oil so scarce now, it was unheard of to give it to anyone other than family or closest friends. "But how will you manage, if you give away your oil?"

"Why, our healers will make more."

"They can do that? You still have your toutile plants?"

"Don't you?"

Dovella shook her head. "There's a blight. This was the last of my father's oil."

The Kaftil brushed his hand against Dovella's cheek. "Then indeed you have done us a great service, to use it as you did. You shall have a cask of oil to take with you. When there is peace enough, we will send someone to restore your toutile fields."

His voice was so gentle, Dovella could only gaze in wonder. How different he seemed now from the stern man she had first encountered in his Council Chamber.

The Goddess demands deeds, Daneel had said, not belief; and tonight there had been deeds to be thankful for. Let whatever gods or Goddess who could, accept the thanks.

As they prepared to return to Vellaban, the Kaftil said, "You must let me know if you get tired on the way." He grinned. "My aunt is quite taken with you. She will be very angry if I don't take care of you. And it is not wise to anger my aunt."

"Your aunt?"

"Yes, the woman who spoke with you. And Tavel is my sister's daughter. So you see, we have much for which to thank you."

Again Dovella stared, astonished by the news. She would never have thought the old woman so important. But then, nothing in Hill country was the same as it was in the Village. She would have to revise her ideas about a lot of things, it seemed.

They got underway at dawn. The trip went quickly, and even the narrow, precipitous trail was less frightening than before, perhaps because she was too tired or too elated to think about it. Or perhaps it was the song that the Kaftil and Bofast sang, a song that gave thanks for a victory. Their voices were strong and blended in perfect harmony.

Dovella leaned over to pat the mare on the neck. "Thank you," she whispered. "Thank you for taking care of me." From the way the mare lifted her head, Dovella could almost believe that her words had been understood.

Back in her room in the Kaftil's house, a warm bath awaited Dovella. It was almost as if they knew how important cleanliness was to her well-being. She slid wearily into the oil-scented water. Thinking of her empty vial of healing oil, Dovella could no longer hold back her tears. The Kaftil had promised to replenish the oil, and provide more, but she had still committed a sacrilege. And worst of all, she, a healer, had caused the death of a man. Even though she had restored the flow of water to the Village and saved the crops of the Hill Folk, that couldn't erase her other transgressions. It was fortunate, indeed, that she had not gone through the Rites.

Covering her face with her hands, Dovella wept. After all the wrongs she had done on this trip, how could she ever face Safir? Dovella wiped away her tears and looked at the Goddess medal, gleaming in the lamplight. She would always treasure it, but it wasn't the same as the medallion of the healer. And she knew now that a healer was what she was meant to be. Had the machine not been ailing, she would not have been drawn to it so strongly. She was glad that she had been able to mend it, but even though the machine had responded to her touch, and she had felt a kind of kinship with it, still she had not felt that bud of joy that she had felt when healing Tavel.

The door opened and Lucella came in with a tray, this time smiling, without her usual shy reserve. "Please come to the Council Chamber when you have finished," she said, and set the tray on the table next to the bath before taking her leave.

Dovella looked at the tray, her throat almost closed with tears, but after a sip of jubana juice, she felt her body begin to relax. She finished the drink and sank back into her bath.

What she had done, she had done. It was well that she had not gone through the Rites, she thought once again. Her deeds would have been unforgivable, had she taken her vows. But she could still be an engineer; she could return here and learn about the machine, put healing behind her. There must be no more tears.

She finished eating the meal, then rose from the bath, dried her body and anointed it with lotions, and dressed in the clothes that had been cleaned while she was away. She would go to the Council Chamber, where no doubt the Kaftil would report on the events at the reservoir, and tomorrow she would begin the return trip to the Village, to her role as apprentice to Avella. Even if she no longer deserved to be called healer, she had won her place as engineer. She would study the Old Books in the Village archives, seek the mysteries hidden there. The workings of the machine couldn't be magic, surely.

Twenty-Three

A s chairman of the Council this season, Pandil usually entered the Council Chambers last, but tonight she came early and took her place at the polished round table. Its central pattern of interlaced cogwheels glowed softly in the weak light from the chandelier and the lamps along the walls.

It had been a mistake, perhaps, for her to have insisted on the full day plus three hours' notice, for now they had to rely on artificial lighting, and with the power shortage that meant a dim room. Havkad was sure to point that out to reinforce his argument that the gods were displeased. But she'd barely had time to get everything ready as it was. She could only hope that Wraller's plan would be worth the time it had taken to set up.

No point in worrying about that now, she thought, tugging at her red-trimmed black tunic. She had taken even greater care than usual in her dress tonight, brushing her dark hair until it shone, then putting it into battle braid. She'd put on her formal uniform as well, and pinned on all her medals. Draped over the back of the chair was the black robe that councillors were required to wear at the meeting. She would put it on later, after everyone had arrived, but when they came in, they would see Master Security Officer Pandil, and know what they were up against. Not that any of them would be intimidated, nor would she want them to be. She did, however, want to remind them of who she was. They might remove her from the Council, but she was still the Security Master unless her Guild dismissed her. The New Schoolers might be able to bring that about, but they'd have a fight on their hands.

Havkad and his people came in first, eager for the battle no doubt, and secure in their certain victory. Well, let them gloat. If Wraller's plan worked, they'd be less happy when the evening was over, even though they had won.

Havkad himself was quiet and unusually restrained, lowering his squat body into the chair with a deep sigh. Perhaps he'd learned what Pandil had discovered in his house. Eilert, on the other hand, was smiling widely. Was the woman stupid, Pandil wondered, or blind?

"Good evening, Councillor Pandil." Eilert stressed "Councillor" as if to emphasize that the title would soon be inappropriate.

"Good evening, Master Eilert," Pandil replied, smiling as confidently as possible.

Havkad's other supporters filed in, some solemn, a couple smirking. The gods preserve us from fools, Pandil thought. She could scarcely contain a sigh of relief when Wraller finally entered. Blaint and Staver were with him. "Evening," they said, almost in unison. Staver smiled, a gentle, sweet smile. "Master Pandil," he said, "this is sad business. Sad business, indeed." He glared at Havkad, then sat down and began a low conversation with Blaint, his fingers continuously worrying at the bruise on his cheek.

With a broad smile that would fool most people, Wraller

walked over to her chair, carrying a thick book. He is still too pale, Pandil thought; too thin. Whatever had been done to him, his full recovery was taking longer than she liked. If only Dovella were here to continue with his healing. Once again she wondered if her young friend had made it safely to Vellaban.

Wraller placed the book gently on the table in front of her. Its red cover was dark with age. She noted with pleasure the puzzled glances that passed between Eilert and Havkad. "Thank you, Master Wraller," she said.

Melkard glanced at her defiantly. He looked startled — her dress, no doubt — but he stiffened his back and turned his attention to his companion. According to Safir, he had been to see Avella, but despite their friendship, Melkard was clearly lost to them. Avella would be disappointed.

Well, that was it. The New School held seven votes to five against, and she had little reason to suppose that any of them could be swayed. Her only consolation was that they wouldn't get away with lies about what happened here tonight.

Havkad was looking at the two empty places across the table, the ones normally occupied by Avella and Plais, a slight smile on his face. She didn't know when she despised him most, when he put on that smug smile, or when he behaved like a pompous bully. She couldn't help grinning at the way his mouth dropped open when Plais walked in pushing a chair that was mounted on a low wagon. He claimed to dislike the contraption one of his apprentices had designed, but he was using it ever more frequently to get his patients out into the fresh air.

Avella lay propped in the chair. Her wan face glistened with perspiration, but her eyes shone with their old spark.

Her being here was of little use, perhaps, but she wouldn't be denied. And perhaps her battered visage would shame the others, if nothing else.

After Avella and Plais took their seats, the apprentices filed in, Carpace among them. Havkad winced when she walked in, as did several others. She, too, had insisted on attending, even though Plais would have preferred that she remain at Healer's Hall. One side of her face was swollen and blue with bruises, and her arm was bound in a sling. She walked stiffly and occasionally drew in a sharp breath and bit her lower lip.

When everyone was in place, Pandil stood and slowly donned her robe. When she sat back down and struck her gavel on the table, Havkad shoved his chair back; but before he could rise, the door at the end of the room was flung open. Maidel and Jael strode in followed by six men.

"What is the meaning of this?" Havkad demanded, rising quickly. His chair clattered to the floor behind him. "Council meetings are not open to spectators."

"Not spectators," Pandil said, trying to disguise her satisfaction at his surprise. "These are our silent witnesses."

"Call them what you like, they've no business at this session."

"But they have." She feigned perplexity. "Are you telling me you did not follow the Founders' practice of inviting silent witnesses to attend this Council session?"

"What are you talking about?"

"The Founders made a provision for witnesses from the Village to attend Council meetings when the behaviour of a member was called into question. You did call this meeting to question my behaviour, did you not?"

Havkad looked at Eilert with a question in his eyes. She shook her head. "I'm not aware of any such practice," he said.

"Then you should be," Pandil snapped. "You are the ones making such a cry to return to Founder ways; you ought to know what they are." She opened the heavy tome that Wraller had brought in. "'Section 27,'" she read. "'And when a councillor invokes privilege to bring charges against another councillor, and if there be great division in Council, then shall each side be granted permission to bring in six witnesses to hear the charges. And though they must keep silence in Council, they shall be free to speak the truth of what they have learned to the citizens at large.'" She looked from Havkad to Eilert. "Are you saying that you are not knowledgeable about the Founders' laws?"

Havkad shot Eilert a poisonous look, then straighted up his chair and turned his attention to the six men.

Although Wraller had disagreed at first, he'd finally gone along with Pandil's suggestion that three of them be devout New School adherents. Bake Master Hovel was no friend of Pandil's and it had taken all Wraller's influence to get him here, but the man was honest; he'd report fairly on what happened here tonight. And the first thing he'd report was that Pandil had been scrupulously fair in choosing her witnesses, while Havkad had been ignorant of the law.

It was Carpace who had suggested Feranc the bookmaker and Lencoln the blacksmith. Although he was still active in the New School, Feranc had recently split with Havkad over the involvement of the sorcerer, and Lencoln hated violence probably as much as Safir. According to Carpace, neither Hovel nor Lencoln knew about the sorcerer, and neither would accept his involvement in New School affairs.

Havkad glowered at them, but he would look foolish objecting to their presence, and he knew it. And if he didn't object to them, he could hardly object to the other three: the knife maker Osten, Lakon and one of Eilert's apprentices.

Melkard frowned on seeing Lakon, knowing that news of what happened tonight would soon be spread throughout the outlands, and Eilert looked none too comfortable at seeing her apprentice.

Well, it might all come to nothing, but as Wraller had said, at least the people would hear the truth about what was going on, and that would be important in days to come, for if Havkad succeeded in ousting Pandil, he would turn on the others who opposed him and spread his lies about their conduct. The Villagers needed to hear how she met his charges.

Havkad turned back to Pandil. Somehow he kept his fury in check, but she could see he was clenching his hands. "I call all to witness," he said, "that the gods have shown their displeasure in the leadership of the Village. For my many warnings, I have been persecuted, especially over the past few days. Our sacred house of worship has been defiled and I and my followers have been shut out by Master Security Officer Pandil and her officers."

When he mentioned the sacred house of worship, Hovel and Lencoln shared a puzzled glance. Wondering why they knew nothing about it, Pandil thought — and none too pleased, if she was any judge. Feranc frowned and compressed his lips. Even Melkard looked surprised. But Havkad was oblivious to everyone now, too caught up in his own pomposity. Pandil smiled. He doesn't need his foulheads, she thought; he could bore people to death.

"Furthermore," he went on, drawing his squat body to its full height, "she has made various accusations against me and loyal New School disciples. No one could be more appalled than I at the attack on the Master Engineer." Here he made a slight bow towards Avella, though he didn't look at her. "And the recent attack at the Engineering Building is even more appalling. Before the gods, I swear that I had nothing to do with these attacks, nor do I believe that they were the acts of New School worshippers. I don't know what evidence Master Pandil has, since she has refused to share it with Master Eilert."

He glanced around the table, looked earnestly towards the silent witnesses. "It is not a light thing to bring an order of dismissal against a fellow councillor," he said, lowering his voice and adding a note of sadness, "but in cases where power has been so clearly abused, I see no other recourse. Secure in the knowledge that the gods have withdrawn their favour from the leadership of the Village, however, I make my petition that Pandil be removed from this Council. I have also presented a petition to her Guild that she be removed as Master of Security, as well."

A hum of whispered conversation went around the table as he sat down. Master Eilert started to rise, but before she could get to her feet, Pandil stood.

"Although I had planned on a public hearing in the offices of court to present my case," Pandil said, giving "public" slightly more stress, "I am quite prepared to submit my evidence here. As chairman this session, however, the rules say I may not speak, nor vote except in cases of a tied vote. It will be necessary, therefore, for me to appoint a temporary chairman for the remainder of this session."

"We waive that requirement," Eilert said quickly.

Havkad gaped at her, but others smiled, amused no doubt that Pandil's strategy had failed, for she would surely have appointed one of them and so evened the vote. Although he frowned, Havkad didn't question Eilert's judgement, but not so the Master of Religion.

"Not so quick, Master Eilert." He pursed his lips and looked around the table. His fleshy hands, fingers interlaced, lay at rest on his round stomach. "Surely that is something we need to consider."

"Would you like to consider being the temporary appointment?" Eilert snapped. "As Master Pandil pointed out, you would not be able to vote in that case."

He looked disconcerted for a moment, then the implication hit him and his cheeks reddened. "No, of course not. No. I take your point."

"If it is agreed, then," Pandil said, "I'll continue. I have laid no charges against Havkad regarding the two attacks mentioned. However, as you well know, I do hold in the Security Building several New School adherents who were involved in those attacks. These men are all closely allied to Havkad, and none of us here are ignorant of the particular teachings Havkad has been espousing, namely that women in high offices are anathema to the gods and should be removed from office — forcibly, if necessary." She paused and glanced pointedly at Eilert and the other female New School supporter, wondering again why they would be so supportive of Havkad.

"Furthermore," Pandil continued, "Havkad has spoken strongly about the machine and has said that the gods have shown their displeasure by cutting off the water. It doesn't take much for people of scant intelligence to jump from that statement to the implication that the gods are against the machine. Therefore, I have said, and I stand behind the statement, that I hold Havkad morally responsible for the attacks. As Master of Security, however, I have made no such charge. I do have evidence and numerous witnesses who can testify that the attackers are New School adherents. And you see before you what Master Avella and her apprentice Carpace have suffered. Master Avella was unconscious for two and a half days."

She paused there, as if considering whether to say more. She glanced at Havkad, who sneered and shook his head. Nonetheless she could see tiny beads of sweat on his upper lip.

"Now, as to the charge that I have kept Havkad from the 'sacred house of worship,' as he calls it. My apprentices and I legally entered the house to retrieve a set of scrolls that had been improperly taken from Archives Hall. While searching for the scrolls, we came upon several cases of weapons, most of which we have determined were stolen."

This caused all the consternation she had hoped for, not only among many of the councillors, but among the New School silent witnesses, who looked as if they were hard pressed to maintain silence. And it was obvious from his gaping mouth that Havkad had not been aware that Pandil had bypassed the trap.

She glanced at Wraller. They had been unable to decide whether or not she should mention sorcery. She had felt that it would be to their advantage to keep Havkad guessing about how much they knew, and Wraller had finally agreed, only insisting that if things went badly, he would be allowed to ask

Havkad questions about the sorcerous trap in his house.

"What weapons?" The Master of Religion demanded, his cheeks puffing out in indignation. "Why should Havkad have weapons?"

"Truth is all the weapon the New School needs," Havkad said, recovering quickly. "If you found any others, you put them there yourself."

"Naturally I can't prove that I didn't — not tonight — any more than Havkad can prove that he wasn't aware of the weapons being there, nor of how they were obtained. I had fully intended to call into the public hearing those witnesses who saw us leaving the house with loaded carts, but this meeting was called before I could arrange that."

Again she stressed the word "public," and again there was a low hum as councillors whispered among themselves. And again the silent witnesses kept quiet, though they fidgeted and looked at one another with frowns and shrugs and lips clamped tight.

"But whatever you may think on this matter," she went on, "there is no doubt that New School people attacked Master Avella and the Engineering Building."

"My father," blurted Carpace. "My own father."

"Be quiet!" Havkad roared. "Apprentices are not to talk during Council."

She stared at him defiantly, then smiled. She had made her point and she knew it.

"Let that be for the moment. I have an even more serious charge." Pandil looked around the table. "I expect that most of you, except for Councillor Havkad, are unaware that the machine relies on source water from a large lake on the other side of the mountain of the Hill Folk. The machine there was set to be automatic after the last war with the Hill Folk, although the Kaftil allowed a few people to stay for maintenance purposes."

She paused. "Also held in the Security Building is a saboteur who admits to being in Havkad's pay."

Mouth agape, Havkad lunged forward as if about to rise. He sat back slowly, his upper lip glistening with perspiration. His eyes darted around, but he met no one's glance, although both Melkard and the Master Trader were staring at him. Interesting, Pandil thought.

"This man, named Konell, had with him a map and written instructions for closing down the flow of water from the source. The flow was to be cut completely by Festival, and then miraculously restored when the New School came into power."

"Lies!" Havkad shouted.

"The instructions for shutting off the water are in Havkad's writing. And they are stamped with his mark."

"Lies!" He jumped to his feet and stared at his fellow councillors.

"I have the documents here." Pandil pulled them from the pocket of her tunic. At her gesture, Maidel came forward, took the parchment from her and carried it around the table.

Eilert scarcely glanced at it. The Master Trader tightened his lips as he read, then stared at Havkad as if in disgust. Havkad wiped a trembling hand across his upper lip. Melkard and the Master of Religion both appeared to be at a loss and, after reading it, passed the sheet on without looking at anyone. Others read carefully and looked quickly at Pandil, then at Havkad before passing the sheet on. None of them had known. No wonder Havkad was sweating.

"The men who had been looking after the source machine were all killed," Pandil added.

"Lies," Havkad shouted again, his voice breaking. "All lies. Everyone knows it was the true gods who cut the water flow. We have prayed earnestly that they would restore power."

"We have all prayed for that," Pandil said.

"But I have been called by the gods to lead this Village back to proper worship. This is all — "

Before he could say more, the door flew open. Engineering apprentice Narlos ran in, waving his bandaged hand. "The water has been restored!" he shouted. "Elder Master Quade sent me to tell you that we'll have full power here momentarily."

Pandil's heart raced. "I would say that the gods have heard us," she said, scarcely able to conceal her relief.

Avella buried her face in her hands and wept, and it was all Pandil could do to keep from joining her. Dovella had made it. She was safe. And she had succeeded.

"The gods have answered our prayers in restoring power," Pandil went on more firmly, "but as I told you, it was not the gods who were responsible for turning off the power in the first place, nor killing its keepers. It was Havkad. You have the proof before you. However, I can bring in the prisoner if you like."

"It can't be," Havkad said. "Master Quade has sent a false message." But as if to disprove him, the dimly glowing lamps around the room blazed brighter, filling the room with light.

He looked around, his eyes wild. "How?" he asked. "How did you do it?"

The other councillors, too, gazed around the room in wonder.

Havkad rushed over to one of the wall lamps and touched it, then snatched back his hand. "How?"

"I've heard enough," said the Master Trader. "I've held my peace, not taking either side, but now the time has come to choose. After hearing what Havkad has done, I'm convinced that his way would lead us to destruction."

"I'm with you," Melkard said. "I've held with Councillor Havkad until now, but I see that I've been badly mistaken in him. I think it's time to vote on the question of relieving Master Pandil of her position." He raised his hand. "I vote no. Who will join me?"

The Master Trader raised his hand as well, followed quickly by Avella, Wraller, Plais, Blaint and Staver. Some of the others smiled contemptuously. Still, it was a majority. Pandil sighed, ran her hand across the tight muscles at the back of her neck. It had been close, but the majority was on their side. "Carried," she said, and tapped her gavel on the table.

"No!" Havkad shouted.

"And now," said Melkard, fixing Havkad with a stare that seemed to hold him in place, "now I suggest that we vote to censure Havkad for placing the Village and the outlands in such danger. And I suggest, Master Pandil," he said, turning to her, "that you bring him to court on a charge of treason and murder."

"I will do so," she said. Though both Melkard and the Master Trader had appeared as astonished as the others, she suspected that they had known about the weapons. But what Havkad had done at the source, that had come as a surprise. And they hadn't liked that. But was it what he had done that they didn't like, or the fact that they hadn't known about it?

From the far side of the room, Havkad glared from

one to the other. Then he seemed to pull himself free from some restraint. His eyes flashing rage, he flung out a hand and began chanting. A black mist, thick and putrid, curled away from his fingers and shot toward Pandil. His chanting thundered in her ears, and she stared, too stunned to moved. Havkad was the sorcerer! She had thought it was the stranger Dovella had seen, but now it all made sense. Of course, she'd known that Havkad had been dabbling in the filthy practice, but even after what she'd learned from Konell, she'd had no idea he was so far advanced. She'd expected something from him, yes; but not this. And she was totally unprepared for a sorcerous attack. She threw up a hand to ward against the strike, but knew it would be futile. She could not protect herself from this.

As if in a dream, she watched Jael yank out the shell he kept concealed in his shirt and put it to his lips. Three notes, soft yet clear, pierced the silence of the room, and then she saw the young apprentice's lips move in a silent chant. His eyes were closed and his fingers moved in an intricate pattern.

As the pure tones of the shell had shattered the silence, so it must also have shattered Havkad's concentration, for he turned quickly to jab a finger in Jael's direction, and as he did so, the black rope of mist recoiled and snapped back, collapsing into a film that shrouded his body. A cry of rage and pain ripped through the room and Havkad fell to his knees as the blackness filled his open mouth, choking him.

Pandil's eyes swept the Council table taking in expressions of horror and dismay. On a few faces she read disgust, but whether that was directed at Havkad for what he had tried or because of his failure was anyone's guess. Quickly she glanced at the silent witnesses and saw the same confusion of expressions. They, too, had been caught off guard. But Pandil suspected that several of the people in the room had known about Havkad's dealings with sorcery, even if they had not known that he himself was a sorcerer.

A few had risen, but as the confusion slowly quietened, they settled back in their seats, some as still as if carved in stone, others fidgeting and avoiding the questioning glances of their fellow councillors.

Pandil glanced back at Jael. Had he suspected? she wondered; is that why he'd insisted on staying in the Village until after the meeting? He and Maidel were now kneeling by Havkad's body. "He's alive," Maidel said, "but barely."

"Take him to Healer's Hall," Pandil said, "but keep him closely guarded." She smiled weakly at Jael and thanked the Goddess that she'd let herself be persuaded keep him in the Village until after the Council meeting.

As Maidel and Jael left the room, supporting Havkad's limp body between them, the Master of Roads leaned forward and slammed his fist on the table. He was one of the most outspoken of the New Schoolers. Everyone jumped and turned to face him. When he had their attention, he hit the table again, this time more softly. "You have gained allies, Master Pandil," he said quietly. "You might ask yourself whether you can trust them." He got up and strode out.

The rest of Havkad's supporters looked at each another. After a moment's hesitation, they also left.

Pandil turned to the silent witnesses. "Thank you for your patience. I think the meeting is over now."

"I must get Avella and Carpace back to Healer's Hall," Plais said.

"Indeed," burst out Bake Master Hovel from his position

with the other silent witnesses. "It was very brave of you to come, Master Avella. And you, Carpace. I deeply regret that New Schoolers were responsible for your injuries. I know we're not supposed to speak in here, and I have fought to hold my tongue, but I am so outraged by what I've heard that I can no longer keep silent. That you should have been injured by one of us grieves my heart, dear lady." He looked at Carpace. "And you, child; I cannot think what possessed your father."

"I have no father," Carpace said.

Hovel's eyes filled with tears. "You need a home," he said, "a place where you will be safe. I can give you that."

Carpace covered her face with her hands, shoulders shaking.

"That is very good of you, Master Hovel," Pandil said. "And it was good of all of you to come as witnesses. I know it was hard to hear these things, but I felt you had to know."

"If I had not heard them for myself I would have had a hard time crediting them," Lencoln said. "Even though I did not always agree with Havkad, I believed that he was devout, albeit misguided. I thank you for bringing us here, for otherwise we might never have known what he was doing."

Ferenc nodded. "And after what we've witnessed here, we have much to discuss."

It was as well that Havkad had made his sorcerous attempt, Pandil thought; now there could be no doubt in their minds that he was corrupt.

One by one they took their leave until all were gone except Pandil and Wraller.

"I can hardly believe it," Wraller said. "We won. The power restored and Havkad defeated." He smiled at Pandil.

"I can hardly take it in. And that Havkad was the sorcerer — it's almost beyond belief. I would never have dreamed he could do the things he has done."

Yes, there was surely cause to rejoice, Pandil thought, but no way to undo the damage that had been done — to Avella and Wraller, to burned-out and terrorized Outlanders and Foresters, to Carpace and other disillusioned New Schoolers who had truly believed, to Safir's peaceful nature, to Pandil herself, who still felt filthy from plundering the renegade's mind. And what about Dovella, who had made it all possible? The young healer would forever bear the scars of causing a death.

As to the Village — it would take years for the breach caused by Havkad's evil to be healed. If it ever was.

Twenty-four

WHEN DOVELLA REACHED THE COUNCIL CHAMBER, THE room was empty except for Tavel and the Kaftil's aunt. The young woman walked toward Dovella and took her hand.

"You should be in bed," Dovella scolded, though she felt the surge of joy that always came with a healing. A joy she had forfeited the right to ever know again.

"I wanted to be here for this." She led Dovella up to the dais where the Kaftil's aunt stood waiting. Dressed now in a robe of pale blue, she seemed very different from the old peasant woman Dovella had taken her to be.

"You are a truly gifted healer," the woman said, "for Tavel's wounds were deep and festered." She drew from her pocket a medallion on a red ribbon hanging from a chain of smaller medals. It was exactly like the medallion Safir wore. The woman started to put it around Dovella's neck.

Dovella stepped away. "That is only given to those who go through the Rites of the Healer. I have no right to wear it."

"It is in healing that you perform the true rites," the woman said, "and Tavel bears witness to your gift."

"But I don't deserve it."

The woman touched her arm. "I am Khanti-Lafta," she said, her voice soft but firm. "I say you have earned the right to wear the medallion."

Khanti-Lafta! Just before Dovella left home, Safir had spoken of the great healers of the Hill Folk, but she had somehow thought that they, too, were only legends. And even if she had known there was still a great healer in Hill country honoured as Khanti-Lafta, she would never have dreamed that it could be this old woman.

"I don't deserve it," Dovella repeated. "I'm glad my work mended the machine, but I misused the sacred oils."

The great healer shook her head. "The oils are given us by the Goddess, and with them we are truly blessed, but they are for the good of all. It was for the good of our people and yours that you used them. There is no sacrilege in that."

"But there is more," Dovella said, determined to be honest. "I caused a man to die on my journey here."

The Khanti-Lafta paused. "Did you seek his death?"

Dovella shook her head. "He sought mine."

"In doing so, he found his own." Then, more gently, she continued: "One must always feel distress at taking a life, any life, but you fought to preserve your own. He could have preserved his at any time by breaking off his attack and leaving. He chose not to do so. His death lies in his own choices. I do not say that you should forget it — you must never forget it — but do not embrace guilt for an action that was not of your making."

She placed the medallion around Dovella's neck. "Had you more time with us," she said, "we would have a full ceremony, and I would carry you through the mysteries of the Rites myself, but as you are returning to the Village, your father and the Master Healer can do those honours."

"I thank you," Dovella said, "but the Master Healer Plais won't allow it."

The Khanti-Lafta stepped back and looked at her, blue eyes flashing. "Not allow it? What right has he to forbid it?"

"We are not permitted to go through the Rites if we miss the scheduled day."

"Which you missed in order to make this journey, to save your people."

"Yes, but that is the tradition, and he will never change his mind."

The great healer stared at Dovella as if she couldn't believe the words she was hearing. She paused for a moment longer and reached out to lightly stroke Dovella's eyes, then trace a pattern on her forehead.

All at once, it was as if Dovella could see for the first time. Now when she looked at the Khanti-Lafta, she knew she was in the presence of a great healer. When she looked at Tavel, she could see the injuries that were healing, could see what she, herself, had done in restoring Tavel. She didn't understand what had happened, but she knew that the Khanti-Lafta had opened up something in her mind. Perhaps this was what Safir had meant when he'd stressed the importance of the Rites.

"The Master Healer cannot deny you now," the Khanti-Lafta said. "He will see you have been touched, and he must accept you and teach you. But, if he will not, come back to us. I will teach you."

Dovella smiled. She felt a tightness in her chest, but this time the tears that threatened were brought by joy. Yes, she would return here. But not, after all, as an engineer, for now that her mind had been opened by the Khanti-Lafta, now that she could truly see, she knew that her gift was indeed a blessing, not a curse as she had so long feared. Knowing this, she also knew that she must use all her energies as a healer; she had much to learn.

You fear what you do not know, her father had said. Dovella smiled. How foolish her fears seemed now. And if she could overcome her fear, surely others could be convinced to do the same. If this trip brought an end to the rift between her people and the Hill Folk, that would be the greatest healing of all.

She looked down at the medallion of the Healer hanging about her neck and smiled as she felt the familiar bud of joy open to full bloom.